THE
WOMAN WHO
STOLE THE
WORLD

Printed in Australia
First Printing: October 2022
Shawline Publishing Group Pty Ltd
www.shawlinepublishing.com.au

Paperback ISBN: 978-1-9228-5052-2
eBook ISBN 978-1-9228-5059-1

 A catalogue record for this work is available from the National Library of Australia

THE
WOMAN WHO
STOLE THE
WORLD

ANDREW HOOD

AWARD WINNING AUTHOR OF THE WEEKLY TIPPING POINT

This book is dedicated to my wife Elizabeth,
and our children Lynton, Harrison & Rose

It is also dedicated to our good friend Danielle Thurgood
who was lost to this world in 2020. We miss you Dan!

ACKNOWLEDGEMENTS

I would like to acknowledge and thank Bradley Shaw and the team at Shawline Publishing, for helping me get through a difficult time in my publishing journey and for all your ongoing support. It is easier and far more enjoyable being an author knowing that you are behind me every step of the way. Thank you.

ABOUT THE AUTHOR

Andrew Hood was born in Victoria Australia in 1973 and now lives in New South Wales with his wife and three children. Andrew is an author, blogger, Sales Director and family man.

Andrew's first book 'The Man Who Corrupted Heaven' has been published across multiple countries and has since been nominated for the 2022 Miles Franklin Literary Award and the New South Wales Premier's Literary Award for New Talent.

His personal blog 'The Weekly Tipping Point' was listed at No.39 in the "Top 101 Best & Most Inspiring Blogs" and he has since been a guest blogger on 'The Guided Mind' and 'Change Your Thoughts - Change Your Life' blogs since 2014.

PREFACE

Welcome to *The Woman Who Stole The World*.

This book is the last book in my *The Man Who Corrupted Heaven* trilogy. If you haven't read the original two books, or can't remember them well, then don't fear because this book is almost entirely self-contained. It is a story all its own and only borrows lightly from the original two books. In fact, you could read it first if you wanted to and you wouldn't be any poorer for it.

While researching for this book I was lucky to stumble across some amazing documentary movies and podcasts. These shows ignited my excitement in the documentary genre, and I knew it was a style that I wanted to capture for this book. That is why I have written this book using a podcast format. I wanted to capture that feeling of 'I can't wait to hear what happens next episode!'.

To those of you who have not listened to podcasts in the past, this book's format may feel a little strange at first. I hope you will stick with it until you can see past the format and just enjoy the story for what it is. For those of you that do listen to podcasts, hopefully you can take to the format of this book right away.

As you will see, I seem to change my writing style with each book I release, but I hope you will always hear my voice behind the words. The people of this world and their motivations fascinate me and while that is the case, I will always find another story to tell and another book to write.

I thank you all for taking time to read this book and I sincerely hope that you like it and get something from it.

Warmest regards always,

Andrew.

INTRODUCTION

[Narrator]

Con woman or humanitarian?

Either way, the questions remain: who was the enigmatic Susan Mitchell, and what happened to the hundreds of millions of dollars that she stole from the investors who flocked to her innovative investment fund?

[Unidentified Male Voice]

'She really had a way of making you feel you were on the very edge of history. And that all you needed to do was take that one step, in faith, and that together we could change everything.'

[Narrator]

Miss Mitchell told anyone who would listen that she had an investment system that would revolutionise how people invested their money. That, in her system, invested money not only gained interest at an incredible rate but would also fund major humanitarian efforts around the world while it did so. She claimed to have invented a new type of low-risk investment vehicle that she called the Human Capital World Fund.

Then, about one year ago – at the height of her success but with major questions being asked – Susan Mitchell disappeared without a trace, along with her fund and all the money that was invested in it.

Over the coming months we will investigate how she went from executive assistant to CEO and creator of one of the fastest-growing investment funds of all time. A fund manager to the stars, with over hundreds of million dollars of her clients' money under her management and her sole control. We will try to understand how this secretive woman, with no formal education, could entertain ultra-wealthy A-List celebrities, People of Power and the everyday mums and dads with fanciful stories of her humanitarian successes.

[Unidentified Female Voice]

'Susan was amazing, really! The way she commanded a room was something that I had never seen before. Men, women, everybody loved her. I was very proud of what she had achieved, and I didn't even know her. I just remember thinking, "Here she is – she will show these men what a woman can do".'

[Narrator]

Join us as we investigate the company that she took over and the fund she developed. We will also peer into the mysterious background of Miss Mitchell herself, by talking to those that knew her best. We will try to understand where she came from, who she was working with, and just how she could disappear so completely with all that money.

Join me, Stephen Grace, as we go on the search for elusive Susan Mitchell – The Woman Who Stole The World.

EPISODE 1: THE PURSUER AND THE PURSUED

[Narrator]

On the 31st October, 2015, Halloween, a timid young woman called Susan Mitchell took the stage for the very first time at an Emerging Markets Financial conference in New York. The speech that she would deliver over the next 24 minutes, which was recorded on an attendant's mobile phone, would one day become a viral sensation online to over five million viewers.

[Unidentified Male Voice]

'It wasn't even on centre stage. They had some boring Deloitte guy up at centre stage. This was one of those break-out rooms – the room you get when you pay to sponsor the event. The only reason I was there was because I had heard the Deloitte guy speak before. I don't think that any of us really knew what we were about to see.'

[Narrator]

In the video, which is still online, we see Miss Mitchell taking the stage in a matte black pantsuit with her chestnut brown hair falling across both her shoulders. At this stage, early in the video, we don't get a sense of the woman that she was about to become right before our eyes. To put her humble beginning into even more context, if you take the time to read some comments under the video, you might notice that many people stopped watching before the two-minute mark, simply because she started so poorly.

[Unidentified Female Voice]

'I still tell people I was there, in that room from the video, when she gave that original speech. I was lucky. She was beautiful, really. So elegant.'

[Narrator]

From such a small beginning she would go on to impress some of the wealthiest people from around the world and they would shower her with their money. Everyone wanted to be part of her exciting new investment fund – The Human Capital World Fund – and to 'change the world'. And then, at what would seem to be the height of her success, and with money still pouring in, she disappeared off the face of the earth. Neither woman nor money were ever to be seen again.

My name is Stephen Grace, and I am a freelance journalist. I specialize in finding and exposing financial fraud all around the world. In my time, I have investigated some of the world's largest financial crimes. From Bernie Madoff ($65 Billion), to Bernie Ebbers ($11 Billion). From Tom Petters ($3.65 Billion) to Susan Mitchell. And although Susan Mitchell is a smaller fish in the scheme of things at only hundreds of millions, none of the other bigger cases prepared me for what I was about to uncover.

Typically, my investigations focus on what drives people to commit these crimes, or frauds. Are they regular people, just like you or I, who were desperate, or got greedy and made a mistake? Are they born psychopaths, people who will say anything to get what they want? Or is there something else? Perhaps they are a small part of something much bigger? In this show, we will explore these considerations and more as we try to uncover the truth.

The story of Susan Mitchell first found me about six months ago when I was approached by one of her clients. This client had lost a sizable amount of money and was keen to track her down. He had heard about the type of investigative work that I had done in the past and wanted to know if I could help him. To get a sense of perspective, I asked him how much money Miss Mitchell had taken from him and to my surprise he was not forthcoming with the amount. He stated that it was substantial, more than a million dollars, but he was not willing to disclose the precise sum. This was interesting to me because, usually, law-abiding victims are comfortable for the enormities of their losses to be known, but not this man. This man said something to me that in all my years of investigating financial fraud I had never heard before.

He said …

[Unidentified Male Voice]

'I don't care about the money. I'd just like to know if Susan is okay.'

[Narrator]

Now, one thing that I know after all these years investigating financial fraud is that it is always about the money. Often a lot of hard work was put into earning that money and it is being invested for a purpose such as to buy a house or for retirement. When that money is taken from them investors often feel like their future has been taken from them and that they would need to start all over again. Many of the fraud victims that I usually speak with feel betrayed by the perpetrator and often threaten to physically harm them if they ever saw them again. The victims rarely care about the perpetrator's wellbeing. Often they just want to regain a little of the pride that they lost in the betrayal of trust. Time and time again I have heard victims say things like "I can't believe this has happened to me" or "I am too ashamed to tell my friends". Many blame themselves for not seeing the warning signs that become so obvious to them only afterwards.

But this man was different. I'll let him introduce himself and tell you his story in the next episode, but for now let me share just a little more of our conversation that day.

[Unidentified Male Voice]

'I don't care about the money. I'd just like to know if Susan is okay.'

[Stephen Grace]

'Why? What do you think has happened to her?'

[Unidentified Male Voice]

'I don't know. Perhaps she has been kidnapped by people looking for money. Perhaps she got in over her head and ran away in fear. Maybe even … maybe she is dead. I don't know, but I would really like to find out.'

[Stephen Grace]

'Have you tried to hire a private detective?'

[Narrator]

He then let out a deep breath, and said something that immediately intrigued me.

[Unidentified Male Voice]

'I did, but he found nothing. How do you find someone that doesn't exist? Nobody even knows her proper name, or anything about her. I figured … you're the finance guy, perhaps there is a trail there.'

[Stephen Grace]

'And you say that it is not about the money?'

[Unidentified Male Voice]

'For others it might be, but I have enough already. And my pride, it is not such a precious thing.'

[Narrator]

In the next episode you will hear more from the gentleman who had approached me on that first day when I heard about this story. You will understand what role he played in it all, and why the money was not important to him. I would meet with this man on multiple occasions over the coming months and every time that I did, this story would take a twist or a turn in a new direction.

We will also discuss the Human Capital World Fund with one of its co-creators and he will explain what made it so innovative. We will also attempt to paint more of the picture of the elusive Susan Mitchell herself. We will try to uncover why she did it and where did she, and all that hard-earned money, go.

In this series of podcasts you will hear from the people that knew her well, the people she worked with and the people she stole money from. We will even have a finance industry expert on hand as we try to piece together the puzzle of Susan Mitchell and her Human Capital World Fund.

At this early stage we would like to invite anyone who has had some involvement with Susan Mitchell to contact us. If you invested money in her fund, know her personally or even if you are Miss Mitchell herself and are listening to this, we would very much like to talk to you for our investigation. Perhaps the one small piece of information that you have is the missing link needed to tie it all together.

It is often said that 'Not everything is as it seems' but with Susan Mitchell – The Woman Who Stole The World – nothing *was* as it seemed.

Now a word from our sponsors …

EPISODE 2: THE AGENT

[Narrator]

Who was the mysterious Susan Mitchell – The Woman Who Stole The World? And how was she able to convince so many people to invest hundreds of millions of dollars into her Human Capital World Fund before disappearing off the face of the earth with everyone's money?

Join me, Stephen Grace, as I attempt to find out.

You may recall from Episode 1 that I was first approached about this situation with Susan Mitchell by a gentleman that I did not know who said to me:

[Unidentified Male Voice]

'I don't care about the money. I'd just like to know if Susan is okay.'

[Narrator]

In today's episode we will hear more from that original interview and how that investor came to be involved with Miss Mitchell. We will see how their chance meeting would open an entire world of fame and fortune for Susan and how she would take advantage of it. If there was ever a spark that lit a bushfire, you could say that this was it.

Now, let's hear who he is and what he has got to say. I was sitting in his small inner-city office when this interview took place.

[Stephen Grace]

'I appreciate you reaching out to me with this story. Can you start by introducing yourself and telling us a little about what you do for a living?'

[Dylan Clarke – The Agent]

'My name is Dylan Clarke and I run a talent agency for up-and-coming singers and musicians. Sometimes, even the talent themselves don't understand what they have. I scout the talent shows, school musicals, or even buskers on street corners and find the diamonds in the rough. I then take them into my care, polish them up, and present them back to the world. I have been doing this work for over twenty years. Sometimes a client - perhaps one in twenty – will have the kind of talent that really stands out. Even on a world stage. These are the ones that become global super stars. With these unicorns that I call them because they are so unique, I will typically call up one of the big global talent agencies that I'm aligned with and they take over the day to day management from me. They are happy to have a new star that they didn't have to find themselves, the talent gets to realise their dreams and I am rewarded handsomely for my service. Within a few months of that exchange that artist becomes the name you see in your newspapers every day.'

[Stephen Grace]

'Could you tell us some names of the people that you have discovered.'

[Dylan Clarke – The Agent]

'I would say "no" usually, as I am not supposed to say their names once they have moved on from my direct management. However, a few of them have referenced their involvement with me publicly so I can mention them. If you search online, you will see that JC Chains, Veronique and Ku-Stom have all thanked me personally in their acceptance speeches. There are many more names I could throw out, but they are not public knowledge, so I won't.'

[Narrator]

I looked about his small office and every wall was full of photos of Dylan Clarke either shaking hands with, or with his arm around, someone important in the entertainment industry. Like him, I could list the names of people in those photographs but my years in journalism have taught me better. I never accept evidence of close association if it is given so freely. I can only imagine a young up-and-coming singer walking into this room and taking it all in. To me everything seems designed to get a young person's signature on a contract. Dylan seemed to sense my hesitation.

[Dylan Clarke – The Agent]

'You are smart. You know not to trust these photos alone and you probably look about and think, this is not such an enormous space; how successful can this guy really be? Well, I don't splash my money around – it's not my style – and, frankly, it scares off some of my potential talent if I do. If I get some kid with a voice like an angel off the street, and they come in here and I've got an expensive gold watch and gold trinkets everywhere, they are just going to think I want to make money off them. I am very honest with them. This wall here on my right is my current talent list. The wall on my left is the talent that has left me to go up the stack. Sometimes it works out well for them, sometimes it doesn't. That wall behind you is the people I admire. It helps me to see them every day when I look up by reminding me of who I want to be. And behind me, always, is my family. You can ask any of them, I make this point clearly.'

[Narrator]

For the record, I looked up a few of his associations and all that I checked out was true. Everyone I spoke to had only good things to say about Dylan Clarke.

[Stephen Grace]

'So, is it just the one in twenty that makes money?'

[Dylan Clarke – The Agent]

'Great, this is an important question. The answer is no. Big-big money, yes. But, just medium-to-big money no. I got some of my guys off the street, and they are now living in their own houses. They paid for them themselves with the money we made together. And I can tell you, that is big money for someone who has nothing. I tell them I have three tiers of talent and each tier comes with its own level of success and money. I've got my A-Grade, Big-Ballers – the sky is the limit for those guys. I have my B-Graders who can have a career; a few albums, a bunch of hits, and if they are smart and we play it right they get enough money to buy themselves a pleasant house and put their kids through college. Lastly, I've got my Struggle Streeters. I feel for these guys: they have all the talent in the world, but some birds never learn how to fly. I support them for a few years, but eventually I got to cut them loose. It's called a talent pool but there are only some that can swim in the deep end. Some of them don't know which end is which so they panic even in the shallows.'

[Stephen Grace]

'Okay, thanks, I understand. Now if you don't mind, I would like to get on to the topic at hand. Can you please tell us about your association with Susan Mitchell?'

[Dylan Clarke – The Agent]

'Yeah, right. Sorry, I could talk about my business all day. I'm proud of what I have built here. Susan – she is why you are here. What do you want to know?'

[Stephen Grace]

'You were there on the day of her very first presentation at the Emerging Markets Financial Conference, right? Can you tell me first what you were doing there and then about the presentation that Susan gave?'

[Dylan Clarke – The Agent]

'Yeah, like I said to you on the phone, I was there. My business doesn't stop when I make my money. I need to be smart about what I do with it as well. I don't leave these things in the hands of others. That is why I was there. It was not even centre stage. They had some boring Deloitte guy up at centre stage. This was one of those break-out rooms. The room you get when you pay to sponsor the event. The only reason I was there was because I had seen the Deloitte guy before. I don't think that any of us really knew what we were about to see.'

[Stephen Grace]

'What did you see?'

[Dylan Clarke – The Agent]

'So, they announce her spot, and Susan walks on stage in that black suit of hers. On some videos they cut out the first few minutes, but I was there. I saw the whole thing myself. I'll tell you now, she wasn't always that confident. There were those first few minutes, where she faltered. Her voice broke a little, and she lost her place. To borrow a line from my industry you could say "she flickered like a candle in the wind". I think it is what first got my attention because I leaned in to listen. I felt bad for her, and I wished that I could help her. But then she found herself another gear and when her flame finally caught, she burned bright.'

[Stephen Grace]

'I guess that this is where I struggle with the whole thing. I have watched the video and read all the comments, and like some people who left comments I don't see it like you do. She is obviously a very educated woman, and there is certainly a pleasant story that she presents around her Human Capital Fund, but I don't see this "flame burning bright", as you say.'

[Dylan Clarke – The Agent]

'Yeah … well, perhaps you see what you want to see. And maybe that is what I saw as well. You've got to remember that this was a finance industry function, with a lot of very smart finance guys in the room. Any of them could have ripped her apart on the spot if they didn't believe her story, but they didn't. We all assumed that for her to be standing on that stage someone had vetted her story beforehand. She was the CEO of an investment company after all. If I had ripped off people and I was up on stage at some event I can tell you now, there would be a lot of hecklers. But on that day, nobody said a word. We just watched and listened.'

[Stephen Grace]

'Okay, well I guess I just don't get it.'

[Dylan Clarke – The Agent]

'When you watched the video online, you already knew that she had disappeared, yes? Well … like I said, you saw what you wanted to see.'

[Narrator]

If you read the remarks left by people online from that very first speech of Miss Mitchell it is clear to see that I'm not alone. Not everyone was sold like Dylan Clarke. However, it is also abundantly clear that there were others that seem to fall under her spell quickly. Some of them are still trying to invest in her fund today, even after knowing that she has disappeared.

[Dylan Clarke – The Agent]

'Anyway, you can see the presentation for yourself, it's not very long. So, afterwards I'm sitting there quite impressed but still a little unsure if I would invest any money with her, when this lovely young woman comes up to me and says, "Excuse me, Mr. Clarke, my name is Jane. Susan Mitchell – the lady who was just on stage – would really love to meet you. She is just debriefing now but hoped that you might wait around a few moments and perhaps join her for a coffee".'

[Stephen Grace]

'Did she pick you out of the crowd randomly?'

[Dylan Clarke – The Agent]

'At the start, this is what I was wondering. I thought, "Here we go – I'm about to get the big sell," but that is not what happened at all. I waited a few minutes for her and when we got together, she knew exactly who I was. She even knew some of the talent that I represented. She didn't sell me on anything. Get this: she asked my opinion. She wanted to know what I thought of her speech and her fund. She even asked me who I thought she should target, and if she was using the right language for that market.'

[Stephen Grace]

'I don't understand. You said yourself, you are not a finance guy. Why would your opinion matter in a room full of financial experts?'

[Dylan Clarke – The Agent]

'That's exactly what I said to her. She said that financial help is not what she wanted. Instead, she wanted help to get her message out to the right people. She honestly believed in the fund's ability to do good in the world. She wanted to know how to talk to regular people about it.'

[Stephen Grace]

'But why you? You say she knew all about you already. Why would she have singled you out in that room?'

[Dylan Clarke – The Agent]

'I still don't know the answer to that question. I got upset and asked her once, but she pushed the question aside like I was missing the point. All I know is, when a beautiful young woman asks an old man his opinion on anything, he is likely to give it. And let me also say that I see a lot of pretty girls in my line of work. Some of them try to sweet talk me, but I see their eyes glaze over whenever I try to teach them anything. I know what they are up to. But Susan – when we were sitting there that day, and she was asking me all those questions she was hanging on every word that this old man had to say. I couldn't stop talking, and she never ran out of questions. She took two pages of notes and I missed the next two conference sessions. In the end I wasn't sure if she was a genius or I was.'

[Stephen Grace]

'Once you gave her all your feedback, what happened?'

[Dylan Clarke – The Agent]

'By that stage I wanted to help her, so I did something that I think changed history. I invited her to a party.'

[Narrator]

In coming episodes, we will hear more from Dylan Clarke about that party and why it would become a pivotal moment in history for Susan Mitchell and the Human Capital World Fund. Before we do, in the next episode we will hear from others that were at the event that day and how they would come to be involved with Miss Mitchell's business from the inside.

This is a reminder that at this early stage we would like to invite anyone who has had some involvement with Susan Mitchell to contact us. If you invested money in her fund, know her personally or even if you are Miss Mitchell herself and are listening to this, we would very much like to talk to you for our investigation. Perhaps the one small piece of information that you have is the one missing link to tie it all together.

It is often said that 'Not everything is as it seems' but with Susan Mitchell – The Woman Who Stole The World – nothing *was* as it seemed.

Now, a word from our sponsors …

EPISODE 3: THE SOCIAL CHANGE ACTIVIST

[Narrator]

Who was the mysterious Susan Mitchell – The Woman Who Stole The World? And how was she able to convince so many people to invest hundreds of millions of dollars into her Human Capital World Fund before disappearing off the face of the earth with everyone's money?

Join me, Stephen Grace, as I attempt to find out.

In our last episode we heard from Dylan Clarke, the talent agent who was at the very first public presentation that Susan Mitchell gave on her Human Capital World Fund back on the 31st of October, 2015. In that episode, Dylan described his very first meeting with Miss Mitchell and how she asked him for feedback on her presentation. He would soon become a major part of Susan Mitchell's campaign, even if he did not realize it at the time.

But, before we return to Dylan, it is important that we hear more from others that were there that day in 2015. In today's episode I will be speaking with another pivotal character in this story. Instead of being a client, this person would become an integral member of Susan Mitchell's trusted members of staff and someone on the inside of the operation.

[Stephen Grace]

'Firstly, thank you for agreeing to be part of this interview. Can you introduce yourself and give a little background on how you came to be there on that day in 2015?'

[Sally Bassett – Social Change Activist]

'Sure. My name is Sally Bassett. I was formally the CSR manager for one of the large global banks. I would rather not give their name, if that's ok. I don't want any further legal problems.'

[Stephen Grace]

'Okay, but could you just elaborate for everyone what a CSR manager is, and why you were there in that room on that day?'

[Sally Bassett – Social Change Activist]

'Sure. CSR stands for Corporate Social Responsibility. My role at the bank was to engage programs internally to drive diversity and inclusion across the many personal backgrounds within the bank's workforce. It was also to ensure that the bank was acting in an ethical and responsible manner, and that we were having a positive impact on the world.

'I was at the Emerging Markets conference that day because I was always on the lookout for new ideas. Completely new ideas are hard to come by, so we often scouted for best practice in our industry and across the world. We then adapted those ideas into the bank. So, I was there to find out how other financial institutions were handling Corporate Social Responsibility initiatives'.

[Stephen Grace]

'And what was it about that session specifically that made you want to attend it?'

[Sally Bassett – Social Change Activist]

'I remember circling Susan's speech in red pen on the agenda that morning because it mentioned "Human Capital", which frankly is the only type of capital that I care about. In every other speech that day there might be a line or two about social impact, but usually they were just finance guys ticking boxes. Susan's speech, to me anyway, stood out above all others, even in the agenda.'

[Audio Archive of the Susan Mitchell Speech]

'Good afternoon, ladies and gentlemen. My name is Susan Mitchell. Today, not only am I going to show you a way to make a fantastic return on your investment, but I am also going to show you that you can help save the world while you do it. We like to think that, one day when you contemplate about your legacy and the positive impact that you have had on this planet, my Human Capital World Fund may be just how you did it.'

[Sally Bassett – Social Change Activist]

'My gosh, those first few lines of her speech. I know others say that she started slowly, but to me, she had me at "Good afternoon". By the end of it I just wanted to find out all I could about her.'

[Stephen Grace]

'And what *did* you find out about Susan Mitchell?'

[Sally Bassett – Social Change Activist]

'That she had been very successful, for one. She had worked her way up from executive assistant to owner and CEO of a funds management company. I found out that she had been involved in a lot of humanitarian efforts around the world. There were photos of her in South Africa, Ethiopia and Singapore, meeting with important men. I was just so impressed with who she was and what she was trying to do. To this day, I still tell people I was there, in that room from the video, where she gave that original speech. Even with everything I know now, I still consider myself lucky to have been there. She was so elegant.'

[Stephen Grace]

'So, how did you come to be involved in her business?'

[Sally Bassett – Social Change Activist]

'After seeing someone like her, who is honestly trying to change the world, going back to my bank job seemed so petty. I had a title next to my name, but I was literally just writing programs to make the bank look better to its shareholders. It wasn't the same as saving orphans in Africa. I came into this line of work because I wanted to have a positive impact on the world. I wanted to get involved. To get my hands dirty, so to speak. So ... one day I just plucked up a bit of courage and called Susan out of the blue. I left a message with her assistant saying who I was and why I would love to speak with her. I honestly thought that would be the last I would hear of it, but I got a call back from that receptionist within fifteen minutes. Susan and I had a lunch meeting scheduled for the following week.'

[Stephen Grace]

'Can you tell us a little about what happened at the lunch?'

[Sally Bassett – Social Change Activist]

'She was late. It's funny when I look back. I was waiting for twenty minutes before I got a call from her assistant, without an apology, saying that she would be another twenty minutes yet. She was forty minutes late all up. It was a long time to be sitting by myself in that restaurant. I felt like

16

I had been stood up for a date [laughs]. Looking back now, I think it was probably a test.'

[Stephen Grace]

'You think that her being late was her way of testing your commitment?'

[Sally Bassett – Social Change Activist]

'Perhaps a test of my personal resolve. I probably would have waited there all afternoon if she had asked me to. I was so keen to meet her. I guess that just made me exactly the sort of person that Susan wanted around her. People invested in an outcome, who would do whatever it takes to get the result they wanted.'

[Stephen Grace]

'It's funny that you are saying you would do whatever it took to meet her, yet you had only ever seen her on stage that one time. I don't understand why you were already so committed.'

[Sally Bassett – Social Change Activist]

'That is because you weren't there that day. You have seen a grainy video of her online and you think you know who she is, but you don't. You watch it and you already have an expectation. I didn't know her at all that first day, but I felt like I had a sense of who she might become.'

[Narrator]

Over the coming weeks I would hear this same rhetoric from many of Miss Mitchell's employees and people closest to her. As far as they were all concerned, I was an outsider. I was one of those that didn't understand the woman, or what she was trying to achieve. I would have to learn to be more understanding of their fanaticism in the future.

[Stephen Grace]

'Okay … but you realize she has disappeared with a lot of hardworking people's money. It is not just super-rich rock stars out of pocket. You might understand why questions are being asked.'

[Sally Bassett – Social Change Activist]

'I can. I just think it is sad that instead of everyone asking, "Is Susan Mitchell okay?" they are all asking, "Where is my money?" They seem to have forgotten that the reason they agreed to invest in the Human Capital World Fund in the first place was to help the people of the world. Now a single person's life is potentially in danger and all they can think about is their money. Their investment suited them just fine when they could post about it on social media to all their followers.'

[Narrator]

There are many theories about what happened to Susan Mitchell and how she disappeared. Many think that she simply took the money and ran. However, there are some who believe there is a bigger conspiracy at play. That it might be mob related or even that someone has kidnapped her for a ransom. We will investigate these theories in future episodes. At that point in our interview I was concerned that I was losing Sally Bassett, and there was still so much more that I wanted to know. I parked the obvious follow-up question, 'What do you think happened to Susan Mitchell?' for another time for fear that it would cut our interview too short.

[Stephen Grace]

'I want to hear more about your first lunch with Miss Mitchell. Do you mind telling us some more about that time?'

[Sally Bassett – Social Change Activist]

'I'm sorry, I get upset because I am honestly worried about her as a person, and nobody else seems to care.'

[Stephen Grace]

'I understand, and you're right when you say that we don't know her like you do. However, I would like to, so perhaps you can help us understand?'

[Sally Bassett – Social Change Activist]

'Okay. So, she finally turned up forty minutes after we had originally agreed to meet. I was actually due back at work from my lunch break, so it took a bit of commitment on my part to still be sitting there at that table. But, having waited so long already, I wasn't about to run off. She looked lovely. I had dressed up, but I still felt under-dressed. She was in another of her pantsuits, which she always wore. Red that time, though. It was just like those ads you see on TV where everyone is wearing brown or gray, and then a beautiful woman walks through the scene in a bright red dress. I didn't know if I was meeting with a CEO or with a model. We introduced ourselves and then she just started asking me questions. Really, they were amazing, some of them. I thought she was joking, but she never took her eyes off me for a second. I will tell you now, in all my years, I have never been under a spell like I was that day.

She could have asked and I would have told her anything.'

[Stephen Grace]

'Can you give us an example of a few of the questions that she asked you, that you thought were a little strange?'

[Sally Bassett – Social Change Activist]

'She asked me about my father, and right out of the blue I told her he had been an alcoholic. I don't tell anyone that! I told her I hadn't seen him since he hit my mother when I was six years old and we both left him. I told her I still sometimes get a little scared when a door opens too suddenly because I think it might be him. We spoke about that for a while, and although she deflected personal questions that I had asked her, it was quite clear that she understood abuse and how it can change people. She asked me about my current job and wanted to know everything about it. I told her I liked it and had a few friends there but felt unfulfilled working for a bank. We would have spoken for two hours, and through it all, she made me feel like I was the most important person in the room. She had an amazing way of doing that.

'Finally, she turned to me, and asked me outright, "Why did you want to meet me?".'

[Stephen Grace]

'And what did you say?'

[Sally Bassett – Social Change Activist]

'I still remember the words. I said to her, "I saw your presentation at the Emerging Markets seminar. I want to work for you. I want to help you make the world a better place".'

[Stephen Grace]

'And what did she say to that?'

[Sally Bassett – Social Change Activist]

'Well… she went silent for a few minutes. Luckily I said nothing, or it would have been over right there. We have rules about that stuff. Then finally, she said that she desperately needed help but wasn't sure if I was the right person for the job. That she needed people she could trust with her life, and not just workers. I tried to tell her that was me, but my word wasn't enough. She asked me to take out my phone and call my boss right there on the spot and resign my position effective immediately.

Which I did. She then suggested that I call my friends at the bank when I got home to say goodbye because it was unlikely that I would see them for some time.'

[Stephen Grace]

'And you did all of this? For a woman you hardly knew?'

[Sally Bassett – Social Change Activist]

'Yep, and you know what? Even after everything I have been through, I would do it all over again. You just can't compare my old life with my new one.'

[Narrator]

I was beginning to wonder if I was investigating a fraud or a cult. On discussing this with one of my colleagues who has investigated cults he mentioned that it is cultlike behaviour to ask new recruits to prove themselves before being permitted entry into the group. It is also cultlike behaviour to remove the influence of the outside world. This case was getting stranger by the moment.

[Stephen Grace]

'What did she offer you for all of that sacrifice on your part?'

[Sally Bassett – Social Change Activist]

'She made me 'Head of Philanthropy' of her business. She also gave me a seventy per cent pay rise from my old job and a new car to get around in. I didn't even ask for the car. I asked her where the nearest bus stop to her office was and she said it wouldn't matter because she was going to get me a car. Two days later, before my car had even arrived, I was on a plane to oversee her humanitarian efforts in South Africa.'

[Stephen Grace]

'Wow, I'm not surprised that you took the job. Did you ever invest any of your own money in that fund?'

[Sally Bassett – Social Change Activist]

'I tried, but she never let me. She said my effort and time were a big enough investment already.'

[Narrator]

We will hear more from Sally Bassett in future episodes, but I had one more question for her that day.

[Stephen Grace]

'What do you think happened to Susan Mitchell?'

[Sally Bassett – Social Change Activist]

'I have been asked that question by many people now, and I honestly don't know the answer. I have a feeling that she is somewhere in a world of trouble, and that keeps me awake at night. I know there were inconsistencies in her story, but you need to understand Susan like I do to understand why that might be. I hope you find her and get your answers. At least then I will know that she is okay. But I have a feeling that the world will never see her again.'

[Narrator]

I didn't get the smoking gun or hot lead that I was hoping to get in that interview. Instead, what I got was an introduction to the cult of Susan Mitchell – The Woman Who Stole The World. Over the coming weeks, stories like this would paint a picture of Susan Mitchell as an intriguing character, who could cast a spell on so many people and demand cult-like loyalty from her staff and customers.

In the next episode we will hear from another pivotal member of Susan Mitchell's team who was swept up into her business in those early days. A man who says he created the financial modelling that the Human Capital World Fund would trade with.

[Unknown Male Voice]

'Yeah, I was there at the conference. There was a minor error in the calculations on one of her slides that she presented. Most people would not have noticed it, but then again, I'm not most people. I rang her up three days later and asked her about it and she offered me a job, on the spot. It wasn't a mistake at all – it was a test. Susan Mitchell didn't make mistakes.'

[Narrator]

We will hear his story and much more next episode.

We are still encouraging anyone who has been involved with Susan Mitchell in any way to contact us. If you invested money in her fund, know her personally, or even if you are Miss Mitchell herself and are listening to this, we would very much like to talk to you. You may be the missing link that could tie everything together.

It is often said that 'Not everything is as it seems' but with Susan Mitchell – The Woman Who Stole The World – nothing *was* as it seemed.

Now, a word from our sponsors …

EPISODE 4:
THE MATHEMATICIAN

[Narrator]

Who was the mysterious Susan Mitchell – The Woman Who Stole The World? And how was she able to convince so many people to invest hundreds of millions of dollars into her Human Capital World Fund before disappearing off the face of the earth with everyone's money?

Join me, Stephen Grace, as I attempt to find out.

So far in this series we have been focusing on the people that either knew or met with Susan Mitchell in the very early stages of her business. Specifically, we have met Dylan Clarke, the talent agent, who would introduce Miss Mitchell to some of his wealthiest clients at a party which you will hear about in an upcoming episode.

We have also heard from Sally Bassett the Social Change Activist who became the Head of Philanthropy for the Human Capital World Fund. Both Dylan Clarke and Sally Bassett were present at the original presentation that Susan Mitchell gave back in October 2015 at the Emerging Markets Financial conference.

Before we can progress with this story, there is one more key member of Miss Mitchell's team that was there that first day and we will meet him now.

[Unknown Male Voice]

'Yeah, I was there – at the conference. There was a minor error in one of the calculations on her slides that caught my attention. Most people would not have noticed it, but then again, I'm not most people.'

[Stephen Grace]

'Can I get you to introduce yourself and give a little background on how you came to be there on that day in 2015?'

[Mathias Lagrange – Mathematician]

'My name is Mathias Lagrange. I am a freelance mathematician. And yes, I realize the irony that my first name is Math-ias and that I am a Mathematician.'

[Narrator]

I'm glad that he did because, until that point, I hadn't. Try to picture an adult version of Harry Potter. His head is just a little large for the rest of his body, which is not all that surprising once you get to know him. He once confessed to me, and I agree, that he could do with a little time in sun. When news of my investigation into the Human Capital World Fund first broke, Mathias Lagrange called me directly. I'm not sure where he got my number from, but he seems resourceful. When he introduced himself over the phone, he seemed upset that I did not immediately recognize his name, or the role that he played in creating the fund itself. In my defence, it was still early stages in our investigations and to that point we still did not know what we did not know.

[Mathias Lagrange – Mathematician]

'I like to go to those finance events because it is the best way for me to find work. I have worked independently for many of the major banks over the past ten years. Usually on a short-term contractual basis because none of them could afford me full time.'

[Narrator]

He must be good if a bank can't afford him. Unlike Dylan Clarke, I did not test Mathias's back story because I got the sense very early on that it wouldn't matter if he was truly the precious resource that he made himself out to be. His story begins for us at Susan Mitchell and not before.

[Stephen Grace]

'Mathias, you say that you saw an error in Susan Mitchell's slides?'

[Mathias Lagrange – Mathematician]

'I usually only pay attention to the slides covered in numbers, because they tell me everything I need to know. However, on this occasion one of her other slides caught my attention because she referenced the name of an algorithm that I once had some experience with. I won't bother trying to explain it to you because we don't have the time, and you probably wouldn't understand it anyway. But later in her presentation, when she finally put up her real numbers slide, I could see that there was no way that the algorithm that she spoke of could deliver the numbers that she had projected.'

[Stephen Grace]

'Did you think about calling her out on it publicly?'

[Mathias Lagrange – Mathematician]

'Understand that I see mistakes in people's figures all the time. First, I ask myself, "Do I care?" which really means, "Is there money in it for me?". If I think that by talking to them offline and offering my services I may get an employment opportunity, then yes, I will make contact. If they choose not to hire me and I see the same mistake again, I go in for the kill. However, If I think that there is a potential that they are purposely misrepresenting their figures to con people, I may just go after them publicly. It helps build my credentials as a giant killer. With Susan's numbers that day though, there was something strange about it. It was less of an error and more of a code, so I held my tongue. Nobody wants to see a smartarse from the crowd destroy the pretty woman on a stage. No matter how right you are. I've learned that lesson before.'

[Stephen Grace]

'So, after you saw the inconsistency in her numbers, what did you do?'

[Mathias Lagrange – Mathematician]

'I rang her up three days later and asked to speak to her financial controller. She told me she did all her own numbers. I thought it was a joke at first, so I challenged her about it. To my surprise, she answered every single question that I put to her perfectly and then asked me a few of her own. She offered me a job, on the spot. It was never a mistake at all on those original slides. Susan Mitchell did not make mistakes. It was bait, to find herself a worthy mathematician. I started working for her two days later.'

[Stephen Grace]

'What job function did you do for her?'

[Mathias Lagrange – Mathematician]

'I think she was tiring of being everything to everyone. She had come up with this financial model for the Human Capital World Fund all by herself. Which I'll admit that, even by my standards, was extremely clever. It was my job to take over that clever model and make it a financial masterpiece.'

[Stephen Grace]

'Do you think you achieved that aim?'

[Mathias Lagrange – Mathematician]

'Absa-fucking-lutely!'

[Stephen Grace]

'Then where is all the money? The hundreds of millions of dollars that were invested?'

[Mathias Lagrange – Mathematician]

'For starters, not hundreds of millions, try billions of dollars. That's how successful my model was. Second, how the hell should I know? I just create the numbers. I don't own the bank accounts or make the trades.'

[Stephen Grace]

'Who specifically did that role?'

[Mathias Lagrange – Mathematician]

'Susan herself. Nobody else had access to the money.'

[Stephen Grace]

'Let me make sure I get this right. You took her original trading strategy and, in your words, "Turned it from a clever idea into a masterpiece". Then you gave it back to Susan and she made the trades and the philanthropic investments around the world?'

[Mathias Lagrange – Mathematician]

'That is correct, yes, I'm not a trader. It takes a special type of skill to crunch the numbers, make future predictions and generate strategy as I do. It is why I earn so much money. I have a unique collection of talents which I bring together. I am writing a book on it at the moment, because I think people will look back on this one day and want to understand how I did it. However, it also takes another type of skill to get the market trades just right and contract the work that we invested in around the world the way they did. I had nothing to do with that part of the business, which is why I always tell people I do not know where their money is.'

[Stephen Grace]

'But once the strategy left your hands, didn't you ever check that she was carrying out your wishes? How did you know if your calculations paid out?'

[Mathias Lagrange – Mathematician]

'I could see that they carried out the investments because you would see Sally visiting sites all around the world. I would say that it makes sense to invest three million dollars in Afghanistan, and two weeks later I see a picture of Sally in Afghanistan cutting a blue ribbon on a new site.'

[Stephen Grace]

'That's okay for the philanthropic investments, but what about the financial trades? That is the money that everyone is looking for right now.'

[Mathias Lagrange – Mathematician]

'Susan kept a computer ledger. At the end of every month, she would print them out and we would sit down and go through them one by one.'

[Stephen Grace]

'So, you are telling me that all you ever saw of the investment strategy that she created and that you "turned into a masterpiece" was a computer printout that she brought to you?'

[Mathias Lagrange – Mathematician]

'… Yes.'

[Narrator]

This is the man that would be by the side of Susan Mitchell in all her Human Capital presentations around the world. He would also be in all her customer meetings and front and centre whenever the fund's validity got called into question. His ability to debate the merits of their fund against the heavyweights of the financial world would earn him the nickname 'The Pitbull'.

I was beginning to wonder if this self-proclaimed 'mathematical genius' was actually all he was cracked up to be. Perhaps in those numbers that Susan presented to him, he simply saw what he, and Susan Mitchell herself, wanted him to see.

I would need to do a lot more digging before I could answer any of these questions. But that day I had one more important question to ask him.

[Stephen Grace]

'What do you think happened to Susan Mitchell?'

[Mathias Lagrange – Mathematician]

'She is dead, or somewhere being held against her will.'

[Stephen Grace]

'What makes you think that?'

[Mathias Lagrange – Mathematician]

'Because if she wasn't, she would have taken me with her. I am way too valuable to her to be left behind.'

[Narrator]

For a man that had been so sure of every word, this last sentence was the only one that did not quite ring true. Perhaps Mathias was questioning how big his impact on the Human Capital World Fund and Susan Mitchell had actually been. Was he really the financial genius that he thought he was? Or, was he just an arrogant fool playing with numbers? It was clear what he wanted to believe.

We will hear more from Mathias Lagrange in future episodes. He was kind enough to talk us through an outline of the financial structure of the Human Capital World Fund, in a way that us mere mortals might understand. Only then can we understand what made it so alluring to investors.

We will also hear from another former employee of Susan Mitchell. Another finance industry veteran who would question the nature of the business that they were in and where the money was going only to be swept up under her spell.

In the next episode we will hear more about Dylan Clarke – the talent agent – and some of his talented clientele. We will hear about the lead-up to the night of the infamous party, where Susan Mitchell and her Human Capital World Fund found fertile ground to grow into her multi-million-dollar investment business.

[Dylan Clarke – The Talent Agent]

'When Susan switched on, her ability to work the room was better than any I've ever seen. They were lining up to talk to her.'

[Mathias Lagrange – Mathematician]

'We came up with a strategy for the party the day before. Divide and conquer. She was in charge of passion; I was in charge of fact.'

[Unknown Male Voice]

'Ha! I grew up on the streets. I know a hustle when I see one. You know what, I invested anyway. I just wanted to see how high she could fly.'

[Narrator]

We are still encouraging anyone who has been involved with Susan Mitchell to contact us. If you invested money in her fund, know her personally, or even if you are Miss Mitchell herself and are listening to this, we would very much like to talk to you. You may be the missing link that could tie everything together.

It is often said that 'Not everything is as it seems' but with Susan Mitchell – The Woman Who Stole the World – nothing *was* as it seemed.

Now, a word from our sponsors …

EPISODE 5:
THE PARTY PLANNER

[Narrator]

Humanitarian, investment genius or charlatan? Who was the mysterious Susan Mitchell – The Woman Who Stole The World? And how was she able to convince so many people to invest hundreds of millions of dollars into her Human Capital World Fund before disappearing off the face of the earth with everyone's money?

Join me, Stephen Grace, as I attempt to find out.

Last episode, we met Mathias Lagrange. Mathias was the self-professed mathematical genius who worked for Miss Mitchell to further develop their ground-breaking financial model for her Human Capital Fund. He would also become one of its most vocal supporters. But looking back now, it is hard to say exactly how many of the recommendations his investment formula made were actually applied to their business investments. We could not find any computer records or paper trails to support his claims or otherwise. Only Miss Mitchell herself would know the answer to that question but she is not answering anyone's calls and is currently nowhere to be found. For now, all we can do is keep searching for answers in other places.

In today's episode we will hear more from Mathias Lagrange, but also from Dylan Clarke, the talent agent that Susan Mitchell plucked from the crowd on her now infamous opening presentation at the Emerging Market Financial Conference back in 2015.

[Stephen Grace]

'Dylan, in our previous chat, you said something that caught my attention. You said "I did something that I think changed history. I invited her to a party".'

[Dylan Clarke – The Talent Agent]

'Ha-ha … did I? I have said it before. Whenever I pluck someone from obscurity and offer them a contract, I feel like I'm changing the course of history. If it wasn't for me, they might never get to the heights that they might get to. Their children may have never gone to college, or receive health care, so you will need to forgive me if I get a little egotistical sometimes. With Susan I may overplay my role in her history, but without me she would not have secured access to the people she did. The people with money. That party was where they all met.'

[Stephen Grace]

'Do you think that is what she saw in you? Access to a network?'

[Dylan Clarke – The Talent Agent]

'Who can know what draws us to people? Maybe I saw something in her as well. I am a busy man after all, but I always made time for her. You think I don't ask myself that question? I did, many times. Even before she disappeared, "What is she doing with an old guy like me?". I will say this: it may have been what she wanted at the start, but I truly believe that I became more to her. She didn't need to keep her contact with me. She had her access by that stage. But she still called me for advice. Even when I had nothing left to offer her.'

[Stephen Grace]

'Like what, for instance?'

[Dylan Clarke – The Talent Agent]

'Well, sometimes she needed personal advice, life advice, business advice. She even came to me in tears a few times. I think I became like a father figure to her in some ways. It was hard for her. She told me she didn't have a family growing up. And she was fast becoming this Wonder Woman Innovator, so she couldn't just have a public meltdown. She needed to vent in private to people she could trust.'

[Stephen Grace]

'Did she ever tell you about the financial workings of her business?'

[Dylan Clarke – The Talent Agent]

'No, not like that. She had her own financial people for that stuff. If she needed financial advice from me, why would I be giving her my money? No, she had some people issues and got a little unwell at one point which I helped her through.'

[Narrator]

At that point in our interview, I desperately want to ask more questions about his personal relationship with Susan Mitchell. But I was also concerned that, given his fatherly attitude towards her, I might make him defensive if I try to get him to share too much personal information too early. So instead, I make a mental note to remember their personal connection and see if I can use it to probe deeper into her mental state in the future. I also want to hear more about the party where everything happened, so I pushed on in that vein.

[Stephen Grace]

'Can you tell me more about the Party you alluded to earlier?'

[Dylan Clarke – The Talent Agent]

'Sure. I have these parties twice a year. I invite all my new talent along and they get to meet my more senior guys. If possible, I try to get some of my global players there. They are the guys that I mentioned earlier that leave me to go off and become big stars. I do that so that they can all learn from each other and help foster a sense of family among my talent. Some of the junior guys become supporting acts for the bigger names and everyone wins. At every party, I try to bring a wildcard guest along that might help them all. For that party I invited Susan along because I wanted to help her business grow but also because I wanted her to help my people get educated about how to deal with their new wealth.'

[Stephen Grace]

'How long was it between you meeting her at the conference and the party itself?'

[Dylan Clarke – The Talent Agent]

'About three weeks. But we met once again before the party so that she could prepare. She said that she didn't want to let me down. So, she asked for a list of exactly who would come.'

[Stephen Grace]

'She was doing her research?'

[Dylan Clarke – The Talent Agent]

'Yes, Susan always did her research. She worked harder than anyone else I have ever met in that regard. Everything planned precisely. Nothing left to chance.'

[Narrator]

We are going to change lanes now to get an insight into the planning itself. Here is Mathias Lagrange, the Mathematical engineer that constructed a new version of the fund.

[Mathias Lagrange – Mathematician]

'It was my second week working with Susan when she called me into her office. I had been going through the financial structure of the fund and I had a few suggestions that I wanted to get her input on. Most of it was still her plan at that stage, but I had suggested a few super-tweaks which would make her algorithm completely market ready. I will add that it also enabled her to squeeze an extra 7 per cent output from the investments, while reducing costs by 9 per cent. With those changes we would call the fund algorithm HCV2 [Human Capital Version 2]. I have dedicated an entire chapter to it in my book, where I break it all down piece by piece to help people understand it.

'Anyway, that is what I wanted to talk to her about, but she had other things on her mind that day. She told me I had one week to make the fund completely bulletproof. "Fortify, then fine tune", she said. She then told me we would go to a party and that we would pitch the fund to potential customers. She then told me that from that point on I had to do everything like people's lives were at stake.'

[Stephen Grace]

'What do you think she meant by that?'

[Mathias Lagrange – Mathematician]

'I don't know. She said things like that sometimes. She told me once that sometimes I got so carried away with the numbers that I forgot that there was a "Human" in Human Capital. To be honest, I never forgot, I just didn't care. It was just a game of numbers to me.

'But I had to be the one to take those numbers seriously because I knew something that they didn't. That if the numbers were not right, then there would be no flying around the world building bridges and getting their photos in the paper with orphans. Without someone always looking at the numbers there would be no company at all.

'So, while I may have forgotten the "Human" in Human Capital, you could say that sometimes Susan and Sally forgot the "Capital" in it. Maybe that is why we worked so well together, the three of us. We were like three legs on a stool, fine if all three of us were around. However, you take Susan out of the equation and me and Sally hardly said a word to each other. Susan was the glue.'

[Stephen Grace]

'What about the planning for the party? Was Sally there for that?'

[Mathias Lagrange – Mathematician]

'Yes, Sally and I started work the same day, so we were both a week in by that stage. Susan brought us both into the boardroom the next morning and sent all the other staff home so we had no distractions. She then told us some of the background of her meeting with Dylan and whoever his clientele was at the time. She then went through a list of everyone that was going to be there on the night.

'Man, some of those names were unbelievable. JC Chains, Veronique, these were the people we heard on the radio every day. Do you even know how hot Veronique is? If not, look her up! Seriously, search "Veronique: Live at the Hilton". Everything you need to see is right there in that video.

'We were so excited just to meet them. Well, me and Sally were anyway. To us, and the world, they were superstars, but to Susan they were just people. That's probably why these people flocked to her with stars in their eyes instead of the other way around.'

[Stephen Grace]

'Knowing who was going to be at the party, how did you prepare for the night?'

[Mathias Lagrange – Mathematician]

'As I mentioned earlier, Susan knew her numbers, which is a big compliment coming from me. But that was never where Susan's real genius lay. For her, it was people. She could read people better than anyone I have ever known. We watched videos of the invitees being interviewed. Never performing, because she said that everyone takes on a persona when they are performing. But she said when they are being interviewed, they were vulnerable. And that is where you learn all about them.

'We would watch them together. She would often pause the footage and say, "You see that? You see how he looked away then? He's lying," and then she would scribble notes. To be honest, Sally and I rarely saw anything. We just nodded or shrugged our shoulders. We didn't know her then like we know her now, and we didn't want to cause trouble in our second week on the job. I will say this though: Susan was right about them almost every time. She read people so well.

'She divided all the invitees up between us and we did our research on them separately. Then, when we had all the facts, we would present them to the group. Sally would even pretend to be the women and I would pretend to be the men. I was embarrassed at first. I'm a mathematician – not an actor. But Susan reminded me yet again that lives were at stake, so I just got over myself and I went with it.

'So, there's me going, [in a deep voice] "You need to feel the heartbreak behind the words", trying to be JC, and then Susan would pitch tailored to my character's style. Now and then she would stop and look over her shoulder like she was having a conversation with herself about it. She did that a lot. It was like she had three minds, all working at once and debating the merits of every single move. It is probably what made her so good at stuff.

'We came up with our strategy for the party. Susan and Sally oversaw the "Sizzle", while I was in charge of the "Steak".'

[Narrator]

We will hear more from Mathias Lagrange in later episodes, but I was keen to hear from Sally Bassett on her recollection of that week as well.

[Stephen Grace]

'Sally, what do you remember about the week's lead up to that first party at Dylan Clarke's house?'

[Sally Bassett – Social Change Activist]

'I remember that in my whole life, I have never worked so hard. I have also never had so much fun. And don't let that ego-on-legs Mathias tell you any different. He had fun as well.

'We must have been at it till 9 pm most days. She would order us dinner and we would just work through. Neither of us had anyone at home waiting for us, so why not. Then, at the end of each exhausting day, Susan would walk us to the door and lock the door after us. We would come back at 9 am the next day and she had done hours of extra work after we left. She would be all excited, like. "Hey, look what I found," and we would be like "Do you ever sleep?".

'We each had someone to focus on. Susan had JC, Mathias had

Veronique, and I had Ku-Stom. There is a funny story about him if you dig deep enough. "They" tell you in all the articles that two years earlier Ku-Stom was living on the streets. That he is a real-life rags-to-riches story. But we found a picture of him from two years earlier. Susan looked it over and said, "People living on the streets don't have six-packs". And you know what, she was right. It was just a story that they created for him. We could construct a complete history of him from high school camps to oboe lessons. The guy had been working at the local McDonalds for god's sake. Not on the streets hiding from mobsters as his people will have you believe. It was amazing how much information we could find about each of them once Susan showed us how to look properly. And for the record, if I see another photo of Ku-Stom's six-pack, I think that I'm going to throw up.'

[Stephen Grace]

'What was your plan with all this research?'

[Sally Bassett – Social Change Activist]

'At the end of each day, Mathias and I would present what we learned about our person back to Susan. She would then present all three people back to us. By the end of that week, we thought that we knew them all intimately. At the party itself, our job was to use that information to find a way to engage and introduce them to Susan. We were then to take our lead from her as the conversation flowed. We didn't have a large team at that point, so it was like the three of us against the world. It honestly felt like we were about to go to war.

'I don't know how she kept so much information in that head of hers, but she did. We would go off notes, but not her. She never needed notes.'

[Narrator]

Now we are getting a picture of Susan Mitchell herself. Highly intelligent, methodical, determined. What we still don't know about her, other than where she is, is what her underlying intentions were at this point. Was she planning to steal money from the people she was about to meet, or were her intentions to build the fund and effect some change in the world? I don't believe we will get answers to these questions from Sally Bassett or Mathias Lagrange alone; we will need to speak to more people that knew Miss Mitchell around that time. People that Sally and Mathias themselves may not even know.

In future episodes we will hear more from the night of the party from people that were there. We will also hear more from Dylan Clarke, the talent agent, and even singer Ku-Stom himself has agreed to speak with us, for which we are very grateful.

[Ku-Stom – Singer]

'Ha! I grew up on the streets, you understand. I know a hustle when I see one. You know what, I invested anyway. I just wanted to see how high she would fly.'

[Dylan Clarke – The Talent Agent]

'When Susan switched on, her ability to work the room was better than any I've ever seen. They were lining up to talk to her.'

[Narrator]

Before we get to the party itself however I think it is best for me to get you an overview of the Human Capital Fund itself from the man who says that he created it, or Version 2 of it anyway. So, next episode we will go back to Mathias Lagrange, and he has agreed to share with us a brief excerpt from his upcoming book 'HCV2 and Me!'

We still have some time left if anyone who was connected to Susan Mitchell in any way would like to get in contact with us. If you invested money in her fund, know her personally, or even if you are Miss Mitchell herself, we would very much like to talk to you. You may be the missing link that could tie everything together.

It is often said that 'Not everything is as it seems', but with Susan Mitchell – The Woman Who Stole The World – nothing *was* as it seemed.

Now, a word from our sponsors …

EPISODE 6: THE HUMAN CAPITAL WORLD FUND

[Narrator]

Humanitarian, genius, or charlatan? Who was the mysterious Susan Mitchell – The Woman Who Stole The World? And how was she able to convince so many people to invest hundreds of millions of dollars into her Human Capital World Fund before disappearing off the face of the earth with everyone's money?

Join me, Stephen Grace, as I attempt to find out.

So far we have learnt about Susan Mitchell, the mysterious CEO, from some of the key members of her foundation team. These people were on the ground with her in the early days of the Human Capital World Fund's success and would help Miss Mitchell to shape her business into the global phenomenon that it would become.

In our last episode we heard from Mathias Lagrange and Sally Bassett, the mathematician and the humanitarian who worked for Miss Mitchell, as they described the meticulous planning that they put into the party that, in Dylan Clarke's words, 'would change history'.

Before we get to the events at the party, I think it is important that we all understand the structure of the Human Capital World Fund itself. What was it that made this product so alluring to investors?

In today's episode, we will go back to Mathias Lagrange. Mathias took the algorithm behind the fund which we were told was built by Susan Mitchell, and he adapted it for a global market. The alternative version of that model he famously calls HCV2 [Human Capital Version 2]. Today, Mathias has kindly offered to share with us an excerpt from his upcoming book 'HCV2 and Me' where he discusses what made it so special.

[Mathias Lagrange – Mathematician]

'She had come up with this financial model for the Human Capital World Fund all by herself. Which I'll admit that, even by my standards, was extremely clever. It was my job to take over that clever model and make it a financial masterpiece.'

[Stephen Grace]

'Do you think you achieved that aim?'

[Mathias Lagrange – Mathematician]

'Absa-fucking-lutely!'

[Narrator]

It is worth noting at this point that there is no evidence at all that Susan Mitchell acted on any of the trades that Mathias Lagrange's fancy calculator suggested for her, or for what happened to any of the money that was entrusted to her. These are all matters still being investigated by me and law enforcement.

Having said that, we still feel that it is important that we explain the product itself, as they sold it to investors.

But, before we discuss the Human Capital World Fund specifically, I thought it was important that I first describe to you all what a standard investment fund is so that you can get some context. Bear with me, this can be a little dry. But don't worry, I will try to tell it to you in a way that my elderly mother might understand.

First, the technical explanation.

A standard 'mutual fund' works by many people – investors – pooling their money together and investing it into a 'portfolio of assets'. A fund usually has a 'fund manager' who will allocate the fund's assets and attempt to create a 'capital gain' or 'income' for the investors. Mutual funds give small or individual investors access to a professionally managed investment that they may not have been able to invest in alone.

Now, to put it more simply, a group of people all give their money to a company. That company pools all the money together and invests in things that they hope will outperform the standard interest that you would just earn by having your money in a bank account. That fund would typically collect a fee or a percentage of the profits for themselves. They do this upfront regardless of if the fund does well or not.

Some of these funds are multi-national institutions that collect billions of dollars. Because they are so large the public assume that they are heavily regulated. We as the public also assume that any wrongdoing by these organizations would have been exposed in the media already. And, because we generally trust the large organizations that we give our money to, we feel comfortable that our money is safe in their hands. However, this is not always the case.

Some investors want bigger returns, so they go looking for more agile and less regulated investment firms. This is where things can get interesting. While there are many fine private investment companies out there, there are some that are not as honest as others in their reporting to investors and regulators.

Some, like the Madoff Ponzi schemes, which made off with up to $65 billion dollars of their investors' money, rely solely on the cultlike leaders of the organizations that they represent.

If you are anything like me, an investment prospectus, the eighty-page document they give you with all their terms and conditions on it may as well be written in another language. It is easy to see why some may just decide to trust the celebrity that they see endorsing it and sign their life away without reading the contract.

Now that we know what a standard mutual fund is, let's find out about the Human Capital World Fund. I know that this is dry stuff but please stick with me because it is important to our story.

Let's return to the interview with Sally Bassett.

[Stephen Grace]

'Sally, most of us know what a standard investment fund is. Do you think you could explain to us what made the Human Capital World Fund so different from all the others?'

[Sally Bassett – Social Change Activist]

'Sure, Stephen. Well, first we were an investment fund like any other. The standard structure of any investment is basically the same: customers give us their money and expect that, when they get it back, it will have risen in value. There were a few things that made us different. Typically, when you give a fund your money, you have very little idea what they will do with it. For instance, let's say that you invest all of your money in a fund called GenericX. And after one year, they get you a glorious return on your money. Many might be happy with that result. That is, if you didn't care what they did with that money. What if they took your money and invested it in a cigarette company that gave people cancer? Some people might still not care, as long as they made a profit. Perhaps they smoke themselves? But others, they might not like the thought that their money is funding a company that gives people cancer, no matter how good the returns may be. These investors have a conscience. It was to cater for this type of investor – those with a conscience – that the finance industry created funds called "ethical funds".'

[Stephen Grace]

'So, you say that the Human Capital World Fund is an ethical fund?'

[Sally Bassett – Social Change Activist]

'Of sorts, yes, but there is still much more than that. The problem with a lot of ethical funds is that they take longer to research, and sometimes some of the best investments, while ethical in nature, don't make a profit. Some of these funds don't perform as well as a standard investment. Moreover, these ethical funds usually have much higher fees that most standard funds because of the research involved. So, you could say that some customers pay through the nose for their conscience.

'Our fund was ethically based, yes, but offered so much more than a standard ethical fund. Our fund had low fees because we didn't want to take money from those in need. Our fund generated better-than-average returns for clients because our payoffs were bigger, financially and in social impact. Our fund changed the world.'

[Stephen Grace]

'But how did it do that? I mean, I've seen all the pictures on the website, and in your brochures. But I still don't truly understand what you were selling.'

[Sally Bassett – Social Change Activist]

'Okay, I will get to the point. Did you know that there was a report done a few years back, that said for every one dollar you invest in a refugee you get two dollars in return through productivity?

'Imagine for a moment that you were very smart, and you created a model – an algorithm – that could find an opportunity like no other and could run projections on what outcomes might come from a small investment. A model that looks at underdeveloped nations and searches for ways to improve a social environment while unlocking true financial value at the same time. True value for the human race!

'Let me explain.

'Let's say that you pick a spot somewhere in Uganda where there is nothing. The people that live there live on the poverty line with no running water. Perhaps our algorithm senses opportunity, raises a flag and we act. So, one day we come along and invest a small amount of our investors' money to build a well or set up a solar water-generator for that village. Suddenly, the people in that village no longer need to march for four hours each day across risky terrain to fetch water. These people now have a life.'

[Stephen Grace]

'I still don't understand how that returns money for your investors.'

[Sally Bassett – Social Change Activist]

'That's because at this point it doesn't, but we have already done a small good for the world. It is the chain reaction that this causes that creates the financial return.

'Now that the villagers have a life, we want to teach them how to be self-sufficient and self-reliant. So, we help them build farms around sustainable crops, or extract resources from their surroundings. Suddenly, for such a small investment from us, these people have meaningful work and an income. They develop industry. Once they have industry, we connect them with businesses that require their goods and services, and through that negotiation we make our return. And I can assure you it is a much higher return than the standard two-dollar return for every one dollar invested in a refugee. It can be up to three, four, five, even ten dollars. The sky is the limit.'

[Stephen Grace]

'Some might say you are setting them up so that you can steal their local resources.'

[Sally Bassett – Social Change Activist]

'No, we are setting them up for their future so that they can generate value from their resources. We don't own their businesses, they do. We might negotiate to buy their goods at a lower rate, but we do it for the long term, which enables them to secure meaningful long-term work, sometimes across generations.'

[Stephen Grace]

'But the research and setup times must take years before you get your returns.'

[Sally Bassett – Social Change Activist]

'Not when you have done it as many times as we have. And not when you have Susan Mitchell making the calls. She has a way of making things happen.

'Mind you, that was just one type of project that we did. We did another where we signed a JV [joint venture] with a sneaker manufacturer to clean up the plastics from the ocean. Almost every little piece of plastic that we pulled out of the ocean together they bought from us to recycle and create a new line of premium sneakers. They win through cheaper raw materials, positive brand recognition, and higher profits. We win through project management and third-party contracting services. The world wins through cleaner oceans and funkier shoes.'

[Stephen Grace]

'Who is this company? Where are those villages in Kenya? Show me proof that any of this actually happened.'

[Sally Bassett – Social Change Activist]

'I can't. I have signed a corporate and personal non-disclosure agreement. These companies want the world to think that it was all their ideas. It would undermine the confidence of a town for me to say that they couldn't have achieved all they have without the white man's money. They deserve better than that, and we have always been okay with letting the world take the credit.'

[Narrator]

It was clear that Sally Bassett was still well and truly under the spell of her former employer, Susan Mitchell. The problem we faced as an investigative team was that there had been early profits. Big ones too. Some of the early investors, who Susan would meet at that party, confirmed as much for me. There were photographs of Miss Mitchell in South Africa, Ethiopia and Singapore next to presidents and people of influence. You can see them all smiling and cutting tape on new building sites.

The problem is that outside of the photos there is no financial paper trail to prove any of it. I still had many questions about the fund that I wasn't sure Sally could answer. So, I put them to Mathias Lagrange.

[Stephen Grace]

'How did you select where to invest? Who made those decisions?'

[Mathias Lagrange – Mathematician]

'Mathematics made those decisions. We simply interpreted the information that the algorithm gave us. As I said to you previously, Susan's initial equations were really quite good. So good, in fact, that it took me a time to even accept that they came from her and not some sixty-year-old male mathematics professor. You may think that I'm being sexist but until that point no other woman had even got close to having a conversation with me on some of this stuff.'

[Narrator]

I could only imagine the number of women desperately brushing up on their mathematics just so they could impress Mathias Lagrange.

[Mathias Lagrange – Mathematician]

'She was not quite at my level, but she was worthy. Remember, this was more than just a financial investment to some. It was a badge of honour. People put their association with us on their websites as a symbol of the type of person they were. They wanted to show themselves as not just some rich dude, but someone who cared about the world enough to put their money where their mouth was.'

[Stephen Grace]

'But how did they track the performance of their investments? We have found no link at all to any of the humanitarian efforts that you say you invested in.'

[Mathias Lagrange – Mathematician]

'They could track every dollar that they invested with us right down to the project. We had an online portal to track it all. You don't realize how powerful that was. For instance, let's say you are Ku-Stom and you give us one million dollars to invest. You can see the investment that we made in a small village in Uganda, but you can also see that it has stalled. Perhaps the local militia are stealing resources, killing anyone who tries to help. Susan makes a few calls and the next thing you know, Ku-Stom flies in on his private just to meet the president of that country and perform in a free concert. The people see their ruler shaking hands with a rock star and the rock star's followers six million social media followers see their star with a president. They get all of that if they guarantee the security of the project. Everybody wins and the value of the investment skyrockets.'

[Narrator]

Once again there is a deflection. We look for proof of investment and they offer online portals, confidentiality agreements, and social media posts. It was getting easier to understand the allure of the Human Capital World Fund. Especially for those who wanted to do something meaningful with their money but didn't have the time or knowledge required to dig into the detail or require any proof.

I want to give the last word to Dylan Clarke, who was the Talent Agent, that Susan Mitchell plucked from the crowd of her now infamous opening presentation at the Emerging Market Financial Conference back in 2015.

[Stephen Grace]

'Dylan, why do you think your clients invested their money in Susan Mitchell's fund?'

[Dylan Clarke – The Talent Agent]

'I guess you have to ask yourself what was missing in the investors themselves that drove them to this product? Maybe getting paid millions of dollars just to sing a song that took you a day to record is not enough for some people. They look for other ways to prove their value to the world.'

[Narrator]

Was it the so-called humanitarian impact, the profits generated for its investors, or simply the magnetism of Susan Mitchell herself, that brought so many investors to the Human Capital World Fund? Whatever it was, when they came, they all brought their friends and their wallets with them. And they couldn't get enough of what Miss Mitchell was selling.

We will resume our story of Susan Mitchell's meteoric rise through the finances of the rich and famous, and hear more from Mathias Lagrange and Dylan Clarke, in future episodes. We will also hear from another former employee of Susan Mitchell who was one of the first people to question the nature of the business that they were in, and where the money was going.

Next episode we will go back to Dylan Clarke and some of his clientele as they tell their stories of the night of the infamous party where Susan Mitchell and her Human Capital World Fund found fertile ground for her future success.

We are still encouraging anyone who has been involved with Susan Mitchell to contact us. If you invested money in her fund, know her personally, or even if you are Miss Mitchell herself and are listening to this right now, we would very much like to talk to you. You may hold the key to unlock all the mysteries that remain unanswered.

It is often said that 'Not everything is as it seems' but with Susan Mitchell – The Woman Who Stole The World – nothing *was* as it seemed.

Now, a word from our sponsors …

EPISODE 7: KU-STOM

[Narrator]

Who was the mysterious Susan Mitchell – The Woman Who Stole The World? And how was she able to convince so many people to invest hundreds of millions of dollars into her Human Capital World Fund before disappearing off the face of the earth with everyone's money?

So far in this series we have been focusing on the people that knew Susan Mitchell in the foundation stages of her fund. We have also learnt a little of the structure of the investment vehicle that she peddled as the future of socially responsible investing.

[Sally Bassett – Head of Philanthropy]

'That would be a true value for investors but also for the human race!'

[Narrator]

We have also heard about the extraordinary lengths that Miss Mitchell went to in her preparations for what would be her introduction to the world of the rich and famous.

In this episode, we will find out about the events of the night that Dylan Clarke said changed history.

So, without further delay, let's cross to Dylan.

[Stephen Grace]

'Dylan, can you please tell us about the parties that you hosted for your clientele?'

[Dylan Clarke – The Talent Agent]

'I am in the business of making dreams come true for talented people, but for that to happen they first need to have a dream to aspire to. When I take them off the streets, with their beat-up guitars and empty stomachs, some of them just think their dreams are to record a song in a studio and have somebody hear it. Now, if I was a charity, I could make that dream come true for them very easily, but I'm running a business so I need to know that they can generate a return for my investment in them over time. Sometimes I have to look past just the talent alone and see a potential in the person. That is my superpower. When everyone else is looking for talent, I am seeing talent before it has had time to develop, And, when others are listening to singers, I'm hearing behind the words. I'm hearing their emotion, their pain, their sentiment. I hear it all. Sometimes I even hear it before they do.

'Anyway, if I was to pluck them off the streets and tell them they could be the next JC Chains or Veronique, they would think that I was trying to hustle them. So instead, I say, 'Let's just make some music together. Record a few songs and see if the magic finds us,' and sometimes it does. I sit there in that cheap studio and I hear them sing that note that matters, and I think, 'I was right!' Sometimes it takes time for them to develop. They need to believe that others started off just as rough as they did.

'So, every three or four months I throw a party. I invite my new talent, and they get to mingle with my more experienced guys. Maybe we even throw in a superstar for good measure, if I can get them to drop by for a few hours.

'Suddenly, these guys that started from nothing stand up a little taller. The boys get their photo taken with JC or Ku-Stom, or the girls with Veronique. Now they have something to aspire to, they have a bigger dream all of their own.'

[Stephen Grace]

'Remind me, what made you invite Susan Mitchell to your party?'

[Dylan Clarke – The Talent Agent]

'Some of these guys are making money – *real* money. Some for the first time in their lives. Often, they do not know what to do with it. What I have learned over the years is that there is nothing more dangerous than a blooming popstar with too much money. They look at fancy clothes, drugs, fast cars, women or men. And it's that short-term thinking that gets them into trouble. If their careers stall or for some reason they can't perform like they could, their fans can give up on them and move on quickly. Some of them will never reach the heights that they could have. They end up right back where they started, hating everyone, including me. If you don't believe me just have a look at how Ferraris are being sold off cheap by ex-rockstars who are struggling to fund ever-increasing drug habits now that their songs are no longer selling.

'I tell my guys that I want them to still have money in their pockets even when they are old, so I try to help them make better choices. I asked Susan to come along because I thought they could learn from her and maybe invest "a little of their money" somewhere that might do some good for the world.'

[Stephen Grace]

'And did they invest in the Human Capital World Fund?'

[Dylan Clarke – The Talent Agent]

'Yes. But I think it is more appropriate to say they invested in Susan.'

[Narrator]

An enigmatic spokeswoman, an investment company designed to help the world, and a room full of the entertainment industry's newest talent with pockets full of money. I believe the saying is: 'shooting fish in a barrel'.

In Episode 5 we got an insight into the amount of research and planning that Miss Mitchell and her two employees invested into that party. Let's now cross back to one of those employees: Sally Bassett. Sally will talk us through how it played out on the night.

[Sally Bassett – Social Change Activist]

'All that research really helped the three of us play our parts perfectly. My job on the night was to speak to the women, especially Veronique. I was to talk to them about Susan as the company's founder, and what an inspiration she was to me. I spoke briefly about my recent flight to South Africa and the people that Susan and I had been meeting with while we were there. I was told to say my piece and then catch myself and stop. Almost like I had a secret that I didn't want them to know. If they asked me questions about it, I just told them they should watch Susan when she finally got up to give her speech. That I didn't want to steal her thunder.

'You could say I was building hype.'

[Mathias Lagrange – Mathematician]

'Susan said my job was to do what I do best: to let everybody know how clever I was. I was to name drop every institution that I'd worked for in the past, in a way that suggested those roles had all just been development for this moment when I finally got to work for Susan Mitchell. To be honest, it wasn't much of a stretch. It is how I felt then, and still feel now.

'I was not to discuss the fund itself before the presentation, but I needed to leave them feeling that the mere fact that I was involved meant that whatever it was, it would be something special. At that point Susan was happy for me to take full credit for the creation of the algorithm. It would be harder later when more people went back and watched her original presentation online. So now I tell the truth, that she started it but I made it a masterpiece. She was funny. She used to pretend to people that she didn't understand all of it, and then they would say something negative and she would shoot them down in flames. I think part of it also was to make me sound smarter. She never wanted any of the credit.

'My job on the night was to give the entire enterprise credibility.'

[Stephen Grace]

'If you were the credibility and Sally was the hype, what part did Susan play?'

[Mathias Lagrange – Mathematician]

'She was the influence. And she was on fire that night. How she carried herself around that room. That red dress! I tried to find a photo of her from that night but all I could find was a snap of Susan and Veronique. The problem was that Susan had positioned herself so that Veronique was the only person who shone in the photo. Go ask anyone who was there. I don't care how beautiful Veronique is, Susan was the only person anyone was looking at that night.'

[Dylan Clarke – The Talent Agent]

'*Has anyone mentioned the dress?* Yes, well, I won't go on about it but that dress was really something. I'm a happily married man so I will leave it at that, but I'm glad my wife wasn't there. I would have been in some trouble.

'The party kicked off and I could see right away that her people were working the room. I thought it was because they were excited to be meeting famous people but when I got up close to them, I could hear them baiting everyone. People were pulling me aside saying, "Who is this woman? Does she sing?" and I'm responding, "No, she's in finance". They thought I was teasing them. JC got angry with me because he thought I was keeping her a secret.

'They were lining up to talk to her.'

[Narrator]

We were lucky enough to get a little time with another person who was there that night and would later invest in the Human Capital World Fund: singer and international recording artist Ku-Stom, otherwise known as Jerome Johnson.

[Recorded Concert Audio]

'Ladies and gentlemen: the king of the jungle, the A-Pex predator; welcome to the stage, KU-STOM!' [Crowd cheers enthusiastically]

[Narrator]

Our interview with Ku-Stom was fifteen minutes backstage, right before a major concert in front of ten thousand people.

We apologize for the background noise in this recording.

[Stephen Grace]

'Ku-Stom, thank you for sharing a little of your valuable time with us. What can you tell us about Susan Mitchell?'

[Ku-Stom – International Recording Artist]

'Yeah, I got beautiful women. You understand? I click my fingers and five appear in five minutes. Five-in-five, you understand? I'd trade fifteen of them for one of her.'

[Stephen Grace]

'Yes, I understand she was very attractive. But what about her speech at the party that first night? What did you think about that?'

[Ku-Stom – International Recording Artist]

'I grew up on the streets. I know a hustle when I see one, you understand? You know what, I invested anyway. What's money to me? Just another track. I just wanted to see how high she could fly.'

[Narrator]

We are going to pause for a moment and get Sally's take on that comment.

[Sally Bassett – Social Change Activist]

'Ha, did Ku-Stom actually say that? Well, if he says that he knew, and he still did what he did, then he is a bigger crook than any of them. I would think that telling your followers to invest in something you *know* is a hustle in the hopes you might get laid would be illegal. Forget prosecuting Susan. You could lock him up right now. Personally, I don't buy any of it. He believed in it just like I did and just like everyone else.

He is just not man enough to admit it.'

[Narrator]

Ku-Stom would play a pivotal role in the whole affair of Susan Mitchell and the Human Capital World Fund. And although he didn't know it yet, on that day we met, Ku-Stom's troubles in relation to the fund were only just beginning. You will hear more about his role in the affair in upcoming episodes, but for now let's return to the interview where, in that brief space of time, he would share some information with us he would later regret.

[Stephen Grace]

'You say that you knew it was all a hustle, and yet you invested a significant amount of money in the Human Capital World Fund anyway? I don't understand why you would do that.'

[Ku-Stom – International Recording Artist]

'That's because you don't have money. I got money. Money's my bitch. When there is something I want to do, I throw money at it. I didn't throw money at that damn fund just because I care about babies in Africa. I got enough people shaking me down for babies that ain't mine here. I invested because I care for the woman.'

[Stephen Grace]

'But you did so much more than just give her money. You shared photos of you both together online. You endorsed her message to others and encouraged them to give her money as well. You didn't just give her money. You gave her credibility.'

[Ku-Stom – International Recording Artist]

'Yeah, well, when you are Ku-Stom there always someone looking for a photo opp and a slice of the pie. I didn't know the woman would disappear. If she had just hooked up with me, like I told her, she would be safe right now and everybody would have their damn money.'

[Narrator]

I didn't want to leave our meeting that day on an unpleasant note; there was still so much that I wanted to speak to him about in relation to his role in the saga of Susan Mitchell and the Human Capital World Fund.

His assistant pointed to her watch to signify that we are almost out of time.

[Stephen Grace]

'Ku-Stom, what do you think happened to Susan Mitchell?'

[Narrator]

It was the first time in that interview that I had seen him uncomfortable. You may also notice the rock star swagger depart from his voice as he tries to answer.

[Ku-Stom – International Recording Artist]

'I don't know. But, when you are talking about sums of money that large – hundreds of millions of dollars – when someone goes missing it is usually not a good sign. I am very worried about her. You are going to post this out to everyone yeah?'

[Stephen Grace]

'Yes, anyone will be able to listen to it.'

[Ku-Stom – International Recording Artist]

'Well, if you are out there Susan, and you can hear this, you have my number. Just call me, any time day or night and I got you.'

[Narrator]

His assistant, and a screaming crowd of adoring fans, now signals more enthusiastically that our time is up. Ku-Stom still had more that he wanted to discuss with us or perhaps he just liked the attention.

He turned to his assistant before dismissing me.

[Ku-Stom – International Recording Artist]

'Kila, I'm going to go one more round in the ring with this man. Set another one of these interviews up so we have more time to talk. See to it, you understand?'

[Narrator]

His assistant nods and my time with Ku-Stom ends abruptly. I never did get that extra interview.

Regardless of if Ku-Stom knew that Susan Mitchell's Human Capital World Fund was a hustle or not, he seems to have fallen for it hook, line and sinker. And right from their very first encounter at Dylan Clarke's party. He would invest millions of dollars of his own money in the fund but he also encouraged others to invest a lot more. He may have even profited when they did so. Stay tuned, as there is a lot more to uncover in this respect.

In our next episode, we will hear from others who were there that night. We will come to understand the complex relationships that Susan Mitchell would develop with the other recording artists that were there, Veronique and JC Chains.

[Mathias Lagrange – Mathematician]

'Veronique even recorded a film clip where she dressed like Susan. The title of the song was "Shameful". I could never figure out if those two loved or hated each other. I guess that is just women for you.'

[Narrator]

If you know something about any of this, it is not too late. We are still encouraging anyone who was involved with Susan Mitchell to contact us. If you invested money in her fund, know her personally, or even if you are Miss Mitchell herself and are listening to this right now, we would very much like to talk to you. You may hold the key to unlock all the mysteries that remain unanswered.

It is often said that 'Not everything is as it seems' but, with Susan Mitchell – The Woman Who Stole the World – nothing *was* as it seemed.

Now a word from our sponsors …

EPISODE 8: VERONIQUE

[Narrator]

Who was the mysterious Susan Mitchell – The Woman Who Stole The World? And how was she able to convince so many people to invest hundreds of millions of dollars into her Human Capital World Fund before disappearing off the face of the earth with everyone's money?

Last episode we heard about the infamous party at Dylan Clarke's house where Susan Mitchell first rubbed shoulders with Dylan's superstar clientele.

In this episode we will hear more from events of that night, including an insight into the tumultuous relationship between Miss Mitchell and the up-and-coming songbird now three-time Golden Microphone winner, Veronique. We have also been lucky enough to get a bootleg recording of Miss Mitchell's speech from that night from an anonymous source. We will be playing part of that recording for you later also.

Unfortunately, Veronique did not agree to be interviewed for this show, so we will need to draw on the recollections and opinions of others to tell her story.

Veronique, if you are out there listening in, and you would like to give your version of events, then please contact us. Our lines are always open.

[Stephen Grace]

'Mathias, you mentioned in our previous interview that you were assigned to Veronique for that night. What did that entail?'

[Mathias Lagrange – Mathematician]

'There were pretty girls all over Ku-Stom, but as far as I was concerned there were only two women in the room that night: Susan and Veronique.'

[Stephen Grace]

'What about your co-worker Sally?'

[Mathias Lagrange – Mathematician]

'She doesn't count.

'I can tell you, though, that when Veronique and Susan finally came together, it was like thunder meeting lightning. And I don't say that shit lightly.'

[Stephen Grace]

'Can you tell us a little about that first encounter and your part in making it happen?'

[Mathias Lagrange – Mathematician]

'As we had planned, I had been talking to Veronique's people in the lead up to Susan's presentation. It was in the weeks before Veronique's meteoric rise, but she still had her minders even back then. Personally, I think they were trying to keep her in cotton wool and away from Ku-Stom.

'As we had rehearsed the week before, I had to get her minders' approval before I could approach her directly. Susan told me it would be the respectful way to approach someone in her position. After they said "yes", I just went up to her and told her I worked for Susan, and that Susan would be honoured if Veronique would be a guest at the speech later that night. Then I asked if it would be okay for Susan to have ten minutes of her time to thank her personally afterwards.'

[Stephen Grace]

'What was it you were trying to achieve?'

[Mathias Lagrange – Mathematician]

'We wanted her to be an objective listener and not just a face in the crowd who was looking at her watch. We knew that if there was already a plan for them to meet afterwards, that Veronique would have no option but to listen.'

[Stephen Grace]

'And did she agree?'

[Mathias Lagrange – Mathematician]

'Yes. I think that we genuinely intrigued her. She seemed curious to know who Susan was and what she had to say.'

[Narrator]

Let's take a moment to hear more from Dylan Clarke, who was Veronique's agent at that point of time.

[Dylan Clarke – The Talent Agent]

'Actually, there is one thing that I regret from that night. I should have handled Veronique better. I am usually quite careful with fragile egos, and that night should have belonged to Veronique.

'I think I got distracted by Susan and it clouded my mind. Susan ended up being a much bigger figure on the night than I thought she would be. You could say she stole a little of Veronique's thunder. Veronique, though, is a good girl. She did everything right, and her time came. As I promised her it would.'

[Stephen Grace]

'Can you give us a brief insight into the type of woman Veronique is when the camera is not rolling?'

[Dylan Clarke – The Talent Agent]

'She is one of a kind. She has it all. The voice of an angel and the body of a bombshell. And to most people that is what they hear and see. But I will tell you what I saw on that high school stage all those years ago. I saw a beautiful young girl who sings with her eyes. There's a reason people cry listening to her songs, and it is not because of her curves. It is because they feel her heart break. They see it in her eyes when she sings.

'The world might think that her fifteen minutes of fame are up, but I can tell you right now, the world is wrong. Her next album is about to drop, and when it does it is going to break the mold. They will be playing these songs on the radio for the next twenty-five years. You mark my words.'

[Stephen Grace]

'Can you tell us if Veronique agreed to invest in The Human Capital World Fund?'

[Dylan Clarke – The Talent Agent]

'No, that is where I stop. That is her business, not mine.'

[Stephen Grace]

'Then would you say that she and Susan Mitchell became friends?'

[Dylan Clarke – The Talent Agent]

'This … this question is tough to answer. And who am I to say. They were friendly if that is what you mean. They may have met once or twice after. But Veronique wasn't like the boys. She didn't flaunt her relationship with Susan like Ku-Stom. Veronique was always a very guarded young woman when she wasn't singing. She gives you nothing for free.'

[Narrator]

I put the same question to Susan Mitchell's employee Sally Bassett.

[Sally Bassett – Social Change Activist]

'Friends? I don't think that term sums them up right.

'Let me try others on for size. Business associates? No. Peers? No. Adversaries? No. How about Frenemies? Yes, I think I heard that once. Friends and enemies at the same time.

'Every time that they met, Susan would go alone, so we never really saw them together. I know Susan gave Veronique some advice once, which I believe really helped her get out of some type of trouble, but Susan would never discuss it. The only reason that I know is because I overheard Veronique say on a phone call to Susan, "I'm sorry, I didn't know who else to call," as Susan ducked into a meeting room once to be alone. I then heard Susan wind up the call as she was coming out saying, "I'm just glad I could help. You have my direct number, call me anytime".'

[Narrator]

Intrigued, I put this scenario to Dylan Clarke.

[Dylan Clarke – The Talent Agent]

'First, I have heard of it. Maybe some girl trouble, maybe Susan's team made it up. I don't know.

'Veronique always had me if she was ever in trouble. She didn't need anyone else.'

[Narrator]

Veronique never publicly acknowledged her relationship, nor any business dealings, with Susan Mitchell or the Human Capital World Fund. The only time she ever mentioned Susan directly was when pressed during an interview.

[Archival audio – Veronique Interview]

'I think what they're doing is important work for the world and for the people within it. But for today, I'm here to discuss my new album.'

[Stephen Grace]

'Sally, if Susan was giving Veronique advice, then surely they had become friends?'

[Sally Bassett – Social Change Activist]

'I would love to just be able to say "yes", but their relationship was just not that simple. The two of them were complex women. For instance, I once saw Veronique dress and act like Susan in a film clip. You only realize it was an insult when you hear the name of the song. I will not bother repeating it here, but Susan knew it was about her.'

[Stephen Grace]

'And how did Susan react?'

[Sally Bassett – Social Change Activist]

'She reacted by sending over a bunch of flowers with a card saying it was her favourite song yet!'

[Stephen Grace]

'Am I right in assuming that Veronique did not invest in the Human Capital World Fund?'

[Sally Bassett – Social Change Activist]

'Actually, she did. That is the issue. I guess what I am really saying is that it would have been much easier on all of us if she didn't. We were a business, after all, not a friendship network.'

[Narrator]

With Veronique flatly refusing all our requests for interviews, and Susan Mitchell nowhere to be found, we may never know what was discussed between these two mysterious women when they were alone. But that didn't mean there wouldn't be more for us to uncover about their tenuous relationship in the coming months of our investigation. You will hear more about that in future episodes.

For now, we are going to rule a line underneath the relationship between Susan Mitchell and the singer Veronique, because we have one more important person who was there that night. Someone that would come to have a profound impact on Susan Mitchell herself and that of the Human Capital World Fund. That was world-wide sensation and three-times-awarded Recording Artist of the Year JC Chains.

[Dylan Clarke – The Talent Agent]

'The bond between Susan and JC was like no other I've seen. To know him like I do, and to have seen them together how they were, is to understand what I truly mean by this.'

[Narrator]

We will hear more about the beginnings of that bond between Susan and JC Chains next episode.

Before we end today's episode, we have a special surprise for you. Although Dylan Clarke had always insisted on a 'no phone or recording devices' policy at his parties, someone who wishes to remain anonymous had in fact smuggled in a recording device. Their intent was to leak some of the juicier content of the evening to the press. They never did air this part of the recording because at the time no one expected it to have any value long term and they shelved it. The good news for us is that when that person heard about this show they sent us a copy of the recording. Well, to be honest, they wanted to sell it to us, but when we declined they sent it anyway. Perhaps they had no other takers.

We ran it past Sally Bassett for her validation and Sally has confirmed that it is an actual recording of Susan Mitchell's speech from that very evening.

This exclusive recording is your opportunity to hear the very words that Ku-Stom, Veronique and JC Chains heard on the night when, as they say, history was made. We hope you enjoy.

We apologize in advance for the inferior quality of the recording. We did our best to improve it, but this was as good as it got.

[Archival Audio – Bootleg Recording]

'Hello, ladies and gentlemen, my name is Susan Mitchell.

'I am supposed to be here today to talk to you about money … but what if I didn't? What if, instead, we spoke about something linked, but completely different?

'As the Chief Investment Officer of my fund, I am supposed to talk about money. A lot. In fact, you could say that, like it is for so many of my peers, it is supposed to be my religion. There is only one problem. I'm not actually very interested in money. I have spent so much of my life without that, personally, I don't need it. Money itself is not important and I'll tell you why. It is because money is not the truest capital of the world. I believe that the truest capital of the world is blood.

'If you have any doubt about it, then ask yourself these two questions. The first question is simple enough: how much of your money would you give to make people happy? It depends on the person, right? For those you love, you might pay a lot. For those you don't even know, maybe not as much. Perhaps you might even have a sliding scale on these parameters? The more that you like someone, the more you might pay, right down to nothing.

'Now for the more difficult second question: how much of your blood would you give to save someone's life? Not so easy to answer, right? Talk about a precious resource? You might give your life for one you love, or perhaps you donate blood to the Red Cross, but at a certain point your own blood is too important to you to just give it away. You can't print more of it like you can with money. You can't dig it out of the ground. It is a precious resource to your body and your life.

The problem with blood is the valuation. The world loses money every day. And people die or are killed every day. So many people die in some countries that we've stopped seeing them. So, what do you think we get more upset about? I don't want to offend anyone, but I can tell you it is not about the people. Why? Maybe because as a society we value our own money over people we don't know. There is nothing to be ashamed about. I get it. You worked hard for that money. You need to be smart about it because you don't want to end up being one of those people in need. But just maybe there is a way of doing something smart with money that can help those in need. Those whose blood gets spilt every day on the streets, in developing nations or even through environmental change. Those less fortunate than you.

'Let me put you all at ease. I don't want your blood, but if you will allow me to, I will take your money.

'You see, we have found a way to take that useless resource money and turn it into something valuable. Valuable to those who have nothing. Those whose precious blood is spilled, but for whom nobody cares. Valuable to people in this very city who inject dirty drugs up into their precious blood stream. Valuable to the very world itself that we all live in.

'I have a special insight. Like many of the unfortunate people in this world, I know what it is like to have nothing. Or, to not know where your next meal is coming from. I know what it is like to question the ulterior motives of a man who approaches you in the street because he was not the first to do so and may not be the last. There are people out there who are hurting. They do not trust easily, and many of them do not want your charity.

'And to be frank, neither do I.

'Because like you, I also know what it is like to work bloody hard for every single dollar you earn. If we wanted to, all of us here in this very room could pool our money right now and send it off to some village in Africa. But what would it do for the people themselves? Would we become just another stranger in the street with an apple in our hand and a dirty smile?

'That is not good enough! Charity does not lift people out of poverty. It just buys them some time at the most. It lifts them up into the air and then drops them again.

'So, instead of charity, I developed an investment fund. I developed it because I want to invest in society, not just throw money at problems. I wanted to invest in the human capital of the world in such a way that it enriches the societies and the people providing the money. Two birds with one stone.

'So I sat down and developed a system where we could do all of that, not just once, but time and time again. We developed a mathematical formula that could assess any social situation and calculate the actual rate of investment and return down to the dollar. With not only human life itself factored in, but a healthy-enough profit margin that my investors would want to keep giving, even when the project is over. I'll be the first to admit that my formula wasn't perfect, but it was unique. That was why I enlisted the help of one of the smartest mathematical minds that you have never heard of – Mathias Lagrange. Look him up if you don't believe me. He has worked for all the major banks and accounting firms. This is the very man they bring in to check the work of the experts. He took my formula and made it so much better than it was. He can answer any question that you might have about our fund. Sally, to my left here, will talk you through the seven investments that we currently have underway around the world. These are real project changing places you may not have even heard of.

'As I said at the start, my name is Susan Mitchell, and I am the creator of the Human Capital World Fund. You worked hard to get where you are. Let the money you earned along the way work even harder for you and let the results of what it achieves add to your legacy.

'Together we can create a new future for the people of the world.

'Thank you.'

[Narrator]

In our next episode we will get an introduction into what would become one of the most influential new relationships for Susan Mitchell: that of the one between her and JC Chains.

[Dylan Clarke – The Talent Agent]

'People would ask me, "Are they friends, lovers, business associates? What is going on with these two people spending so much time together?" And I would say, "I don't know. Ask them. I certainly never did. It would be like me asking you about the relationship you have with your wife. None of my business".'

[Narrator]

We are still encouraging anyone who was involved with Susan Mitchell or the Human Capital World fund to contact us. If you invested money in her fund, know her personally, or even if you are Miss Mitchell herself and are listening to this right now, we would very much like to talk to you. You may hold the key to unlock all the mysteries that remain unanswered.

It is often said that 'Not everything is as it seems' but with Susan Mitchell – The Woman Who Stole The World – nothing *was* as it seemed.

Now a word from our sponsors …

EPISODE 9: JC CHAINS

[Narrator]

Who was the mysterious Susan Mitchell – The Woman Who Stole The World? And how was she able to convince so many people to invest hundreds of millions of dollars into her Human Capital World Fund before disappearing off the face of the earth with everyone's money?

In Episode 8 we learned about Susan Mitchell's tenuous relationship with singing sensation Veronique. We also got to hear a bootlegged recording of the very speech that she gave to the superstar clientele at the party hosted at Dylan Clarke's house.

In this episode, we will get an introduction into Susan Mitchell's blossoming relationship with the world-famous JC Chains. The two of them were often seen together in the year after that party and before Miss Mitchell's disappearance, but neither would ever discuss the nature of their relationship. So, in the absence of any information from either of them directly, we will try to piece it together from the scraps of information available to us through witnesses. This was not a simple task, given we are talking about two of the most elusive personalities on this planet.

[Dylan Clarke – The Talent Agent]

'JC doesn't even do promo. I could not have scripted it better if I'd tried. He does all of his talking through his music and the less he talks the more the people want to listen.'

[Narrator]

For those that don't know of him – those few who have been living under a rock – I am going to take a minute to give you some background about JC Chains.

Josiah Charnas, known professionally as JC Chains, is a world-renowned singer, songwriter and businessperson of note. His adopted parents assume he was born around 1976, somewhere in the Middle East because, as far as anyone can tell, no one really knows for sure.

Given some of the fabricated backgrounds seen in the entertainment industry from the likes of Ku-Stom who trump up stories of survival in the ghettos, and because of his importance to our story, we have done our own research into the history of JC Chains. And I can tell you that, on this occasion, reality really can be stranger than fiction.

To kick things off, here is an excerpt from an interview we did with a sibling of JC Chains who, although not a blood relative, was part of the foster family that brought him up. They have asked that we do not disclose their name as part of this program for their own privacy reasons, but I can assure all listeners that we have seen photographic evidence of their relationship with a young Josiah Charnas, JC Chains, and can confirm that this person is who they claim to be.

[Anonymous]

'He was such a strange little boy. He had this thick curly brown hair with those big blue eyes. Even back then, those eyes had all the intensity that they have now. They burned like a blue flame.'

[Stephen Grace]

'Can you tell us what else you remember from the first time you saw him?'

[Anonymous]

'Yeah, I remember he didn't speak any English at all. And, when they brought him in, he was dressed like a Middle Eastern farm boy. I can say that now, but I didn't know what I was looking at back then. It was two days before anyone even knew what language he was speaking. To put it into context you need to understand where they found him and where we lived at the time. We lived in the middle of one of the whitest suburbs in the state. It was a time before the world had been shaken and stirred like it has now. I remember we had only one Asian boy and one Indian boy at our entire school, and you would not have wanted to be either of them if you had the choice. Now every street is like the United Nations, but back then, people here were mostly the same in our community. Everyone looked like they could be each other's cousins. Then suddenly this strange little boy turns up out of nowhere.'

[Stephen Grace]

'When you finally found out, what language was he speaking?'

[Anonymous]

'It was Hebrew! Seriously, I couldn't make this shit up. It was like somebody had plucked this little Hebrew kid up off some farm in Israel and dropped him here in the middle of suburbia.'

[Stephen Grace]

'Did anyone ever come looking for him?'

[Anonymous]

'That's the thing. No one ever came looking for him. And he didn't seem to look for anyone either. No crying "Mummy" or "Daddy". He just sat himself down on the floor with the rest of us foster kids and flicked through a picture book.

'I know that some people have come out of the woodwork now that he's rich and famous, claiming to be his biological parents. But I don't believe any of them. And even if they were his biological parents, he would owe them nothing for how they left him.

'There were twelve kids in total in that house. Eight of them were foster kids like me. We were lucky to have a roof over our heads. And while we weren't blood, you could say that we were at least all a product of our upbringing. All except him.

'Josiah was always just part of another universe. I think that is what the world sees in him now. Something displaced, and unique.'

[Stephen Grace]

'Do you like his music?'

[Anonymous]

'It is very difficult for me to listen to it without thinking of that little boy that was found wandering the streets. He may not have been sad that night, but he would be for years to come. I hear it all in his music, that's why I can't listen. I cried for him many times before the rest of the world ever did.'

[Narrator]

As I said previously, we cross-checked as many facts as we could in this story and can confirm that it seems to be correct. Our anonymous source did not want any recognition or money for their interview, so we have no reason to question their motives in sharing their story other than 'To set the record straight', as they said.

Before we return to the night of the party where JC Chains first met Susan Mitchell, I would like to give just a little background into the man he was when Dylan Clarke first met him.

[Stephen Grace]

'Did you discover JC Chains originally? Can you give us a little background on how he came to be at your party?'

[Dylan Clarke – The Talent Agent]

'Did I discover him? For anyone else it would be easy to say "yes", but not with him. It is like asking a hiker if he discovered the mountains. The mountains were always there. Maybe the hiker put the mountains on a map but that is about all. To say I discovered JC is the same stretch. Now, if I'd found some kid with half his voice on the side of the road, given him a few singing lessons and a few strategically placed tattoos, I might claim them as a discovery. I could at least say that, yes, I chiselled them from the rock. But Josiah, he discovered himself.'

[Stephen Grace]

'In what way was he different? Can you give the listeners a little more information?'

[Dylan Clarke – The Talent Agent]

'You know, I can tell by your questions that you don't listen to his music.'

[Stephen Grace]

'Well, I have heard a few of his songs, but I wouldn't say that I am an avid listener. It is not really my style.'

[Dylan Clarke – The Talent Agent]

'Let me guess, it makes you uncomfortable, right? Too personal, too emotional. Some say that it cuts too close to the bone. It's okay. I can see that I'm right. I have had this conversation many times.

'Let me tell you about the man I found in the car park of a hospital.

'I had just been there to see my father leave this world. It was the night he died, but it was no surprise to me. It had been coming for some time, so I was terribly sad but it was almost a relief at the same when he finally went because he wouldn't be suffering any more. So anyway, after Dad passed, I finish all the paperwork and I'm walking to my car when I hear this... ah... singing, in the car park. I hesitate because it is like nothing I have ever heard before. Emotional, gospel like, beautiful in its pain. Like I said, my father had just died, so I was emotional already. It was not a

THE WOMAN WHO STOLE THE WORLD

good time for me to be scouting for future superstars, but that is not what this was about.

'I found him not as a talent scout but as a man in the state I was in. I needed to find the source of that voice, and I needed to see that face for myself. It was a multi-story car park, and its source wasn't coming from my level, but he couldn't be too far because I could hear him. So, I go down a level first to search for him, but it gets quieter. I panicked. I can't let this voice go or it will haunt me forever, so now I run up a level, and then another level to the roof. That was more running than I had done in ten years. That's when I saw a small crowd all standing around this little covered stairway with him standing underneath it, singing with his eyes closed. Where he was standing was like a natural megaphone. It amplified the sound, which is why I heard it so well downstairs.

'So, I run up to the group and there are like fifteen people all standing around, watching this skinny young guy sing, like they are in a trance. Normal people, nurses, patients, cleaners, all sorts, just spellbound. I turn to the guy next to me and say, "Who is he?" and his response is, "No idea. He comes here every day to the hospital and sings for three hours and then goes home".

'Now, usually younger singers grow up mimicking other singers and song writers so the first thing you need to do is strip them of it. But not him. His voice was his own from day one and his songs were the same. I didn't know any of them. I just listened and cried about the loss of my father.

'Can you imagine Ku-Stom making anyone cry over a song? No. Because he is a creation, a personality built on talent. Josiah is not like that at all. He is talent built on heartbreak.'

[Stephen Grace]

'So how did you come to work with him?'

[Dylan Clarke – The Talent Agent]

'I just sat down and listened until he finished. My father was a tough man; I never expected to cry as much as I did, but JC's music enabled me to do it. His music, to this day, has that effect on people. Anyway, the others had walked away, so we were alone. He came sat next to me and he said, "Thank you for sharing your pain with me tonight. I felt it all, and I did my best to give it voice". I couldn't talk, I just kept crying. He just sat there with me, like he was soaking it all up.

'I finally pulled myself together and asked him why he sings in a hospital car park. He said that it was the place where he felt the most pain. That singing is his way of helping the world, and that it was all that he had to give. I asked him if he would like to help people all over the world and he said, "Yes".

'It was getting a little cold that time, so I told him that if he came back the next day I would show him how he could use his talent to help people around the world. He agreed.

'We didn't even exchange names. He said he would come and so I just needed to have faith that he would.

'I will admit that I was very nervous that I would not see him again.'

[Stephen Grace]

'And did he come, that next night?'

[Dylan Clarke – The Talent Agent]

'Yes. And he signed that contract on the spot. I don't think he even read it. I told him to take it home first. I told him to show someone who knew about contracts, but he said that I'd shown faith in him and now it was his turn to have faith in me.'

[Narrator]

You may not hear it in our voices in the recording, but at that point in our interview it was becoming clear that Dylan Clarke was emotionally exhausted after sharing this story with us. Perhaps it was the death of his father, or simply sharing a story he had not shared before, but he was keen to change the topic of our conversation. So, even though our interest in the life of Josiah Charnas or JC Chains was only just peaking, in the interests of politeness, we agreed to move on.

However, it was becoming clear to us that Susan Mitchell was not the only person of extreme interest involved in this entire affair. We hoped we might get the chance to pick up more of this thread in future interviews.

Having said that, we still needed to hear about the first meeting of Susan and JC Chains on that evening of the party.

So, we aimed our questions back at Sally Bassett.

[Stephen Grace]

'Sally, did Susan and JC Chains meet at the party? Do you know if there was any exchange between them there?'

[Sally Bassett – Social Change Activist]

'Yes, they met at the party, although it was a little strange. In person, away from the cameras, he is exactly like what you see on TV. He really doesn't say much, but when he does people can't help but listen. He was sitting front and centre during Susan's speech, and he never moved the entire time. He just sat there watching, thinking. I think he distracted Susan with his intensity, but she rallied and continued on. I don't know if he was more spellbound by Susan, or if she was by him, but there was something there between them for sure.

'Perhaps that is what got Veronique so wound up that night? Maybe she was jealous of Susan's connection with JC. I don't know.

'Anyway, Susan finished her speech and answered a few questions from the crowd. I then took some questions on our humanitarian efforts and Ku-Stom threw a few bullshit questions to Mathias, just to make himself try and look smart. They were nothing we couldn't handle, so slowly the presentation broke apart and we all mingled once again.

'That's when I saw JC walk up to Susan. He handed her something small and whispered in her ear.'

[Stephen Grace]

'Do you know what he gave Susan or what he whispered?'

[Sally Bassett – Social Change Activist]

'Like I said earlier, when JC talks, people listen. Everyone wanted to know the answer to that question. Susan would never tell me.'

[Stephen Grace]

'So, you don't know?'

[Sally Bassett – Social Change Activist]

'Ah … but I never said that, did I? I was the only person within a metre of them both when it happened. And I also happen to be blessed with exceptional hearing, especially when two of the most intriguing people in my world are just about to meet.'

[Stephen Grace]

'So, what did he say?'

[Sally Bassett – Social Change Activist]

'I'm almost sure he said, "Do you have faith?" and I think he gave her a data key.'

[Stephen Grace]

'Do you know what was on it? Or what her response was?'

[Sally Bassett – Social Change Activist]

'Yes. She said, "It's all I have left". I remember being quite shocked when I heard her say that. Here was this beautiful woman, who was independently wealthy, and in the prime of her life. A woman who never said things she didn't mean and with no religious connection that I knew of, and she said that faith is all she had left.'

[Stephen Grace]

'Do you think that she just said it to endear herself to JC Chains?'

[Sally Bassett – Social Change Activist]

'Well, I thought about that later and yes, it is JC Chains and there are millions of women around the world that would say anything to get close to him. But it was also Susan Mitchell, and that was not her style at all. Whatever she meant by it, she meant it.'

[Stephen Grace]

'Did you ever discuss it with her directly?'

[Sally Bassett – Social Change Activist]

'Hell no. It was not my business. I feel like I'm betraying her now just by telling you. I'm sure it would surprise her just knowing that I had overheard. When I think back now, it is easy for me to think that she considered me a friend. I certainly hope she did. That doesn't mean my intentions weren't good, it's just that I never got to the inner story with her and I'm not sure many did. God knows, she needed a good friend from time to time. But I don't know if I ever was. We shared a female bond, but I was certainly not her confidant. There were a lot of things that she didn't tell us.'

[Narrator]

I truly want to believe what Sally Bassett says, but I know also that there are legal proceedings underway to recover some of the lost money that was invested in the fund. Maintaining a line of 'Susan was in charge and we knew nothing' may be the only defence that Sally Bassett and Mathias Lagrange have left to keep them out of jail.

[Stephen Grace]

'How about the data key you mentioned? Do you know what was on that?'

[Sally Bassett – Social Change Activist]

'No. Some of his newest music, maybe? I know she was playing it in her office later that week. Perhaps his contact details but I'm just guessing. They spoke over the phone a lot in the weeks after that night.

'I only know that because when one of the most beautiful men in the world calls you for a chat, you still need to tell someone or it didn't happen. And there was no one else around, so she had to tell me. She was smiling like a schoolgirl after her first kiss that day.

'Those two became inseparable – not physically, because JC was off touring the world, but emotionally. They were always whispering to each other on the phone. It was like they had a secret. I could see what was happening, but I don't know if anyone else did.

'Maybe it was their common backgrounds. Both orphans after all. There is a romance in that I guess.'

[Narrator]

We will uncover more in the coming episode about the relationship between Susan Mitchell and JC Chains. This last comment from Sally Bassett, however, reminded us that there is still so much to know about the woman Susan Mitchell herself and her background.

So, we decided to ignore the biographies we read about her in her company's own literature and hired a private detective to delve into who she was before the Human Capital World Fund.

Some of the things we found out during that investigation would leave us to wonder if this wasn't just a woman on the run from investors. Perhaps there were even bigger pursuers that she may have been hiding from.

[Unidentified Male Voice]

'Trying to get a sense of this woman's life from the information I found is like trying to force pieces of different jigsaw puzzles together into one cohesive picture. All of her pieces are different shapes and colours and none of them seem to fit anywhere. I think she is the only one who would know what the final picture should look like.'

[Narrator]

Because of the early success of this series, we are being overwhelmed by the amount of people offering information for us to work though. However, we would still like to talk directly with anyone who has any information about the actual whereabouts of Susan Mitchell herself. If you do, please contact us immediately.

Your information may hold the key to unlock all the mysteries that remain unanswered.

It is often said that 'Not everything is as it seems' but with Susan Mitchell – The Woman Who Stole The World – nothing *was* as it seemed.

Now, a word from our sponsors …

EPISODE 10: LAUNCH

[Narrator]

Who was the mysterious Susan Mitchell – The Woman Who Stole The World? And how was she able to convince so many people to invest hundreds of millions of dollars into her Human Capital World Fund before disappearing off the face of the earth with everyone's money?

In our last episode we got an insight into another character that played a pivotal role in the rise of the mysterious Susan Mitchell: the world-famous singer-songwriter JC Chains. And although we never clearly mentioned it in our last episode, we must now legally state that JC Chain never publicly endorsed Miss Mitchell herself or her fund to anyone. It is hard for us to believe that his personal association with Susan Mitchell played no part in her success, but for legal reasons we must state that he never went public like Ku-Stom did. We will leave it up to you as our story unfolds to make up your own minds on his culpability.

In this episode we will investigate what came next after the party changed history. We know from the financial reporting of the fund, which admittedly was supplied by the company itself, that this was a pivotal point in the company's growth. The point when serious money started to roll in. What is unclear is where all of that money actually came from.

That information, and a lot of other curious facts is what we focused on in this episode.

[Stephen Grace]

'Can you tell us a little about the days after the party? Was Susan Mitchell happy with the outcome of the night?'

[Sally Bassett – Social Change Activist]

'I wouldn't know. She disappeared. In fact, we didn't see or hear from her for three days after the party. It was so unlike her.'

[Stephen Grace]

'Where did she go?'

[Sally Bassett – Social Change Activist]

'I still don't know where she was. Mathias and I actually got a little scared on the third day and rang Dylan to see if she had been partying with any of the guests, but he didn't know where she was either.'

[Stephen Grace]

'So what happened?'

[Sally Bassett – Social Change Activist]

'At the end of the third day she walked into the office like it was no big thing and asked us for an update.'

[Stephen Grace]

'She offered no explanation into where she had been?'

[Sally Bassett – Social Change Activist]

'No. I could have insisted, I guess, but you need to remember that *we* work for *her* and not the other way around. If Einstein walked away for three days, would you question where he'd been? Or would you just trust in his genius that it was likely time well spent?'

[Narrator]

That was the first time I had ever heard of Susan Mitchell compared to Einstein, but it would not be the last time that people would compare her to major historical figures. To her staunch fans, she had a position on a higher plane than that of the everyday man or woman.

[Stephen Grace]

'Mathias, where do you think Susan went in the three days after the party?'

[Mathias Lagrange – Mathematician]

'Who knows? Maybe she needed a rest. In the week leading up to the party, I'm sure she wasn't sleeping more than a few hours a night. And it is not like she had done nothing at all. She had been working.'

[Stephen Grace]

'What gives you that impression?'

[Mathias Lagrange – Mathematician]

'She told us. She said that she had refunded all the money that her previous customers, from before the party, had invested in us. And that she had matched the total of those funds out of her own money so that our business was no better or worse off.'

[Stephen Grace]

'But why would she do that? Surely she would try to bring in as much money as she could and keep it there?'

[Mathias Lagrange – Mathematician]

'I think it was her way of purifying the business. I didn't know the existing customers when I got there, but I could tell that she wasn't especially proud of many of them. She wanted this business to be pure, unencumbered.'

[Stephen Grace]

'Did she ever tell you why?'

[Mathias Lagrange – Mathematician]

'No, but she didn't need to. This was her baby. She wanted to build something that she could be proud of on a world scale. You can't build anything on a world scale without a sound foundation. I think she was cutting out the rot out of the foundation and filling the gaps with her own money. I guess that is why I don't agree with the rumours that she simply ran off with everyone's money. I saw firsthand how much of herself she put into that business.'

[Stephen Grace]

'So, what happened when she came back?'

[Mathias Lagrange – Mathematician]

'She asked us for updates on everyone from the party. We told her that some of their money people had been in touch and wanted to set up meetings. Susan told us to tell them she would only attend personally if their clients themselves would be present. For anything that was pure money she would just send me.'

[Stephen Grace]

'Is it standard practice that the head of an investment fund would not talk to the investment representatives of their clients without them being present?'

[Mathias Lagrange – Mathematician]

'No, it wasn't standard, especially given the amount of money being discussed, but we weren't a standard investment company, and these weren't standard clients. You need to remember that we weren't out there pimping ourselves to every investment fund that would take our call. We were talking directly to clients, our competitor's clients. We changed the entire game.

'In our world, they would be lucky to give us their money. Susan gave us specific instructions that we should walk out of any investment meeting if we felt like we weren't being respected. We would answer every question they had, as long as there was respect in the room.'

[Stephen Grace]

'And how did the clients themselves deal with this attitude? Surely they would not have accepted it?'

[Mathias Lagrange – Mathematician]

'It's funny you say that because in those early days many of them would only accept the meeting if Susan herself would be there. So those end clients were more than happy to come, the money people hated it because that was supposed to be what they were getting paid to do. It became our thing.

'Later, when we got bigger, they would come in hoping to see her. They would walk into our office with their eyes big like saucers, looking about to glimpse the famous Susan Mitchell. But by that stage we were too big for her, or even me, to be doing all the investment meetings.

'We eventually hired a team of four just to handle the standard objections from so-called money experts. You have to remember that these weren't all smart finance industry people. Some of them were just celebrity entourage. High school friends of the famous, with bullshit business degrees who were also fun to party with. Many of them understood nothing about what we were about, but they didn't want to go back empty handed. My guys shut all their questions down in seconds, and they ended up throwing their money across the table at us.'

[Stephen Grace]

'How was Susan in those early days before it all changed? Was she different at all?'

[Mathias Lagrange – Mathematician]

'She was more serious. She was like that saying, "the tuna fisherman that caught a whale" and then doesn't know what to do with it.

'I think she was still coming to grips with the power of the investment vehicle that I had created for her and how much money we could make.

'It all got very serious from that point on, and not just for her but for all of us.'

[Stephen Grace]

'And how about yourself? Were you excited to be part of it all back then?'

[Mathias Lagrange – Mathematician]

'Back then I was, yes. But given everything I know now, I would be happy just to go back to that week we had together before the party, when it was just the three of us in that boardroom working crazy hours. She was our secret back then. But, from the party onwards she belonged to the world.'

[Narrator]

Until that point, I had only ever seen Mathias Lagrange get emotional when he was discussing his own self-proclaimed genius. On that day he was a man who had been to the top of the mountain. Higher perhaps than he had ever dared to dream. Yet you get a sense that he longed to go back to a lower point. A time before, when his life was simpler.

This would become a common occurrence with many of the people that I spoke with. They would all have their own special moment with Susan Mitchell etched into their memories.

[Stephen Grace]

'Sally, were you excited in the weeks after the party?'

[Sally Bassett – Social Change Activist]

'Yes, I was, but sometimes reality can steal a dream right from under your feet. I think I preferred the planning stage. Even though I had to spend so much time with Mathias and we really did not like each other much back then, it was still fun to be in that room together. Sharing that dream. I guess Susan didn't have that luxury. She had reality to deal with.'

[Narrator]

It is unlikely that we will ever know where Susan Mitchell was in those days after the party. For the record, we tried to track down some of her former customers that Mathias Lagrange mentioned earlier, but Miss Mitchell alone kept the record of her customer list. We placed calls to a few people we thought might have had a previous association with her fund, but every person flatly refused to speak with us.

All we know, from a leaked bank statement of that time, is that around two million dollars' worth of withdrawals left the company to go somewhere. And that, less than three hours later, the same value was then replaced into the account in one hit from what looks to be Susan Mitchell's personal account. We do not have enough information at our disposal or the means to track where that money went.

But Susan Mitchell wasn't the only one putting money into her accounts. Money started coming into the business from other places also, and it came in fast. Perhaps faster than any of them expected or were ready for. The next growth phase of their business would bring additional issues, which would then need more people to fix those issues. And more big personalities to throw into the mix.

You will hear more about all of it next episode.

At this point we would like to thank you, our listeners.

Because of you, this show has skyrocketed up the charts at a rate that might impress even Susan Mitchell herself. That growth trajectory has brought its own exciting challenges for us. We have been receiving information from you faster than we can investigate it. So, because of your overwhelming support, we will need to close our information lines until we've had time to sift through everything you have all brought to our attention. But we don't want to cut ourselves off from you completely. We would still like to talk with anyone who has any direct information as to the actual whereabouts of Susan Mitchell herself. For that purpose only, we will leave one of our information lines open.

If you know where Miss Mitchell is, please contact us immediately. We would very much like to talk to you! Your information may hold the key to unlock all the mysteries that remain unanswered.

It is often said that 'Not everything is as it seems' but with Susan Mitchell – The Woman Who Stole 'he World – nothing *was* as it seemed.

Now, a word from our sponsors …

EPISODE 11:
SOCIAL EXPLOSION

[Narrator]

Who was the mysterious Susan Mitchell – The Woman Who Stole The World? And how was she able to convince so many people to invest hundreds of millions of dollars into her Human Capital World Fund before disappearing off the face of the earth with everyone's money?

Last episode we investigated the early money that flowed into the Human Capital World Fund. And while we cannot confirm exactly where it came from, we believe that Susan Mitchell, or some of her backers, may have injected the funds into the business to pay out less desirable pre-Human Capital investors. Perhaps Miss Mitchell intended to wash her business clean of the dirty money that pre-existed within the business. You may recall that Mathias Lagrange even gave us a few names to investigate. We did try to contact these pre-existing investors but none of them would speak to us. In fact, since our last episode aired, two of the people we reached out to have threatened to sue us for defamation if we ever mentioned their names in our show.

Normally these threats would be a good sign that we were on to something big. However, in the absence of any actual evidence they were involved, our lawyers have advised us that mentioning them by name would not be worth the legal exposure.

In this episode we will introduce you to some new members of Susan Mitchell's team that were brought in to help facilitate her rapidly growing business.

As you will come to see, every new person we speak to about this enigmatic woman only seems to deepen the mystery about her and gives us more questions to chase answers for.

[Stephen Grace]

'Can you please tell us who you are and what your relationship was with

Susan Mitchell and the Human Capital World Fund?'

[Allison Bailey – Social Media]

'My name is Allison Bailey. Susan brought me in to the business to be her head of social media. But in reality, my job went way beyond that.'

[Stephen Grace]

'Can you please elaborate for us on what other ways you were assisting Miss Mitchell?'

[Allison Bailey – Social Media]

'Well, first you really need to understand the mess she and the business were in when I arrived. She brought me in for social media, but it was quite clear that the social genie was already out of its bottle by the time I got there. People were already sharing her launch speech online, so she had a small presence. Not much, but every fire starts with a spark and she had her spark. Then Ku-Stom posted that picture of them together at the party with a comment, "This woman's gonna change the world, you understand. And I'ma help her do it". He had obviously turned off his spell check, but that didn't stop it getting an audience. It got over five hundred thousand likes. So, she called me in the very next day and made me an offer I could not refuse. The only condition was that I had to drop all my other clients and work for her exclusively, starting the following day. I took over social media, as well as corporate and personal branding.'

[Stephen Grace]

'Is that standard practice in your industry?'

[Allison Bailey – Social Media]

'Lol, nothing is standard practice in my industry. This industry has only existed for ten minutes.'

[Stephen Grace]

'Right. And do you mind if I ask: how old are you? You seem quite young to be an expert on social media and corporate branding.'

[Allison Bailey – Social Media]

'I'm 22. I will admit that I have no formal qualifications, but I had helped three small businesses generate several million dollars' worth of sales by the time I was nineteen. I know what I'm doing. I just wasn't expecting the circus that was about to come.'

[Stephen Grace]

'What was the mood when you first joined the team? They must have been very excited to be getting so much attention so quickly?'

[Allison Bailey – Social Media]

'Well, Sally and Mathias certainly were excited. They had gone from almost no social footprint to being snapped in the background of megastars. Sally spent over half the day taking calls from friends saying that they had seen her in the Ku-Stom photo.'

[Stephen Grace]

'How about Susan Mitchell?'

[Allison Bailey – Social Media]

'Ahh, Susan was not excited at all. You could say she was in a panic. The very first thing that she did was show me the photo and ask me if I could take it down!'

[Stephen Grace]

'Why? Surely all the new attention would have been great for her business?'

[Allison Bailey – Social Media]

'It's strange, but she never really told me why she wanted it taken down. I tried to change her mind of course. I thought she looked amazing. I even tried to get her assistant to back me up. That dress that she wore was beautiful and the way the camera angle caught the side of her boobs was perfect click bait. No wonder that photo got so much attention. I joked with her that the photographer must have had an erection when he took it and now half a million teenage boys probably had the same.'

[Stephen Grace]

'I have seen that photo that you are referring to, and you are right in that she looks elegant. Do you think perhaps she was embarrassed?'

[Allison Bailey – Social Media]

'Susan didn't get embarrassed. Well … I'm sure she did, but not outwardly. I just don't think that she ever wanted to be the public face of the company. I sort of got the impression that half a million teenage boys ogling her photo did not worry her, but perhaps there was someone in particular that she did not want to see it.'

[Stephen Grace]

'Right. Any guess on who that might be?'

[Allison Bailey – Social Media]

'Who knows, abusive ex-husband, estranged father, people she owed money? It could be anyone. She never spoke to me about her past, and I never asked.'

[Stephen Grace]

'So, what did you advise her to do?'

[Allison Bailey – Social Media]

'I told her it was too late and that she now had a choice. Spend months trying to get him to take it down, which, given the amount of traffic it had received, they would never have done. Or she could take control of the narrative and change the story. Which luckily is what she allowed me to do.'

[Stephen Grace]

'And how did you go about that?'

[Allison Bailey – Social Media]

'Well, this is where I go to work. We analyzed the photo that Ku-Stom posted and his text. It was quite territorial. It was like he was saying, "This woman is amazing and she's mine, so back off". We had to respond in a way that wouldn't hurt his ego but allow Susan the capacity to stand alone as a personality. I also put together a plan to siphon some of his followers to our page, but I didn't tell Susan that. The plan I was developing was to social proof the business in her image.'

[Stephen Grace]

'What exactly does that mean?'

[Allison Bailey – Social Media]

'Her fund was still in its early stages, so it didn't yet have a credibility of its own. However, if I could develop a substantial personal brand behind Susan, her brand would give the fund an enhanced credibility. New fund, but hot, trusted leader. I never formally told her of this, but once she accepted the fact that she was going to have a personal identity alongside the business, she gave me the green light. In the end, I pumped that photo for all that it was worth.'

[Stephen Grace]

'And what was the outcome?'

[Allison Bailey – Social Media]

'I'm very good at my job, Stephen. For Susan, I had a social media platform that movie stars would envy. Within one week she had over two million personal followers and we didn't have to pay a cent for any of it.

We simply got Ku-Stom's followers to follow Susan, and a whole bunch of new followers on top of that.'

[Narrator]

We will hear more from Allison Bailey in future episodes, but for now I think it is important to call out Allison for the independent thought and action that she would bring into Susan Mitchell's business. She was the start of the new breed of talent that would be brought into the company to help deal with its meteoric rise over the coming months, and she would come to have a massive impact on the success of the Human Capital World Fund.

As more people joined the business over the next few months, Miss Mitchell's vice-like grip on the world around her would strain under the pressure. Rogue internal actors like Allison Bailey and unknown foreign influences would soon be a constant concern for Susan Mitchell.

But before we meet more of the new team, something Allison Bailey said in her interview got our attention and we felt it needed further investigation.

You could say that it was a major investigative oversight on our part, but when we heard Allison Bailey refer to Susan Mitchell's 'assistant' in her interview we believed she was referring to Sally Bassett. It was only after reviewing a small part of our interview with Dylan Clarke, which did not make it to air, we realized he had referred to Sally Bassett and an assistant in the same sentence. At the time of that interview, we had assumed that both references were about Sally Basset, but hearing the term 'assistant' again got us questioning our assumptions. So, we put a quick call in to Sally Bassett to clarify the situation once and for all.

[Stephen Grace]

'Hi, Sally, thank you for taking our call at such short notice. We just came across something and hoped that you might shed some light on it for us.'

[Sally Bassett – Social Change Activist]

'No problem, Stephen. I'm always happy to help. What's up?'

[Stephen Grace]

'So, we have now met Allison Bailey and spoken with her.'

[Sally Bassett – Social Change Activist]

'Oh yes, I can only imagine what she had to say.'

[Stephen Grace]

'She gave us a lot of interesting information. One thing she said did get our attention on listening back after we had concluded the interview. It might be nothing, but we then heard a similar reference from one of our interviews with Dylan Clarke, so we thought we should check with you to be sure. Both of them refer to Susan Mitchell's 'assistant'. Now, we don't want to insult you, but we thought they were referring to you at the time because of the closeness of your relationship with Miss Mitchell. Now we are not so sure. Was there someone else in that office working with Susan Mitchell in that capacity?'

[Sally Bassett – Social Change Activist]

'It's okay, I don't get insulted easily. You could say that in some ways we were all just Susan's assistants. But, in this case, your new hunch would be right. Susan had an assistant. She was a young lady called Jane.'

[Stephen Grace]

'Right! It's strange: there doesn't seem to be any record of her anywhere in the documentation that we have on the company. Given her immediate access to Susan Mitchell and her daily activities, we would really like to talk to her. Do you have a last name for Jane?'

[Sally Bassett – Social Change Activist]

'Hmm … no, actually. Susan introduced Mathias and I to her with just her first name. Even when I think back now, I remember her email address as simply Jane at the Human Capital World Fund.'

[Stephen Grace]

'Great, we will try it, thank you. Do you also have a phone number for her, by any chance?'

[Sally Bassett – Social Change Activist]

'I do, but it no longer works. Like Susan's, it was disconnected when she disappeared. I would try the email though because out of all the email addresses for the company it seems to be the only one that still works. I'm not saying that she is getting them, but that is the only address that doesn't get immediately rejected. I'm sure it is just an oversight but worth a shot.'

[Stephen Grace]

'Thanks, Sally, you have been extremely helpful.'

[Sally Bassett – Social Change Activist]

'Anytime. I am always happy to help.'

[Narrator]

For any of you listening in who may have lost money in the Fund or have considered emailing Jane, we can confirm for you that someone has now shut her email address down like all the others. However, at the time of the recording of that call with Sally Bassett, it was still live. We sent two separate messages to Miss Jane, no current last name, and believe that they have been read by someone. However, we cannot be completely sure. There has been no response to date.

To Miss Jane, if you are out there and you are listening to this, you are not in any personal legal trouble for the actions of Susan Mitchell or the fund she controlled. We have spoken to the authorities and can also guarantee your personal safety in return for any information that may lead to Susan Mitchell's whereabouts, if that is the reason that you are currently in hiding. We would very much like to talk to you.

That is all for today's episode. In our next episode, we will meet another new player in this enterprise. Someone who would be brought in to deal with a new set of challenges that no one seems to have seen coming, including Miss Mitchell herself. Also, will get an insight into how Miss Mitchell, a woman who is so used to calling the shots, deals with the unexpected and an unwanted change to her plans. Stay with us, and we will tell you the incredible story of what Ku-Stom did next.

[Sally Bassett – Social Change Activist]

'I remember Susan standing there staring at me with her mouth open. I think it was the only time I ever saw a crack in her composure, in all the time I knew her.'

[Narrator]

More on that topic in the next episode.

As always, we would still like to talk directly with anyone who has any information about the actual whereabouts of Susan Mitchell herself or her assistant Jane (last name unknown). If you have any information that may help us, please contact us immediately. We would very much like to talk to you and would be happy to keep your information confidential if required.

You may hold the key to unlock all the mysteries that remain unanswered.

It is often said that 'Not everything is as it seems' but with Susan Mitchell – The Woman Who Stole The World – nothing *was* as it seemed.

Now, a word from our sponsors …

EPISODE 12: THE KU-STOM TRUST

[Narrator]

Who was the mysterious Susan Mitchell – The Woman Who Stole The World? And how was she able to convince so many people to invest hundreds of millions of dollars into her Human Capital World Fund before disappearing off the face of the earth with everyone's money?

Join me, Stephen Grace, as I interview those closest to her to answer the questions on everyone's mind. Questions such as: who was she? why did she do it? and where did Miss Mitchell and all that hard earned money go?

Last episode we met Allison Bailey who joined the Human Capital World Fund to assist with social media and corporate branding. They called Allison in right after singer Ku-Stom posted a photo of himself and Susan Mitchell together, telling his online audience of millions that Miss Mitchell was about to change the world, and that he was going to help her do it.

[Allison Bailey – Social Media]

'It was quite clear that the social genie was already out of its bottle by the time I got there.'

[Narrator]

Last episode we also stumbled upon an intriguing new character in this saga, Susan Mitchell's personal assistant, Jane (last name unknown). We are reviewing our recordings over again to see if there is any more information that we may have missed about Jane and hope to bring it to you in future episodes.

In today's episode, we will hear more about the rapid expansion of their business. How did they grow so quickly, from a clientele of just a few popstars to hundreds of thousands of people from around the world, amassing hundreds of millions of dollars?

Once again, we will be joined by Sally Bassett, one of those closest to

Miss Mitchell during that crazy time of expansion.

[Sally Bassett – Social Change Activist]

'I remember Susan standing there staring at me with her mouth open. I think it was the only time I ever saw a crack in her composure, in all the time I knew her.'

[Stephen Grace]

'This is a major development in the story, but I would just like to understand the mood within the business first. Can you bring the listeners up to date on what had been happening since the party?'

[Sally Bassett – Social Change Activist]

'Okay, sure. Well, it had been about four months since the night of the party, and we had received our first serious run of investment money. I had just returned home from a business trip to Kenya where were sponsoring a project to build a small bridge, so I was exhausted. It wasn't a major project, but it would cut the time a villager took to get water each day down from six hours to under thirty minutes. A massive impact on their lives. I remember it well because I couldn't wait to get back and debrief Susan. That's when I took the phone call in my car. As soon as I hung up, I remember thinking to myself that no one is going to be interested in my little bridge story now.'

[Stephen Grace]

'Who was it that called you that day, Sally, and what did they say?'

[Sally Bassett – Social Change Activist]

'It was Ku-Stom's people. We had money, but we were still a small company at that stage. Susan had brought in Allison to run social, but we still had only about six or seven full-time staff. At that point, I still managed the Ku-Stom account personally. Within weeks of that call, we would have an entire team on it.'

[Stephen Grace]

'I am keen to understand the flow of events here because Ku-Stom's involvement in everything Susan Mitchell gets very blurry about this time. Were they ringing to invest money?'

[Sally Bassett – Social Change Activist]

'Yes, but not like you might think. We already had some of his money. I won't say exactly how much because that would not be professional, but I will say that it was under a half a million dollars. He had made a big statement about supporting Susan online, and he had to back it up, or we would have called him out about it. So he sent us a cheque one week after the party.'

[Stephen Grace]

'What was it about the fund do you think got him so excited?'

[Sally Bassett – Social Change Activist]

'Susan! Everything he did was to get her attention. Personally, I think it drove him crazy to see her with JC, and he wanted to dominate her attention with big acts of support.'

[Stephen Grace]

'So, after his initial cheque, and his post on social media linking himself to Susan, what was it that his team called to tell you that day when you were returning from Kenya?'

[Sally Bassett – Social Change Activist]

'They said they had "put the word out on the street" and that Ku-Stom had "made some calls" – all their words, of course. They were trying to sound super cool about it like it was no big deal, but I could tell that for them it was. I thought to myself, "Okay … so maybe they raised another fifty thousand. I can do something with that". But it wasn't anywhere near that figure and when they finally said it, after all their jive talk, I had to pull over the car to collect myself.'

[Stephen Grace]

'How much money had they raised?'

[Sally Bassett – Social Change Activist]

'Well, without even checking in with us, Ku-Stom's people had set up an investment trust and raised over fifteen million dollars from thousands of backers online.'

[Stephen Grace]

'How did you react to that?'

[Sally Bassett – Social Change Activist]

'To say that we were not ready for it would be an understatement. We had no intention of ever being ready for that! We catered for a small clientele of wealthy customers, and maybe a corporate fund or two, but not for over five thousand individual retail investors. Some of them were kids, fans of Ku-Stom, with money they had been given for Christmas presents. Others were mums and dads who had been saving for college funds and didn't trust the banks. I still can't get my head around how what they did could be legal, but somehow, they assured me it was. In the coming weeks, more money would come. Later, we would learn that even within the individual units of their investment, people had pooled their own money together to be part of it. I think Ku-Stom may have been pressuring his own people to dig into their own pockets.

'In a single moment, we had gone from a socially responsible investment company to a multi-level marketing organization.

'I went straight to the office and told Susan.'

[Stephen Grace]

'And what was Miss Mitchell's response once you told her? Was she excited?'

[Sally Bassett – Social Change Activist]

'Not at all, Stephen. She thought I was joking. She asked me to repeat it for her three times and swear to her it was true. I remember her face like it was yesterday. She just sat there with her mouth open, blinking.

'I felt terrible about this later, but I think I said something like, "I didn't sign up for this, Susan".'

[Stephen Grace]

'And what was her response?'

[Sally Bassett – Social Change Activist]

'She looked at me and said, "Neither did I". Then she said to hold all her calls for the afternoon and locked the door to her office.'

[Narrator]

'The legalities of the "Ku-Stom Trust", as it would come to be known, are still being debated through legal channels. We will hear more about that battle in future episodes because, at this stage in our story, its legal status was not the issue. Putting money into a fund is easy enough, but trying to get it back out again, as investors in the Ku-Stom Trust would one day find out, would be another thing altogether. And it is in those times, on the exit, that legal status can become very important.

I think it is important to understand the framework of how they raised the money, so that we can understand why it was such a problem.

To do that, I have asked a financial expert Peter Lana from Lana Consulting to explain it simply to us. For the record, Peter would come to work for Susan Mitchell within days of Miss Mitchell finding out about the fifteen-million-dollar Ku-Stom Trust investment. We will hear Peter's full story in the next episode.

For now, here is his explanation of the Ku-Stom Trust.

[Peter Lana – Lana Consulting]

'Stephen, the difficulties with the Ku-Stom Trust has a lot to do with how his people went about raising the money. A normal investment company might go through a lot of legal work to set up protections for itself – and its customers – before it gets an approval to trade.

'However, for the Ku-Stom Trust, Ku-Stom's people didn't do any of that. Instead, with no thought for the future, they used a global crowd-funding platform to raise the money. It is the sort of platform someone might use to raise funds for a musical project, or a piece of art that they couldn't afford to do on their own. These types of platforms also sometimes get used to collect money for charity cases, like for the family of a dead police officer or a town's flood relief or bushfire appeal. These platforms can raise money ranging from hundreds of dollars to millions of dollars like it did in the Ku-Stom case. Some of them are more secure and have strict conditions about what happens to the money afterwards – they don't want to it be used for funding terrorism, for example. But other platforms simply don't care what the money is used for. They just act as a collection plate and take a cut on the way through.'

[Stephen Grace]

'And how long do you think it would have taken Ku-Stom's people to set this collection platform up?'

[Peter Lana – Lana Consulting]

'That is an excellent question, Stephen. He had used that service before to pay for his first and second albums, so it was not new to him. It probably would have taken all of fifteen minutes to set it up and write a few messages on social media to get it moving. I could almost imagine him doing it on a whim. Then, as the money rolled in, he started having fun with it on social media. Allison showed us the lead-up to it. In his posts it was quite clear that he was cultivating a "fear of missing out" mentality. This is often how fraudulent funds raise lots of capital in a very short time.'

[Stephen Grace]

'Right. So was the Ku-Stom Trust money the same as the standard

Human Capital World Fund money?'

[Peter Lana – Lana Consulting]

'Another good question. Absolutely not. Let me explain.

'The people that invested directly with Susan had a legal right to ask for their money back. However, the Ku-Stom Trust people gave their money to Ku-Stom. Whether or not they realised it, they donated it to him. What he did with it was his business. In my professional opinion, Ku-Stom has a personal claim for the Trust money that he gave to us. But all those individual people really need to take up their grievances with him. I'm sorry, I know they don't want to hear that, and I certainly don't want to inflame the situation by saying it, but we don't even know who they are.

'Of course, this is all clear now after the fact. At the time, though, we were all just scrambling around trying to figure out what was happening. I was just as mystified by it as everyone else. I should have known better. I'm supposed to be the bloody expert.'

[Narrator]

We will hear a lot more from Peter Lana and his role in the next episode. For now, it is important to keep in mind that he played a role in the financial structure of the company after that first influx of funds. He would try to make sense of the mess that was Mathias Lagrange's mathematical formulas, Sally Basset's socially responsible projects, and Ku-Stom's un-invited capital injection. The only reason that he can talk with us now is because of his own legal prowess in his employment contract. He had requested one simple clause which allowed him complete isolation from any litigation that may come to the company. And while it and his full cooperation with the authorities may have kept him out of jail, it hasn't done anything to protect his brand reputation in the industry that he loves.

It makes you wonder why he was so insistent on that clause. What did he really see happening in those early days?

You won't have to wait long because we will hear his full story in our next episode.

[Peter Lana – Lana Consulting]

'They publicized my joining the organization as a validation of their credibility. In the end, I'm not sure if I was a target or an accomplice. Trust me, this question keeps me up at night. Often!'

[Narrator]

As always, we would still like to talk directly with anyone who has any information about the actual whereabouts of Susan Mitchell herself or her assistant Jane (last name unknown). If you have any information that may help us, please contact us immediately. We would very much like to talk to you and would be happy to keep your personal information confidential if required.

You may hold the key to unlock all the mysteries that remain unanswered.

It is often said that 'Not everything is as it seems' but with Susan Mitchell – The Woman Who Stole The World – nothing *was* as it seemed.

Now, a word from our sponsors …

[Peter Lana – Lana Consulting]

'My name is Peter Lana and I should have known better.'

[Stephen Grace]

'What exactly do you mean by that?'

[Peter Lana – Lana Consulting]

'So, let me explain. I make my living as a private forensic accountant. Which is just a fancy way of saying financial private investigator. I'm the guy that the government, news organizations, or high net-worth individuals call in to investigate embezzlement, money laundering or financial crimes. Sometimes I have even worked for the likes of investigative journalists like yourself and programs similar to this one.

'More recently though, and because of their huge rise in popularity, I have been investigating the claims of ethical or socially responsible managed funds. Which is what the Human Capital World Fund claimed to be.'

[Stephen Grace]

'Were you working for anyone else when you started investigating the Human Capital World Fund?'

[Peter Lana – Lana Consulting]

'I was freelancing. You could say that was part of my problem because at that point, I had not discussed my suspicions with anyone. I had no one to bounce my thoughts off. Which can cause issues for people like me.'

[Stephen Grace]

'Should you even need it? Aren't you the expert?'

[Peter Lana – Lana Consulting]

'Yes, but everybody makes mistakes, Stephen, even forensic accountants. I'm sure that even you, with your years of reporting experience, still have someone to read over your work before you report it. Someone to catch those minor spelling mistakes or rounding errors that you might have missed.'

[Stephen Grace]

'Yes, I have an editor.'

[Peter Lana – Lana Consulting]

'Right, well, imagine you write a story and even though you have been reporting perfectly for the past twenty years, this one time you miss something very early. Perhaps you fully intended to show it to your editor, but somehow the story got out of control and they pressured you to publish your story unedited. How much damage do you think that one error could cause?'

[Stephen Grace]

'Well, in my industry it could cause millions of dollars' worth of damage or legal battles.'

[Peter Lana – Lana Consulting]

'Right. Well, for me it was a mistake that may be closer to hundreds of millions of dollars' worth of damage. Would you be able to sleep at night with that much damage hanging over you? That is why I started this interview by saying I should have known better. I feel partly responsible for this mess, but I want it stated clearly that I never took anyone's money. You search my bank accounts if you don't believe me. I can assure your listeners that I have nothing. Not even my own self-respect after this whole saga.

'I'm sorry, I'm going to need a moment.'

[Narrator]

While Peter takes a moment to collect himself, I want to assure you all that we have checked into Peter Lana's background, thoroughly. We can report that we have found no evidence that he has ever been involved in anything of a questionable nature in the past. In fact, in the years preceding his involvement with the Human Capital World Fund, Peter had twice received awards from the National Board of Accountants and Auditors for his services to their industry.

I can also tell you that, throughout his interviews with us, Peter was always extremely open and cooperative with us, even when discussing his own failures and shortcomings.

[Stephen Grace]

'Peter, could you please tell us how you came to be involved with Susan Mitchell and the Human Capital World Fund in the first place?'

[Peter Lana – Lana Consulting]

'Sure, Stephen. Like you, I am an investigator. Now and then something unusual sparks my interest, that I want to know more about. Typically, I want to see if there is any financial impropriety that may affect the public and thus needs to be exposed. I should say that, at that early stage, they were still much smaller than the companies I usually investigated. But they had one thing that stood out to me early as a red flag.'

[Stephen Grace]

'And what was that?'

[Peter Lana – Lana Consulting]

'Their sales pitch was too good! There are unwritten industry standard rules in this industry about the way you market a managed fund. Most of the corporations want their fund to stand out, to differentiate themselves from the others. But they also want to work within their industry framework. Mostly, they market themselves as "just like the others – only better". Being part of the herd gives them a credibility. It also makes their customers feel like their money is in safe hands, even if they don't believe all the promises the funds make. But then the Human Capital World Fund and its popstars came along. And these guys are not even pretending to be like the others. They don't care about "credibility by association". It made my job very hard because how do you compare them to the industry standard funds. It is not like you are comparing apples with oranges. It is more like comparing apples with bicycles.

'Like I said before, at that stage there wasn't a lot of money yet invested. The only reason I started investigating them at all is because another project finished and I thought to myself that if I didn't investigate them, I wasn't sure who else would.

'So, I knocked on their door one day out of the blue and started asking questions.'

[Stephen Grace]

'Did they try to hide anything from you?'

[Peter Lana – Lana Consulting]

'Not at all. Quite the opposite. Mathias invited me in and gave me a tour of their office. It was quite small in those days, but you could see that they were already running out of desk space. Sometimes there were two or three people at a single desk. Mathias explained to me they were experiencing hyper-growth, and that they were looking for a bigger office location. For the record, we never left that office. We just kept cramming everyone in there.'

[Stephen Grace]

'Did Mathias answer all of your financial questions?'

[Peter Lana – Lana Consulting]

'Sort of. He had answers for everything. I'm not sure if they were to the questions I was asking, but he seemed to have a lot of answers. He was one of those "smartest guy in the room" type people. He seemed keen for me to know that, but I've had experience with these types of guys before. Often, once you get past the initial flurry of information, there is actually very little substance behind them. I guess you could say that he was smart in a way that makes you regret asking your question. You end up confused and unsure if you got the answer you were looking for. I even tried asking a few questions a second time, using other words, so that I could be sure that I hadn't confused him. He just maintained his same answers with a smile on his face. It was like he had absolutely nothing to hide.

'Full credit to Mathias, though. I have been stonewalled by smart guys before, but he was different. He seemed to thrive in the combative nature of our discussion. Maybe he had spent too much time talking to dumb popstars and was glad to have someone from the industry that he could spar against.

'It was all a bit too much for me in the end, though. I wasn't happy with any of it. I think that if I had walked away at that point and gone back to my office to take it all in, I would have written it all up as a potential scam that day. But I didn't.'

[Stephen Grace]
'Why didn't you?'

[Peter Lana – Lana Consulting]
'Because that is the moment Susan walked in.

'Let me tell you first, I rarely get to address a CEO directly. Because of that, when I do, I really want to be ready for the meeting and have all my information at hand. But on that day especially, I was not ready to talk to Susan because I had so little to work with. I had comprehended nothing that Mathias had told me, so I was still in my information discovery phase. All I really knew at that stage was that I didn't understand the structure of the company, and that something didn't feel right about Mathias's approach to answering my questions. I will admit that I was worried. I didn't want some high-pressure CEO picking a fight with me before I had all my ducks in order, so to speak. But she didn't do that at all. She just thanked Mathias and invited me into her office. In the end, I hardly asked her anything – she was asking me all the questions.'

[Stephen Grace]

'Questions about what?'

[Peter Lana – Lana Consulting]

'Remember, I had told no one that I was coming to their office, but she seemed to know a lot about me already. She told me she was really pleased that I dropped by, like she had been hoping for it or expecting it. She already knew my background and asked me questions about that. We discussed an article of mine that she had read, one that I had published two years before. And I can admit that it was not the sort of material that the public reads. Come to think of it, I can only think of a handful of people that might have cared about it, or even understood that article. Susan, however, had not only read it but she seemed fascinated by it. It was all very unexpected.

'It was like I had knocked at a stranger's door, and they had answered by saying, "Peter, what took you so long?".'

[Stephen Grace]

'Did she talk to you about the Human Capital World Fund?'

[Peter Lana – Lana Consulting]

'Yes, she did. After about thirty minutes, it was her turn to talk. She said that she had grown up in adversity but had been lucky in the more recent part of her life. She wanted to do her bit to help the world which is why she started the fund. I really wanted to believe her.'

[Stephen Grace]

'But you didn't?'

[Peter Lana – Lana Consulting]

'No, that's not quite right. I believed her, but I just wasn't sure it should matter.

'You must remember, Stephen, I deal in numbers, not in stories or emotions. If companies lie in their numbers, I can see it for what it is.

'The other thing you need to remember is that Susan Mitchell did not invent socially responsible or ethically managed funds. If you watched some of her presentations and you didn't know any better, you might believe so. But that is not the case. They have been around for a while.

'Many of the modern institutional funds say they are ethically or socially responsible now. Given the amount of them, the public might assume that a guy like me has looked over their books and given them a green tick that they are doing the good they say they are, but that is not always the case. These types of funds are growing so fast now and there are only so many of the likes of me. Even fewer, now that I'm out of the game.

'Most people just take them on face value. They give them their money and do not know what they do with it. They check their responsibilities at the door, so to say. Susan Mitchell's contribution to the industry was to show pictures of new bridges, new wells and refugees and provide visibility and connection to the actual dollar that was invested. She then mixed in a few popstars, and Allison plastered Susan's pretty face all over the marketing. You could say she made these funds sexy.

'Can we delete that last line from the interview? Even now, I don't want to be disrespectful to Susan. She was always very nice to me.'

[Stephen Grace]

'So, knowing everything you already knew about how the industry worked, you still joined her company? How did that happen?'

[Peter Lana – Lana Consulting]

'I won't say that I was tricked, because she never tried to hide anything from me. She told me all the business's shortcomings, and I knew that there were a few that I could help her fix.

'The way I explain it to people now is to say that I was just tired of being a voyeur into a business. I was always on the outside looking in. Looking for weaknesses and then picking them apart. I just wanted one time to come inside and help her build something special. I thought that was what I was doing.

'I figured that even if she was half as good as she appeared to be, that this company could be truly amazing. I loved her vision, and her energy.'

[Stephen Grace]

'What happened next?'

[Peter Lana – Lana Consulting]

'They publicized my joining the organization within days. It was like I had validated their credibility. So, from that point on I had no choice but to work super hard for them because they tied my name to it. Susan told me I didn't need her permission for anything that wasn't going to be company-changing. She told me to just go and do what needed to be done.'

[Stephen Grace]

'Knowing what you know now, having spent time inside of the machine, were they what they claimed to be?'

[Peter Lana – Lana Consulting]

'It is a question that I still ask myself every day.

'Yes, I was on the inside, but the company had layers to it. I was just an employee, like everyone else you have interviewed. I told the authorities about our challenges. Every new company has those. If you look at any amazing company, you will see that it was in complete chaos at one stage of its growth. Until Susan and the money disappeared, I thought that is what we were going through. Going through hell to build something amazing.

'I was on the inside and supposed to be the expert, and yet I got conned like everyone else. She took their money, but she took my credibility, which is something me and the people in my industry always value highly.

'I don't expect people who have lost money to care about me, but for the record, I'm not handling this all very well. Every night when I try to sleep, I ask myself if I was a target or an accomplice in all of this. It's a question that I don't have an answer for.

'Having said all of that, if she walked through that door now, I couldn't guarantee you I wouldn't fall at her feet all over again.'

[Narrator]

It seems that Peter Lana has a lot to get off his chest, so we will hear more from Peter in future episodes.

As for us, we were starting to see a psychological pattern amongst all of Susan Mitchell's employees, which made us re-evaluate what her core skill set might have been. There is little doubt that Miss Mitchell was a truly gifted saleswoman, but we believe her understanding of people may have been what really set her apart. She hired people that were passionate about their beliefs and skills. People she knew would act on instinct and then she gave them license to do so freely. These were not nine-to-five workers but self-propelling entities. It can be a brilliant strategy to enable a business to grow fast; however, while this is good in an early stage of business, excessive growth in multiple directions can also stretch a business to a point where nobody knows what anyone else is doing. This would become a very real problem for Susan Mitchell in the future.

'Next episode, we will bring you more of our interview with Allison Bailey as she explains how the company could rebrand itself as an industry innovator and propel Susan Mitchell's personal brand to ever greater heights.

[Allison Bailey – Social Media]

'It was so successful that there even came a point where people recognized Susan's face in the street. Many just assumed that she was going to be an A-list actor, but some also saw her as the next Steve Jobs.'

[Narrator]

There will be more on that interview next episode.

As always, we would still like to talk directly with anyone who has any information about the actual whereabouts of Susan Mitchell herself or her assistant Jane (last name unknown). If you have any information that may help us, please contact us immediately. We would very much like to talk to you and would be happy to keep your information confidential if required.

You may hold the key to unlock all the mysteries that remain unanswered.

It is often said that 'Not everything is as it seems' but with Susan Mitchell – The Woman Who Stole The World – nothing *was* as it seemed.

Now, a word from our sponsors …

EPISODE 14: THE SCANDAL

[Narrator]

Who was the mysterious Susan Mitchell – The Woman Who Stole The World? And how was she able to convince so many people to invest hundreds of millions of dollars into her Human Capital World Fund before disappearing off the face of the earth with everyone's money?

Join me, Stephen Grace, as I interview those closest to her to answer the questions on everyone's mind. Questions such as: who was she? why did she do it? and where did Miss Mitchell and all that hard-earned money go?

Last episode, we met Peter Lana from Lana Consulting. You might recall that Peter made the jump from contract financial investigator to full-time employee of Susan Mitchell and the Human Capital World Fund. It was clear from our interview with Peter that he was aware of some of the early company growth issues but believed that he was joining a legitimate investment company with a bright future. What was unclear was if they recruited Peter to help the company grow, or if they simply brought him in to add a financial credibility to the company and silence its critics.

In this episode, we will talk to Allison Bailey, who ran branding and social media for Susan Mitchell, to unpack that question just a little more. We will also hear from Allison about the 'Ku-Stom vs JC Chains' campaign that she started and the major implications that would come from it in the coming months.

Let's hear from Allison.

[Stephen Grace]

'Allison, can you tell us about the time when Peter Lana joined the company? You seemed to make a big deal online about that.'

[Allison Bailey – Social Media]

'Poor Peter. He was a nice guy. A bit naïve, but I liked him. I don't think he knew what he was getting himself into.

'At that point in the business, I had little to work with. I was still fanning the flames online to keep the fire building. We had the eyes and ears of the world on us, so we had to keep talking and sharing stories of our success. When I heard Peter had joined us, I had to figure out how I could spin it. Now, if you searched online for Peter back at that point, you would have found a few boring articles and a few photos of him in a sweater. Very un-sexy indeed. I wanted something sexy, and newsworthy. So, I had to create it myself.

I found a photo of him that was okay from the head up, so I got a friend of mine to superimpose his head on a model in a tailored suit. It really was quality work. It embarrassed him at the start but, to be honest, he never ever looked so good. I'm sure he knew as much so he finally let it go. Nobody ever guessed that it was a fake.

'I then created a story around him that suggested the entire financial industry took his word as gospel. And that his validation alone was enough to seal our fate. The article had the headline "God Has Spoken – And He is all in on Human Capital!".'

[Stephen Grace]

'Did Susan Mitchell ask you to do that?'

[Allison Bailey – Social Media]

'Not likely. She hated it. She immediately called Peter to apologize.'

[Stephen Grace]

'So, did you pull it down?'

[Allison Bailey – Social Media]

'You have got to be kidding. I paid extra money to get it in front of another million people. I kept telling them, if you have something that you truly believe in, then you must get it in front of as many people as possible. This fund puts food on the table in Third World countries and builds solar powered power stations in deserts. Wouldn't you want to build that fund as big as you can? Even if it makes just one boring finance dude a little uncomfortable. That is what she paid me for. To amplify our message. Not to play nicely and make friends. At that point, it was our best message to the world, so I ran with it full steam ahead. There was no way I was going to shut that down.

'Anyway, she didn't have long to be angry at me for that because I upset her even more not long after. This one she got over, but I'm not sure she ever forgave me for what was to come next.'

[Narrator]

We will hear about that next encounter in just a moment, but before we move on, we just wanted to clarify that we have evidence that Peter was quite embarrassed about how Allison Bailey portrayed him as a god of the financial world. We have spoken directly to two of his industry peers, and both recall his frantic apologies to them about it. They describe him as a humble man who has worked quietly in the shadows of the financial markets for years. It is worth noting, however, that Peter never publicly denounced the article. Perhaps for the first time in his career, he not only believed in a cause enough to join the company, but also saw a moment where he might come out of the shadows into the spotlight as a public figure for the first time.

Now we will return to Allison Bailey and the unforgivable act that she committed that would so upset Susan Mitchell.

[Allison Bailey – Social Media]

'It would have been about a week since I had broken the news that the great Peter Lana had joined us, and I started looking for my next headline. Sally was off finding new ways to spend the new Ku-Stom Trust money and Mathias was busy making sure that everyone knew how clever he was. I was getting bored big time, so I wanted to create something special. A story that would have legs for weeks to come, not just another press release that people would forget in days.'

[Stephen Grace]

'Just before you tell us all what it was specifically, how do you do that? How do you create a story from nothing that has potential to generate news for weeks?'

[Allison Bailey – Social Media]

'You need to force people to pick a side on a topic and hope that they do it so emotionally that they will continue to argue amongst themselves from that point on. It is like dropping a lit match into a firework factory. At the start you just need the flame to catch one wick, and then for that banger to set all the others alight. Once it does you just sit back and enjoy the show. I had tried this strategy once before but had nowhere near this type of success.'

[Narrator]

It was another opportunity for us to get an insight into the mental motivations of Allison Bailey.

[Stephen Grace]

'So what was this "lit match" that you dropped into the firework factory?'

[Allison Bailey – Social Media]

'I got Sally drunk over a lunch one day and got her to tell me everything that had happened the night of the party at Dylan Clarke's house. The night when Susan met Ku-Stom, JC and Veronique for the first time. To that point, I did not know about the little love triangle between Susan, JC and Ku-Stom.'

[Stephen Grace]

'Was it a love triangle, though? We haven't really heard any evidence of them meeting since the party. Let alone anything about any personal relationships Susan Mitchell may have had with the two men.'

[Allison Bailey – Social Media]

'Stephen, you are missing the point. No one really cares if it is true. Do you think they sell all those women's magazines based on truth? If they were based on truth, they would sell three copies. Scandal, on the other hand, sells big. So, I threw a scandal into the firework factory of public opinion.

'I rarely like to give away my trade craft, but I'm quite proud of this one so I will share it this one time. I got a friend of mine to write a juicy article pretending to be someone who was at that party that night. We amped up the love triangle story by adding a few snapped sideways glances from JC and Ku-Stom which were taken completely out of context. I then got him to disclose the million dollars that Ku-Stom had raised for the fund and got him to question that, if JC loved her so much, where was his contribution? It fundamentally asked the reader to pick a side – are you team Ku-Stom or team JC? Do you want the flamboyant boyfriend who does unnatural things to win your heart, or the introverted boyfriend who looks pretty but says very little? I know who I would want and that is just the point of it.

'The moment the story broke, I released a press statement denying all of it immediately. In fact, we denied it so many times, on purpose, that anyone reading it would have been sure that it was true. It may have helped that I put a link to the story in every denial as well. In doing so, we drove more traffic to that story than any other means. Our little flame had found a hungry wick and the first firework had exploded. Soon after, there were headlines like "The Human Capital Queen and her two Rockstar suitors" and "Three's a Human Capital Crowd" popping up everywhere. I had my burning topic for people to pick sides on and now we had fireworks exploding all over the firework factory floor.'

[Stephen Grace]

'How did Miss Mitchell respond to the article?'

[Allison Bailey – Social Media]

'To say that she "lost her shit" would be a colossal understatement. She blasted me in the office out in front of everyone. I tried to deny it, but she knew it had been me. She is quite good at seeing behind things like that.'

[Stephen Grace]

'Did she fire you?'

[Allison Bailey – Social Media]

'Well, that is the funny thing, Stephen: she didn't fire me. I think everyone there thought that she was about to, but she didn't. She finished her little rant and then sent me straight back to work. She never once asked to check any of my work from that point on. Here is the real scoop for you. I believe she was happy with it and that she was pretending. She might not have liked that it caught her by surprise, but again, that is the role she paid me to play.'

[Stephen Grace]

'How do you know this?'

[Allison Bailey – Social Media]

'There is a saying in my game which is, "You can't bullshit a bullshitter". I'm not convinced that her little rant in front of everyone was for my benefit. She could have dragged me off and done it in private if it was for me, but no, she positioned us in front of everyone first. I think she was fine with my little game but wanted to be seen to be publicly furious about it. The team was growing at that point and many of them were being called by reporters for comments on the story, so I suspect she was putting on a little performance for everyone else. Like I said, "You can't bullshit a bullshitter" and I saw right through her little performance. But I don't believe anyone else did. They ate it up, hook, line and sinker.'

[Narrator]

I wanted to get a second opinion on this before I moved on, so I put a question to Sally Basset about it.

[Stephen Grace]

'Sally, were you in the office that day that Susan lost her temper with Allison around the "Team Ku-Stom vs Team JC" story?'

[Sally Bassett – Social Change Activist]

'Oh … yes. I don't think that I have ever seen Susan so angry. She was furious that day. I didn't think that she had it in her. It really put everyone on notice.'

[Stephen Grace]

'Did she often get frustrated by things?'

[Sally Bassett – Social Change Activist]

'Everybody does, Stephen, we all just do it differently. You could say that was a big surprise which came right after the surprise of the Ku-Stom Trust money. So maybe the two things together tipped her over the edge that day. I think she was embarrassed as well. I know that her and JC had been talking to each other, so I assume that they had become friends. Maybe she didn't like that he had been dragged into it all.'

[Stephen Grace]

'Do you have any idea on how the story was received at the Ku-Stom and the JC camps?'

[Sally Bassett – Social Change Activist]

'Yes, I know a little. The Ku-Stom people loved it. They are entertainment industry people after all, and they deal with that sort of thing every day, and it made him look good. They called wanting to stage candid photos of Ku-Stom and Susan attending events together and having dinner at fancy restaurants. Susan didn't want any part of it.

'JC's people reacted differently. I don't know for sure, but I don't think JC was happy.'

[Stephen Grace]

'What gave you that idea?'

[Sally Bassett – Social Change Activist]

'A look on Susan's face after she took a call from him. She looked devastated. Having said that, it could have been anyone on that phone.

I'm just assuming it was him. She said nothing about it of course.

'Look, I'm sure that Allison thinks she did her job wonderfully but, when I look back now, I see that time as the beginning of the end. Things were about to get very difficult for us in the coming months, and she started it all. She can congratulate herself all she likes, but she just kept making things worse. From that point, it all just got out of control.'

[Narrator]

Was Allison Bailey being a renegade employee or was she simply doing the work that Susan Mitchell paid her to do? We may never know the truth if we don't get to ask Miss Mitchell directly.

The one thing that we know is that the 'Team Ku-Stom vs Team JC' campaign was a complete success in all the parameters that Allison Bailey set for it. Its online posts were commented on hundreds and thousands of times by people picking their sides and then arguing their positions amongst themselves. That original article that Allison Bailey commissions and the denials afterwards were shared thousands of times. This dramatically increased the amount of people that saw it worldwide. It even made a crossover into mainstream press when three tabloid newspapers included the story in their gossip sections.

It is becoming increasingly clear to me that, in a digital age, Allison Bailey had a bigger impact on the growth of the Human Capital World Fund than just sharing a few pictures of water wells and bridges in Third World countries. Allison made Susan Mitchell her product and sold Susan to the world extremely effectively. We just don't know if that is what Susan Mitchell, who is an extremely private person, wanted. What is clear is that, in hiring Allison Bailey, she opened Pandora's box and she would have to spend months dealing with the outcomes of Allison's actions.

Next episode, we will hear about Susan Mitchell's next public engagement. It was at an exclusive charity event where once again she would rub shoulders with the rich and famous, including Veronique, Ku-Stom and JC Chains once again. This time there would be dramatic ramifications, which would inflame the headlines even further.

We also have a surprise to share with you next episode. New information and resources have come to light, which are very interesting indeed. We are unpacking it all for you now and trying to make sense of what exactly it means for this story. Stay tuned!

It is often said that 'Not everything is as it seems' but with Susan Mitchell – The Woman Who Stole The World – nothing *was* as it seemed.

Now, a word from our sponsors …

EPISODE 15:
THE CRYSTAL BALL

[Narrator]

Who was the mysterious Susan Mitchell – The Woman Who Stole The World? And how was she able to convince so many people to invest hundreds of millions of dollars into her Human Capital World Fund before disappearing off the face of the earth with everyone's money?

Join me, Stephen Grace, as I interview those closest to her to try and answer the questions on everyone's mind. Questions such as: who was she? why did she do it? and where did Miss Mitchell and all that hard-earned money go?

We are getting to the point in our story now where things get complicated for Susan Mitchell, a woman we still know very little about in the scheme of things. Sure, we have the public persona of Miss Mitchell which we can easily see in any search engine, but what of the woman herself? Who was she really? Was she working alone, or were there people behind her pulling the strings? To help us answer these questions, we have enlisted a little outside help. I can announce now that we will bring in a professional to help us investigate her personal background. You can expect to hear more about that next episode, and you won't believe what he will have to say.

For today's episode, we are going to stick with the story at hand. It was a story created by Allison Bailey who thrust it into the public consciousness. That story being the burning rivalry between the two powerful men vying for Susan Mitchell's affection: Ku-Stom and JC Chains. If you were going to be fought over by any men, even if it was just in the tabloids, these two would be as good as any. Both men have released multiple number one hits. Both men have millions of adoring fans. Both are extremely rich and powerful in their industries. A while it may sound romantic to some, to Miss Mitchell this story was a storm cloud ominously brewing. Luckily for us, when the perfect storm broke, it would play out at a public event in front of hundreds of witnesses, and paparazzi who were pre-warned to be ready with their cameras.

It was a charity event for the rich and famous called 'the Crystal Ball'.

[Stephen Grace]

'Sally, can you please tell us about the night of the Crystal Ball?'

[Sally Bassett – Social Change Activist]

'I felt like Cinderella at the start of that night. Out of the blue one day, Susan told me to meet her outside our office at about noon. She then drove us to a ritzy shopping plaza and told me we needed to both get an amazing dress for a charity event that we would go to that night.'

[Stephen Grace]

'Too bad if you already had plans for the night.'

[Sally Bassett – Social Change Activist]

'Stephen, I would have cancelled dinner with the queen to go. Susan paid for everything. Designer dress, designer shoes, hair, nails – everything all on her card. We then went to her home and got ourselves ready before she got a limousine to take us to the event. I know I mentioned earlier that I never knew if we were friends or if she was just my boss, but that day it was different. We were friends that day, and each other's date for the night. I can say this now confidently because we were giggling like schoolgirls on the way.'

[Stephen Grace]

'Did you have any sense at all, of the drama that would unfold?'

[Sally Bassett – Social Change Activist]

'None. We were just excited to be dressed up for the party. Thinking back now, I feel quite sad for Susan. I know that you all think she is some type of conman who ran off with everyone's money, but I've seen how hard that woman works. You don't work as hard as she did just to run off at the first sign of trouble.

'If anybody needed a night out, she did. She'd earned it. And they stole that from her.'

[Stephen Grace]

'Who stole it from her?'

[Sally Bassett – Social Change Activist]

'Mostly Ku-Stom's people, and the paparazzi. But I'm almost certain that Allison Bailey's fingerprints were all over it as well. JC played a part, but I think he was just reacting to everything else. If there was a conspiracy at play that night, then I'm sure he knew nothing about it.'

[Stephen Grace]

'So how did it all play out?'

[Sally Bassett – Social Change Activist]

'We walked up the red carpet like movie stars. There were even people taking pictures of us like they do on TV. Susan seemed quite surprised that they all knew her name, but they did. Nobody knew me but that's to be expected. They kept asking Susan for a photo by herself, but she flatly refused to let my arm go. I think she was worried that they might try to fake the photo somehow, or maybe she just didn't want me to feel left out. I'm not sure.

'Anyway, we finally walked into the Crystal Ball and everything was just beautiful. It was all lit up like a fairy-tale. They showed us to our table, which was out on one wing, but we didn't care. The super-rich and famous were being positioned directly in front of the stage for the auction. We thought we could just sit at the side and have a few happy drinks together.

'JC was already there and sitting at another table, surrounded by people. As soon as he and Susan locked eyes, I could tell that Susan knew he would be there. Everybody was waving to Susan like they were friends. I was getting a feeling that I would be alone most of the night, but to her credit, Susan did not run off and leave me. She just gave JC a brief nod as if to say, "I'll come and find you later".'

[Narrator]

I am going to cross for a moment back to the interview I did with Allison Bailey when we spoke about this event.

[Allison Bailey – Social Media]

'Of course I knew about it. Who do you think got her the invite? I was so pissed off when she took Sally instead of me. I was her head of social, and the Crystal Ball was the biggest fucking social event of the year. If she knew that I had arranged it she didn't say, because she was still pretending to be upset with me. Taking Sally was such a waste of an incredible opportunity. I will say this: if she had taken me, it would have played out very differently. I would have had her on the front page of every paper the next day.'

[Stephen Grace]

'How did you arrange for her invitation?'

[Allison Bailey – Social Media]

'Easy, I cooked up the scheme with Ku-Stom's people, and they arranged the invite. We then tipped off the press and suggested that they might want to get three shots if they can. The first with Susan and Ku-Stom, the second with Susan and JC, and the third photo, which would be the holy grail, would be if they could get all three of them in the one shot. Ideally, it would have been with one of them looking angry, but as they say, beggars can't be choosers. They were close to getting all three but, unfortunately, they couldn't quite get that last one.'

[Stephen Grace]

'Why were those photos so important?'

[Allison Bailey – Social Media]

'Because Ku-Stom's people knew that romantic rivalry was good for business. So they were more than happy to pull a few strings. I also think Ku-Stom was sick of all the "Mysterious JC Chains" bullshit and wanted to pull him down a peg or two to his level. Scandals will do that to people.'

[Narrator]

Now, let's go back to Sally, who will tell us more about how the night played out.

[Sally Bassett – Social Change Activist]

'We met some lovely people. Some of them had heard of us and were very interested in what we were doing around the world. Businesswise, I made some fantastic connections that night, but I always felt that Susan's mind was elsewhere.

'After about an hour, I said to her, "Can you just go see JC already?". It was quite obvious that's all she could think about. She was reluctant, but I told her, "It's okay, I'm a big girl. I can look after myself," so she finally went over to him.

'I watched them greet each other out of the corner of my eye. It surprised me to see him immediately leave the three people he was with, greeting her with a kiss on the cheek. Now, I don't know him at all, but it did not look like the second time that they had ever met to me. I have thought about this a lot since. There was a special look about the two of them that has been hard for me to define. I wouldn't say they looked like lovers, or associates, or even business partners, but there was an element of all of it in there somewhere. The closest that I could come to describing them would be to say that they looked like conspirators. And I don't mean that in a bad way. I am certainly not saying they looked guilty or criminal, but they had a secret they kept together of some sort. Perhaps it was love, but it seemed more complex than that. They weren't giggling like teenagers; it was more serious. I can't explain exactly how, but it felt to me like there was a secret in the air. And I am almost certain that it had absolutely nothing to do with Ku-Stom.

'Unfortunately, the photo that someone took of them at that very moment tells another story. It basically tells the story that they wanted it to tell, when they later superimposed Ku-Stom into the background.'

[Stephen Grace]

'Was Ku-Stom there?'

[Sally Bassett – Social Change Activist]

'Yeah, he was. I knew right away because the moment Susan and JC met everyone's eyes crossed the room to see the reaction on his face.'

[Stephen Grace]

'And?'

[Sally Bassett – Social Change Activist]

'Ku-Stom was furious. There was no acting, and no doubt about it. And thinking back now, he probably had a right to be angry. He had just raised all that money for us. I think that there was an expectation on his part around that – you know how men can get. I'm not saying that he expected her to sleep with him, but it had been such a public act and I think he was expecting Susan to make a big deal of it in front of everyone. Perhaps everything would have been fine if she had thanked Ku-Stom first, but she didn't. My fault, I guess. I'm not good with that stuff.

'I know for a fact that she was planning to thank Ku-Stom. We spoke about it on the way. But she had her mind on JC, and she went to him first. It was a minor mistake, but it had big ramifications for our night.

'When she did finally make it over to Ku-Stom to say thank you for the money, it was too late. He was cold and angry towards her. She played him well though. I could see that this was not the first powerful man that she'd needed to manage the anger of. I also know this because she later told me that sometimes the most dangerous thing that you can tell a powerful man is that he can't have something. Because, from that point on, they will stop at nothing to get it.

'Luckily, I saw Veronique there. I had only met her the one time at the party and I'm sure that she didn't remember me, but I approached her anyway. I introduced myself and told her I worked for Susan. As I mentioned in a previous interview we had, I was sure that Susan had helped her somehow a few weeks before, so I hoped Veronique might return the favour on this occasion. I said to her, "Susan seems to be trapped over there with Ku-Stom. I can't get near her but perhaps someone at your level might. I was hoping that you might rescue her?".'

[Stephen Grace]

'Did she help?'

[Sally Bassett – Social Change Activist]

'She didn't want to. I don't think she wanted to get caught up in the whole love triangle thing, but then her sense of sisterhood kicked in.

'She told me to stay there and went right over to them. She smiled and said something like, "Enough business talk, time to dance". She then grabbed Susan's hand and dragged her off to the dance floor. Ku-Stom started after them, but one of his people stopped him in a way that seemed to say, "No, boss, the women come to you. You don't chase them". So, he let her go like he didn't have a care in the world. But he was not happy.'

[Stephen Grace]

'You said on a previous occasion that at the party you were tasked to manage Ku-Stom, but I get the sense you don't like him very much. Is that right?'

[Sally Bassett – Social Change Activist]

'Stephen, I'm going to be very careful about what I say here.

'I don't like his music and how it demeans women. Although I will admit that it's fun to dance to. I don't like how he has a family and had a fine education but pretends that he grew up on the streets. I find that disrespectful to those that raised him. But, mostly, I don't trust him. He lies about who he is and where he has come from. And he will say or do almost anything to keep his name in the headlines.

'I wouldn't trust any of those crocodile tears from Ku-Stom that you see on the TV. If people weren't screaming at him for money, would he even be looking for Susan? Perhaps he already knows what happened to her?'

[Stephen Grace]

'Sally, are you saying that you believe Ku-Stom was involved with Susan Mitchell's disappearance?'

[Sally Bassett – Social Change Activist]

'Like I said before, powerful men don't like to be told "no".

'He wanted Susan, and she said "no" to him. Multiple times. I know that for a fact. But it never stopped him trying to get her.

'That is all I am going to say on that matter.'

[Narrator]

This was the first time that anyone had directly suggested that Ku-Stom might have an involvement in Susan Mitchell's disappearance. So, we thought we might run that scenario past Dylan Clarke, who had discovered Ku-Stom and was his former manager.

[Dylan Clarke – The Talent Agent]

'Is that what Sally said? Ku-Stom, huh? Well, she's upset that Susan is missing and, like me, she doesn't believe that she just took the money and ran. So, we are both left looking for people to blame. And, he is an easy man to dislike, if you get close enough to him.

'You need to understand the psychology of some of these stars. There is a reason that I don't look after them anymore once they get to a certain level of fame. Their ego grows to a very unhealthy level. You could say it needs to. If you want to shine brighter than the sun, then first you need to believe that you already do. It is all part of their evolution.

'The reason I hand them off at that stage is because I can't cater to that sort of ego. They need yes-people around them, and I won't give them that. I learned this lesson very early in my career. It was with an exceptional but young talent that I discovered. I won't say his name because I don't want that mess brought up again, but as his success grew, his ego grew as well. He wanted drugs and things that I would not give him, so he went and got them himself. He felt very entitled to take whatever he thought was his by right of his stardom. One night, they arrested him for drugging and raping an underage girl.

'Now, I'm not saying that happens with all of them. I know JC and Veronique to both be very fine people. But there are some that shine just as bright but whose fundamental characters are not as stable as those two. Often, these people stay at the top because they have a team of yes-people around them that are paid to take the fall for their drug possessions and indiscretions. There is another team at the record companies that pay off injured parties to ensure their silence. I flatly refused to do any of that. That specific person was not considered a star in jail. They don't take kindly to men who rape young girls in jail. They killed him only weeks into his sentence.

'It left me with an enormous decision to make. I love my job and I want to be the one that helps them rise, but I don't want to be there for the tantrums when they get there or for the fall. I decided that there should be a time when I let them go.

'Getting back to your question, was Ku-Stom involved in Susan's disappearance? I don't believe so. I'm sure that he is regretting the whole saga, but what most people don't know about him is that he is actually a coward. There is a reason that there are always so many people around him. He can't stand to be alone. I think Susan knew that. Forget what you see on TV, he is a man that loses his nerve, not his temper.

'If he ever hears what I just said, he will never speak to me again. But I have had enough of him now. After this whole affair. I don't care if I never speak to him again.'

[Narrator]

When stressful situations happen, like somebody dying or disappearing, it is common that people can turn on each other. In the light of these events, it makes sense that some of those involved in Susan Mitchell's life might blame each other for her disappearance. Sometimes it is easier to blame others than it is to accept that you didn't dig deeper into a vague answer or obscure reference when you had the chance. I can assure you that it won't be the last of the finger pointing.

Sally Bassett will now continue to describe the rest of the evening at the Crystal Ball.

[Sally Bassett – Social Change Activist]

'I think it was the only time I have even seen Susan reduced to someone else's level. That was Ku-Stom's contribution to her life. He may have been responsible for all that money and her new popularity but, in the end, he just dragged her down to his level. I once heard someone talk about him like he invented the Human Capital World Fund. But regardless of what some people may think, he invested very little of his own money in it. It was all other people's money. If he truly cared for her like he once said he did, maybe he could have invested some more of his own damn money in it.

'Getting Susan to the dance floor got her out of the immediate trouble but was just a staging area. The night just went from bad to worse as his representatives approached us, trying to get Susan back to his table. We also had other men there keen to get their photos taken with Susan. Basically, the Crystal Ball spell was broken, and we just wanted to get out of the place and away from it all. At about 10 pm, Susan got a call from someone and told me she had to leave immediately.'

[Stephen Grace]

'Do you know who the call was from?'

[Sally Bassett – Social Change Activist]

'No idea, and I never asked. It was supposed to be such a special night but, in the end, I was just happy to get the hell out of there. I told her on the way home that I didn't want to have anything more to do with Ku-Stom.'

[Stephen Grace]

'And what did she say to that?'

[Sally Bassett – Social Change Activist]

'She agreed and instead got Allison Bailey to step up and manage that relationship from that point on. It makes sense, I guess. She seems to speak their language.'

[Narrator]

I have never met her personally, but Susan Mitchell must have been something special. Enormous amounts of other people's money were being traded for her attention. Famous popstars acting like spoilt teenagers. Invitations to the Crystal Ball, a charity event for the mega-rich. What was it about Susan Mitchell that created so much attention? We are going to attempt to find out.

Earlier this episode you may recall that I said that we were going to bring in some help to dig up some personal information about Susan Mitchell's background. I can now give you a little more information about that.

We were recently contacted by someone who would not disclose their name to us but said they would like to help us find Susan Mitchell. So much so, that they offered to help pay for a professional investigator to help us find her. Unfortunately, we had to decline their initial offer when they stipulated that they wanted to be the first to speak to her. Given the nature of their anonymity, or of their motives, we had no choice but to decline. After all, if they wanted to do her harm, we did not want to be leading them right to her.

In the end, they conceded their 'first contact' clause and gave us the money anyway. They said that to them, it was more important that we found her. They just wanted to be sure that she was okay. As there were no other conditions, we were clear to take their money and bolster our chances of finding Miss Mitchell. That is assuming, of course, that she is still alive.

Next episode, we will hear from the private investigator that we hired to help us track her down. He will share with us lots of new information and some interesting theories we had yet to consider.

It is often said 'Not everything is as it seems' but with Susan Mitchell – The Woman Who Stole The World – nothing *was* as it seemed.

Now, a word from our sponsors …

EPISODE 16:
THE PRIVATE EYE

[Narrator]

Who was the mysterious Susan Mitchell – The Woman Who Stole The World? And how was she able to convince so many people to invest hundreds of millions of dollars into her Human Capital World Fund before disappearing off the face of the earth with everyone's money?

Join me, Stephen Grace, as I interview those closest to her to try to answer the questions on everyone's mind. Questions such as: who was she? why did she do it? and where did Miss Mitchell and all that hard-earned money go?

We are very excited to bring you this episode. It is the first time that we have been able to bring in external investigative help to assist us in the search for Susan Mitchell and the missing money.

You may recall that last episode we told you that we were contacted by someone anonymously who told us he had a vested interest in finding Miss Mitchell. Such a vested interest that he was willing to pay for a private investigator on our behalf to help us find her. Why he did not hire his own private investigator, or what his intentions are with Susan Mitchell once she is found, is still unclear to us. For this reason, we only agreed to do it on the proviso that if we find Miss Mitchell, we will give up her location if she expressly gives us her consent to do so. They agreed, and here we are.

So, without further delay, and because we are as excited to hear from him as you may be, let's dive right in and see what he has got to say.

[Stephen Grace]

'Could you please start by telling the listeners who you are and what you do?'

[Dirk Rockford – Ford Investigations]

'My name is Dirk Rockford. I am the owner and chief investigator of

Ford Investigations. I am in the business of finding people. People that can't be, or don't want to be, found.'

[Stephen Grace]

'Like an old-fashioned bounty hunter?'

[Dirk Rockford – Ford Investigations]

'A bounty hunter chases criminals. They only get paid when they find them.

'Many of the clients that hire me have family members who have either left of their own accord or are suffering mental difficulties or illnesses. Some also have drug, physical abuse, or financial problems. So, unlike a bounty hunter, I'm not always looking for criminals. For me, a missing person just means that someone wants them found.

'The other difference between me and a bounty hunter is that I get paid upfront. It is either that or I don't take the case.'

[Stephen Grace]

'Can you tell us how you would normally go about finding someone in a case like this?'

[Dirk Rockford – Ford Investigations]

'First, you need to find out why they went missing. We need to determine if they disappeared of their own free will or was there a cause, or stressor, that caused them to leave. This will have a big impact in the approach that I might take to find them.

'Another of the early steps in an investigation is to make sure that the person is not injured, dead, or in jail. We go about this by checking in with hospitals, medical facilities, morgues, and law enforcement, to see if any of them have seen them or anyone matching their description.'

[Stephen Grace]

'Have you been able to do that for Miss Mitchell?'

[Dirk Rockford – Ford Investigations]

'I did, but unfortunately, they had no one by that name or matching her description. I checked out a few Jane Doe cases, but none of them turned out to be her. Which I will say, given the condition of the bodies they presented to me, is a good thing. For her, anyway.'

[Stephen Grace]

'Having done that, what would the next step in your investigation be?'

[Dirk Rockford – Ford Investigations]

'I would typically need to ask a lot of questions with my client. Determine what may have transpired before the person went missing. It is a key part of our process usually, but in this case you have already shared all of your recorded material with me, so that was not necessary.

'Having said that, some of the interview questions you asked people, to build your narrative and entertain your audience, are not necessarily the same questions that I would ask when trying to find a missing individual.'

[Stephen Grace]

'How did you fill in the gaps between the information I provided and the information you would usually require?'

[Dirk Rockford – Ford Investigations]

'To start with, I went back and conducted a more thorough interview with her oldest colleague, Sally Basset, to ask some more personal questions about Susan Mitchell.

'I then went and conducted another interview with Dylan Clarke, because I was keen to explore the nature of their relationship further. With him, I was trying to understand if he was the friend of Susan Mitchell he claimed to be, or was he just cleverly manipulated by her to gain access to his clientele.

'As per the terms of our agreement, and with everyone's approval, I will share some of the more interesting parts of those interviews with you now.'

[Narrator]

We would like to assure listeners that, although it may sound like these interviews were recorded on a hidden microphone, they were not. The microphones that we use for our show are broadcast-grade equipment and Dirk was using a Dictaphone for his recordings. We apologize for the quality of the recording you are about to hear.

[Recorded Audio – Dirk Rockford]

'Sally, you mentioned Susan Mitchell's rules in your recordings with Stephen. You said that everyone there had to follow "her rules". Can you please tell me a bit more about those rules?'

[Recorded Audio – Sally Bassett]

'Oh … those. I'm sure that anyone who works for a boss with a brilliant mind like Susan's also has some quirky behaviours to work around. She only had three rules that we had to work by and if we followed them, we could do whatever we liked. They were: don't question her if she gives you a direct command; don't interrupt her if you can see she is thinking; and, the biggest of all, never enter her office without her inviting you in. She was extremely firm on that one. She instructed us to knock and wait. Even her assistant Jane had to follow that rule, but I think she understood it better than the rest of us.'

[Recorded Audio – Dirk Rockford]

'Why do you say that?'

[Recorded Audio – Sally Bassett]

'Jane never made a joke about it. We all used to joke that it gave Susan time to remove the bodies of her enemies, but Jane would just sit there stone faced like she was trying to hide a response. Her knock on Susan's door was different also, apologetic in a way. It was like she knew how serious it was to interrupt her, or something. It is hard for me to explain, but it was just a sense I had back then.'

[Recorded Audio – Dirk Rockford]

'Why do you think she had that rule?'

[Recorded Audio – Sally Bassett]

'I don't know. And I didn't care. It was an honour, if not always a pleasure, just to work for her. She always came out smiling, so it seems a tiny price for all of us to pay for Susan's privacy.'

[Recorded Audio – Dirk Rockford]

'And this "Jane" – you still can't remember a last name? Or have a photo of her in the office that you can give me?'

[Recorded Audio – Sally Bassett]

'No, I'm sorry. I have looked, and she is not in any of our office photos.'

[Recorded Audio – Dirk Rockford]

'Getting back to Susan, did she ever say anything else of a personal nature to you that you thought was surprising, or strange?'

[Recorded Audio – Sally Bassett]

'She said one thing that made me sad once. I had just lost a distant uncle to cancer which I was a little sad about. I remember she said to me "You are lucky you weren't close. I carry my dead around with me like a scarf". She said no more about it. However, it gave me the sense that she must have had a very sad life, early on.'

[Recorded Audio – Dirk Rockford]

'Do you think that she may have lost someone that she loved?'

[Recorded Audio – Sally Bassett]

'I think that she may have lost everyone that she loved. She had a way of saying things sometimes that clarified that the one sentence you just got would be the very start and end of the same topic. By the time I had looked up at her with a sad look on my face, she had already moved on.'

[Dirk Rockford – Ford Investigations]

'Stephen, as you can hear from the recordings, Susan Mitchell gave away very little information away about her life before the business. Even to those who were closest to her. Typically, this could mean a lot of things, but usually it alludes to a created identity. Perhaps she was part of a witness protection program or perhaps she was running from an abusive spouse. Although, I don't get that sense here.'

[Stephen Grace]

'Can I ask why?'

[Dirk Rockford – Ford Investigations]

'This woman commands too much control over her world for me to jump to that conclusion. If you listen to the recordings – which I know that you have – it is clear to see that she seems to control men well, as an attractive woman. I think that piece about "carrying her dead as a scarf" was a slip. I think it was a part of her past life, slipping its way through her defences before she had the chance to grab it and push it back down again. Slips happen all the time and they help me a lot. I don't get the sense that she is hiding from anyone specific, though. More that she is hiding *something* specific from everyone else.'

[Stephen Grace]

'Did anything else slip through the cracks as you were speaking to Sally Bassett?'

[Dirk Rockford – Ford Investigations]

'Not in her interview, but she contacted me the very next day with some important information.'

[Stephen Grace]

'Such as?'

[Dirk Rockford – Ford Investigations]

'She had been re-watching some of Susan Mitchell's old presentations, and in one video you get a glimpse of her assistant, Jane. I had seen that video also, but I had just made an incorrect assumption that the woman in it must have worked for the venue and not Susan Mitchell directly. It was exciting because that video clip is the only video footage or photo that we have of her to date. Because I have it and it is new information, I decided that I will focus more of my investigation into this young woman, "Jane". I suspect they may still be together somewhere. If they are still alive, that is. It just makes little sense any other way. The only reason no one is looking for Jane is because nobody even knows if that is her real name, and she is not holding anyone's money. I checked in with the police and nobody has launched a missing person's case with them about her. Jane sounds like another made-up name for another made-up identity to me. Another Jane Doe, so to speak.'

[Narrator]

Dirk replayed for us one of the Susan Mitchell presentations that we had seen over a hundred times looking for clues. Sure enough, at the twelve-minute mark, as Susan Mitchell's voice cracks, a young woman approaches her from the right-hand side of the screen and hands her a glass of water. She is on the footage for a total of three seconds. In that time, we only ever see her profile, left profile as she approaches and right profile as she leaves. Dirk created a crude composite image of this 'Jane' face-on by digitally gluing her two profile pictures together.

What we can tell you is that, like her employer, she is an attractive woman who is approximately twenty-five years old. She is about five foot and three inches tall, with light brown hair and a face that seems to be remarkable in its lack of individuality. I don't say that to be nasty, it is just that there is no defining feature that I can use to help you imagine what she might look like. When you look at her, you have the sense that you are looking at a good friend's much younger sister – someone mostly ignored because she said very little outside of what she absolutely needed to.

We shared the email address that we had for her with Dirk before he left us. We had still not received a response from her to that point, but we hoped maybe he could trace it back somewhere.

We are going to return you now to some more of the recorded interviews supplied by Dirk Rockford. This time we will hear a recording of Dirk with

Dylan Clarke, where Dylan will share more details about his relationship with Susan Mitchell.

[Recorded Audio – Dirk Rockford]

'How do you think she knew so much about you that first time you met her? No disrespect, but I have looked you up online and I couldn't find out a lot about you. Yet she seemed to know who you were even then.'

[Recorded Audio – Dylan Clarke]

'You think I was her mark? You think she set the whole thing up just to trap me and get to my clients? It is a fair assumption. Perhaps if I was on the outside looking in, I would think the same thing. I have asked myself these same questions. When someone of this standing, and this amount of money goes missing and your name is one of the first on the list of people to talk to, you ask yourself these tough questions.

'I spent days rolling them over in my mind. Looking at them from every angle.

'Having done that self-reflection, I think that the reason people like you ask me this is because you never met her. You underestimate her – and maybe me also. You never saw how hard that woman worked. They have lists of the conference attendees, you know. Perhaps she looked out on that audience and saw three of seven people she had researched beforehand. Maybe I was just the one she liked the look of at that moment. If that was the case some may call it a con and others might just consider it incredible salesmanship.

'And let me be clear, she didn't know everything about me. She just knew some. Enough to start a conversation, you might say. We became friends in our chats, and I wanted to help her, yes, but it was always at my insistence, not hers. As I said, you never met her. You think you know her, but you don't.'

[Recorded Audio – Dirk Rockford]

'But why did you want to help her so much?'

[Recorded Audio – Dylan Clarke]

'Because sometimes I rescue people. Singers busking on the street with nothing. Addicts with a story to tell and half a voice to be able to tell it. I clean them up and help them find their feet. Sometimes there is money in it for me, but sometimes there isn't. I can always tell when people come from nothing, no matter how flash their clothes are. I can see it. We formed a friendship not because she lied to me but because she didn't need to. I'm sure of that now.

'Maybe I was a bit of a father figure to her. It felt that way sometimes, but I don't know for sure. You will have to ask her if you find her, but I hope you don't.'

[Recorded Audio – Dirk Rockford]

'Why do you say that?'

[Recorded Audio – Dylan Clarke]

'Because you want to find her for the wrong reasons. You want the crown of having found "The Woman Who Stole The World". I'm thinking differently these days. I'm thinking that perhaps the longer she is missing, the safer she will be.'

[Recorded Audio – Dirk Rockford]

'Safer from who?'

[Recorded Audio – Dylan Clarke]

'Safer from the circus back here waiting for her. It doesn't matter what her intentions were. If you find her, they will rip her apart in the courts. I don't want to be a part of that. I'm done here.'

[Narrator]

It was at that point that Dylan Clarke ended his interview with Dirk Rockford.

[Stephen Grace]

'Dirk, after conducting those two interviews, can I ask what conclusion you came to?'

[Dirk Rockford – Ford Investigations]

'Well … for a starter, I'm not completely convinced that Dylan Clarke was any more than just an easy target. Susan Mitchell would not be the first woman to treat an older man like a father figure to get something she wanted. I also think the fact that he got upset with me and closed the interview is because he may have felt a little ashamed that he had allowed himself to be used so easily. It is very common.

'Sally's interview was much more interesting to me because we can piece together some new information. There is a history there, before her time with the Human Capital World Fund. A time where we believe there were some deaths to multiple loved ones. She used the words "I wear my dead around my neck like a scarf". That sounds like multiple people to me, and maybe even a little guilt. This is all good information. I now know that this history exists. I just can't quite see a path to it yet. But if it is there, I'll find it.'

[Stephen Grace]

'Is there anything else of interest that you might like to share with us in this episode?'

[Dirk Rockford – Ford Investigations]

'There is one last thing that troubles me. How does a personal assistant get to be the CEO of a company? Of any company, let alone a funds management company with millions of dollars under management. She seems to have had no experience, or money of her own when she started and yet she disappeared with millions.

'I wanted to investigate that more, so I have done a little homework. What I know so far is that the company was founded by the great (her words) Isaac McGlynn and his adopted brother John Hannebery. Both men have a clear history that is traceable and checks out. And while Susan Mitchell may call Isaac McGlynn "the great Isaac McGlynn" there were not any other people that I could find who would agree. In fact, all ex-customers of the brothers say that the only reason that they did business with them in the first place is because they were bullied into it. One of them only spoke to us openly because he was under the assumption that they were now both dead. When I informed him that I believe John, the second brother, was still alive, he turned white and did not want to continue with the interview.'

[Stephen Grace]

'What happened to the two brothers?'

[Dirk Rockford – Ford Investigations]

'That was the question I wanted answered as well. I know from publicly available records that Isaac McGlynn died of pancreatic cancer. I have seen the death certificate with my own eyes, and it has a still-practicing doctor's signature on it. I have confirmed with police that they have Mr McGlynn registered as deceased. The crematorium also confirmed that they did their job cremating his body. Everything checks out on Isaac McGlynn.

'John Hannebery, the other brother, is a little harder to pin down. We know he ran the company on his own for a few months after his brother's death. Then, one day, he signed the business over to Susan Mitchell and then he disappeared. When he did, he was worth millions. And, from what I can tell, most of that money is still there waiting for him. People are still being paid to maintain his house even though he hasn't been back for months.

'As I said earlier, I believe he is still alive, and would love to talk to him directly, but so far, I cannot track him down. I have a few leads I am following up, but to this point, he has not returned my calls or messages.

'If I do ever get in contact with John Hannebery, I would be very keen to ask him about Susan Mitchell. Especially what she might have said, or done, to entice him to leave the entire company to her and walk away from the very business he started with his brother.'

[Stephen Grace]

'So, given everything you know so far, what are your initial thoughts on Susan Mitchell and her whereabouts? If you had to make an educated guess.'

[Dirk Rockford – Ford Investigations]

'There is a lot about this woman that makes little sense. Perhaps she is a genius, as I've heard some say. Perhaps she is just a fantastic actress who has fooled everyone.

'Every action she took seemed to be deliberate, but often either out of order or disconnected. It was like she was putting together a jigsaw puzzle, but instead of connecting adjoining pieces, she was laying down precise pieces amongst space so that people looking on could not make out the complete picture until it was already too late.

'Given all of this, and that she and all the money are missing, it is much easier to believe that she was an actress. It is even easier to believe that she could have pulled it all off if there was a team behind her. A team creating the scam from the ground up. Financiers, mathematicians, groomers, all preparing her for the big show. A plan to steal money from a group of mega wealthy popstars. She doesn't seem to have any background, so she could be Russian for all we know. There are a lot of mafia type activities and scams coming out of that part of the world these days.

In my experience, the term 'genius' gets bandied about too easily and often to those who simply know just a little more about something than the person awarding them the title. And I hate to say it so openly on your show but if it is the case that she is the front for some type of mafia activity, then they have either changed her appearance, or they have simply killed her off to clear up the loose ends. Either way, she could be anywhere in this world, and in any condition. I'm sorry, I know that a lot of her supporters listen to this show, but you asked me for my educated opinion, so I gave it.'

[Narrator]

We took this theory to Sally Bassett.

[Sally Bassett – Social Change Activist]

'He was right about the jigsaw puzzle. She was building something amazing, and I'll admit that I didn't always see the big picture. But I know what I saw, and I knew her intent. She wanted to do something special for the world. Something amazing. And I still believe that to this day.

'I would like to make one thing clear, if I if may. In all the time I knew Susan Mitchell, she never once took a single order from anyone else. I am not in the least bit surprised that a man like Dirk could not bring himself to think that a woman might be capable of great things. He sees a puppet because he can't bring himself to believe that there is not a man pulling the strings.'

[Narrator]

We are at the end of another episode and once again we are scratching our heads about this mysterious woman.

We will hear once again from Dirk Rockford after he has had more time to investigate the leads that he had uncovered during his interviews. We hope we get that chance to speak with the elusive assistant Jane as well. Her photo and that of the former CEO and co-founder John Hannebery are now on our website for all to see. We encourage you to view their photos and see if you recognize them. If you have any information at all that may help us locate them, please get in touch. You may hold those joining pieces of the jigsaw puzzle that brings the entire picture into focus.

It is often said 'Not everything is as it seems' but with Susan Mitchell – The Woman Who Stole The World – nothing *was* as it seemed.

Now, a word from our sponsors …

THE NURSE (377)

Against all her internal pain the patient managed to squeeze out a few words. 'Tell me again about the plan.' She then sunk back into her pillow.

The young woman who had been her only companion shifted in her chair uncomfortably. 'Nothing has changed,' she replied.

'Tell me anyway,' the patient said through a laboured breath. 'It makes me feel better.'

The nurse checked the patient's chart. Whatever it was that they were planning was not her business, but she couldn't help herself in wanting to know what it was. For weeks this had been her only patient and yet she knew so little about her. Mainly because they spoke so rarely when she was in the room.

That face, she thought to herself as she took a quick glace back in her patient's direction. *Where have I seen that face before?* It was not the exact face but the likeness of it that was just out of her reach. *A sick mother, or grandmother, of somebody famous?*

She took another look at her patient's companion, but her face was different again. If the companion was the patient's daughter, she must have taken completely after the father because she seemed to be cut from a different cloth altogether. Attractive also, but in a brand all her own.

The nurse had been given strict instructions not to ask questions of the women in this room that were not immediately health related. And to never discuss her patient with anyone else, other than the doctor presiding. These conditions in themselves told her enough. Whoever this patient was, she valued her privacy and was prepared to pay an outrageous price to die in peace.

Who would I tell?

The nurse had been in these types of situations before in her private hospital, but never like this. The one thing that she knew for sure was that it is much easier to keep a secret when you don't know what that secret is. It would be in the best interests of the nurse's continued employment if she left the recognition of this patient in the back recesses of her mind.

Let it stay safely out of reach for now.

Perhaps one day, after she dies and this bed is empty once again, the nurse will see the ghost of that face again on a television screen somewhere. It will be at that point that she might think to herself, *that's her, poor thing. She was very sick, but I helped her to die with dignity.* If her patient was famous enough the nurse might even wish that she had someone else in her life that might care to know.

The patient and her companion had stopped talking and there was now an unnatural silence in the room.

They are waiting for me leave, the nurse thought. *Whatever little time they have left together it should not be wasted by my curiosities. Better to give them their privacy.*

As the nurse was leaving the room, she heard a whisper over her shoulder.

'Tell me again, about the plan.'

EPISODE 17: MONEY

[Narrator]

Who was the mysterious Susan Mitchell – The Woman Who Stole The World? And how was she able to convince so many people to invest hundreds of millions of dollars into her Human Capital World Fund before disappearing off the face of the earth with everyone's money?

Join me, Stephen Grace, as I interview those closest to her to try to answer the questions on everyone's mind. Questions such as: who was she? why did she do it? and where did Miss Mitchell and all that hard-earned money go?

In today's episode, we will hear more from Peter Lana, a finance industry expert and independent consultant who, in his own words, 'should have known better'. You may recall from Episode 13 that, after starting his own investigation into many financial inconsistencies that he uncovered with the company, Susan Mitchell was able to recruit Peter to join them – just another example of how persuasive Susan Mitchell can be. In this episode, Peter will tell us about his early days with the company and some of the challenges that he saw early on.

With no further delay, let's hear from Peter.

[Stephen Grace]

'Peter, I am interested to hear what happened right after you joined the organization. We know that you already had concerns going in, but I am keen to know what happened next.'

[Peter Lana – Lana Consulting]

'It was like jumping on to an already burning platform!

'We had all these kids running around cheering about saving the world, and yet, when I looked around, all I could see was litigation. They were all getting excited about going to parties, and I was worried about going to jail.'

[Stephen Grace]

'Did you take your concerns to Susan Mitchell?'

[Peter Lana – Lana Consulting]

'Not immediately. I wanted to compile a list of all the legal and compliance issues first and then present them to her in priority order. So, I told her I had found a lot of problems, but I needed time to work through them first. I asked for two weeks to investigate everything and bring her a report and she agreed.'

[Stephen Grace]

'And then you presented the report to Miss Mitchell? How did she respond?'

[Peter Lana – Lana Consulting]

'Yeah, I did. When I took her through it, she wasn't surprised. In fact, some of it she knew about already. She said that she had not had the time, or the team, to rectify many of the issues because the company had grown much faster than she had expected.

'We discussed the top five issues in depth, and then she asked me to stop. It had been over two hours by that time, and she looked exhausted. We had not discussed it all, but I think that she also knew that, as the CEO, it was better that she did not know all the problems yet.'

[Stephen Grace]

'What makes you say that?'

[Peter Lana – Lana Consulting]

'Because I asked her if she wanted me to send the full report through and she said no. She instead asked me to send her the top items that we had discussed only. She said that there were only so many problems she could shoulder in one day. She asked me to set up a round two of the meeting where we could discuss the next five items. Which I did for the same time the following month.'

[Stephen Grace]

'Do you think she took your concerns seriously?'

[Peter Lana – Lana Consulting]

'Yes, I honestly do. At that point, anyway.

'We came up with a plan to address the first two biggest issues together, and she delegated the other three to me. She gave me full power to fix them with no need to involve her. She said she hired me to fix issues, so that's what she wanted to empower me to do. She didn't want to become the bottleneck.'

[Stephen Grace]

'Is that typical, that a chief executive would empower a staff member to just fix things, as important as some of those things sound like they were? Without the need to go to her for approval?'

[Peter Lana – Lana Consulting]

'Maybe not, but how much can a single woman control? Even one as brilliant as Susan Mitchell. She can't be in control of everything, so I just got on with it.

'The very next day, I took the number one issue and worked eighteen hours straight trying to fix it. I wasn't sure it would even be possible. But I put a plan together and worked at it step by step. I surprised myself with that one, and it gave me some energy to go after the rest, but they wouldn't all be that straightforward.'

[Stephen Grace]

'Did any of the other staff get involved with your work at all, or know what you were working on?'

[Peter Lana – Lana Consulting]

'No. Everyone had their own fires to put out. I don't think anyone outside of Susan knew the size of some of the problems I was working on. They were all too busy running about saving the world and trying to convince popstars how clever they were.'

[Stephen Grace]

'Can you give us an example of the issues that you were working on?'

[Peter Lana – Lana Consulting]

'I don't want to bore your listeners, but the problems were all business or financial structure. I guess that is the reason they hired me: to deal with the boring stuff.

'For instance, when I got there, she had company money, investor money, the Ku-Stom Trust money, even Susan's own personal money, all just thrown in together like it didn't matter. In one bank account! This is like ... basic stuff. I had to separate it all out into different accounts for compliance reasons and set up basic business reporting. I mean, they had reporting, but it was investment reporting not business reporting. I don't think she had a lot of previous business experience.

'Then I created a retail fund for our direct customers and a wholesale fund for the Ku-Stom Trust money. I deemed it wholesale because we didn't know who the end customers were. We didn't even know if it was all the money that he had raised, or if Ku-Stom had kept some as a commission or fee. His team refused to answer that question when we asked them. He flaunted himself as a philanthropist, but for all we know, he could have raised thirty million and kept fifteen. If I'd been there when it happened, I would have advised Susan to return every cent of the moment they got from him. But, of course, that was before my time, so that horse had already bolted.'

[Stephen Grace]

'You mentioned you had Susan Mitchell's personal money tied up in the fund as well. Are you able to tell us anything about her personal financial position?'

[Peter Lana – Lana Consulting]

'All I can tell you is that Susan was not poor when this started. By the time I got there, she was already very wealthy. I can also confirm for you that it wasn't investor money. I know this because, at that stage, we didn't have that many investors. She could have hired someone full-time just to manage her millions and never have to work again. That's why this "running off with the cash" theory makes little sense to me. From what I could see, she never needed the money.'

[Stephen Grace]

'She was already rich?'

[Peter Lana – Lana Consulting]

'Yes. You could say she was comfortably rich. She could have spent the rest of her life on a beach anywhere, living it up. Instead, she spent her time with us, all cooped up in that little office. That's where she was when we could find her, anyway. She disappeared a lot.'

[Narrator]

The news that Susan Mitchell was independently wealthy was new to us. Sure, we had seen footage of Miss Mitchell driving around in expensive cars and wearing expensive clothes. The problem with that is, in our line of work, it is usually just a sign that someone is about to go broke. Or that they are flippantly spending someone else's money. It is often how confidence actors attempt to trick new investors. They show them a seemingly attainable level of opulence before running off with their invested money.

I will say that it put a small dent in the theory that she was just an actress working for the mafia – that is, unless it was seed money from them. Instead, she now seemed to be a woman of substantial means with a plan. One that she went to great lengths to make sure that nobody else could see.

We could no longer be so sure that the money that she had disappeared with was her sole motivation.

An oversight on our part which we would be keen not to repeat.

[Stephen Grace]

'Where do you think she went when she disappeared during those days?'

[Peter Lana – Lana Consulting]

'No idea, and not really my place to speculate. I guess she could have gone home at some point. That would have been fair. I can't remember a time that I didn't see her working. She was there at all hours when she was there, if that makes any sense. But, when she went dark, she went dark. She wouldn't answer the phone, email, or anything. It was like she didn't exist.'

[Stephen Grace]

'Let's go back to all the issues that you were dealing with at the company. Did you honestly believe you could work through them all? That you could fix everything?'

[Peter Lana – Lana Consulting]

'I can honestly say "yes". At that specific point in time, with all that I could see, yes. I knew it would be difficult, but I thought we were going to pull through and become the company that Susan promised everyone it would be. A company that would forever change the ethical investment world and the lives of some of the poorest communities around the world. And when I say this to you now, you must remember that I'm no sucker. I was supposed to be one of the so-called experts because of my extensive financial knowledge and sceptical mindset. Given another six months, I still believe that I could have had our business much more solid and ready for anything that could come our way. Unfortunately, we don't get to choose when and where things happen in life.'

[Stephen Grace]

'So, what turned it all upside down?'

[Peter Lana – Lana Consulting]

'The same thing that got her into trouble the first time. Money.

'In the same week we first received the fifteen-million-dollar investment from the Ku-Stom Trust, we got another five-million-dollar donation from JC Chains directly. His personal money.

'Let's unpack those two transactions for a minute. Ku-Stom, for whatever reason, is out there waving the flag of our cause. He is generating an unknown amount of money and then passing it on to us. We don't know if he was passing on one hundred percent, or ninety percent, or even fifty percent of the money he was collecting on to us. If you believe even half of the people that have come forward since, it was seem very unlikely that we got it all.

'JC Chains, on the other hand, apparently decided that he liked what Susan was doing for the world and wanted to be supportive. So, he just digs his hand in his own pocket and hands over five million dollars. No expectation, no fanfare, no public notice. His people did not ask for any paperwork and have not made contact in any effort to retrieve that money.

'When you look at the two transactions in that light, Ku-Stom wants to make a buck, JC makes a donation.'

[Stephen Grace]

'So, you think Ku-Stom was using this as a money-making venture?'

[Peter Lana – Lana Consulting]

'I do, but Ku-Stom's people – his real supporters – may not. I don't have social media myself, but I understand he has been out there crying poor like he is the victim in all this. His internal people are not money people – they are hustlers. I'm not surprised that it has ended badly for him. It always does for these types of guys. They luck into a scam, and it blows up in their face. Professional scammers would have done much better for themselves.'

[Stephen Grace]

'Can you put your consulting hat back on for a moment and help us understand the scam? Surely, they would know that people would expect to get their money back at some stage. What would they do then?'

[Peter Lana – Lana Consulting]

'I play a game. It's called, "How would I do it, if I was a scammer". If I were Ku-Storm's people, I would raise the money for the good cause and take my cut. Let's put some imaginary figures in to help me explain. Let's say they raise ten million in this fashion for a nice round number. Without letting on, I might then keep thirty percent of that money for myself as an upfront fee. They always pay themselves first. Then I might give the remaining seven million to the Human Capital World Fund to give it some legitimacy. You would then plaster it all over social media to let everyone know that legitimate money was exchanged. You might then hope that the fund earns over the thirty percent that you already took out. If it does, people get their money back and maybe even a little more, but you don't care because you've already made your money upfront. If it ends up being a negative return, you might say something to your clients like, "We should all hold our heads high. We tried to do something good for the world". Or you do what he's doing right now and simply blame us for everything. Susan disappearing is actually a good thing for him. He doesn't have to worry about any of it. He can now just blame her for everything.

'That's how I would do it.'

[Stephen Grace]

'Let me then ask you a question that one of our listeners put to us. Do you think Susan Mitchell and Ku-Stom may have been working together?'

[Peter Lana – Lana Consulting]

'That is just ridiculous. If that was the case, then she must be a phenomenal actress because she didn't want to have anything to do with him by that stage. She even asked me if there was any way we could give every cent of his money back. I'm no public relations expert, but I'm smart enough to know that if we did, we would upset many people who had invested in us, through him. The backlash would've been incredible.

'The mere suggestion of it sent Allison Bailey into a panic.

'That was when I knew there was no going back. The only way forward was into chaos.'

[Stephen Grace]

'Did Susan Mitchell share that opinion?'

[Peter Lana – Lana Consulting]

'She did. She knew what was ahead, just like I did. We were growing faster than she could control and it wasn't just Ku-Stom and JC money, it was coming to us from everywhere. All these New Age millennials started sending us their saving and posting online for the world to see.

'It was a disaster.'

[Stephen Grace]

'Do you have any sense of Miss Mitchell's mental state at that time?'

[Peter Lana – Lana Consulting]

'As far as everyone else could tell, she was fine. But I've seen people battling business problems before. I know what that stress looks like between the smiles.'

[Stephen Grace]

'Did she ever openly admit to you she was worried about the future of the business?'

[Peter Lana – Lana Consulting]

'No, but she was fragile at that point. She started talking to herself all the time. I think she was trying to work things out in her head.'

[Narrator]

The mounting pressure that would come to Susan Mitchell and her entire team would stretch them all to their limits. We will hear much more about over the next few episodes as we count down to the big finale.

If you think you know what is yet to come from what you may have read in the tabloids, then think again, because things get worse again in the mysterious tale of Susan Mitchell and the Human Capital World Fund.

It is often said 'Not everything is as it seems' but with Susan Mitchell – The Woman Who Stole The World – nothing *was* as it seemed.

Now, a word from our sponsors …

EPISODE 18: CHAOS

[Narrator]

Who was the mysterious Susan Mitchell – The Woman Who Stole The World? And how was she able to convince so many people to invest hundreds of millions of dollars into her Human Capital World Fund before disappearing off the face of the earth with everyone's money?

Join me, Stephen Grace, as I interview those closest to her to try and answer the questions on everyone's mind. Questions such as: who was she? why did she do it? and where did Miss Mitchell and all that hard-earned money go?

In today's episode, we will explore the dynamics of the company Susan Mitchell owned as the money started pouring in. Some commentators saw that money as a validation that the company was doing the good deeds that they promised they were doing. Some would see it as evidence of the genius of Susan Mitchell and Mathias LaGrange. Others would come to see the success of the Human Capital World Fund as one of the most successful frauds ever created.

In this episode, we will try to unpack all of that and more as we take you back into the life of The Woman Who Stole The World.

[Stephen Grace]

'Sally, can you please tell us about the time when the second influx of money came in from Ku-Stom, combined with JC's money not long after?'

[Sally Bassett – Social Change Activist]

'That time was the very definition of chaos for me, Stephen. So much so, that if I hear the word "chaos" now, parts of that time pop back into my head. I will tell you about it, but you will need to forgive me if I cry in the process.'

[Stephen Grace]

'I don't want to upset you, Sally. If you would rather not …'

[Sally Bassett – Social Change Activist]

'No. Let me do it and I will try to get it right. That way, it will be on record and I will never have to speak of that time again.'

[Stephen Grace]

'Okay. Well … in your own time, and at your own pace, if you please.'

[Sally Bassett – Social Change Activist]

'First, when I talk about that time, it is important to note it wasn't just the money of Ego-Boy and Sleepy-Eyes – sorry, Ku-Stom and JC Chains. It was all the other money that caught me by surprise. It was the envelopes from twelve-year-old girls who wanted to save the world. The ones sending in their pocket money. It was the big money and the small money all at once. I think I even giggled at the first one I saw. It was cute back then. One even had a picture of a tree with me standing next to it. Not Susan – me! Somehow, somewhere along the line, we had captured the imagination of teenagers and the younger demographic. Perhaps once again, Allison had something to do with it? I don't know.

'But, like I said, it was cute at the start. Those first few handwritten letters. But then, there were just so many of them. And they just kept coming, day after day. Some had cash folded in a birthday card, like a grandmother might give on a child's birthday. Others would just come in with handwritten letters about how they wanted to be like Susan when they grew up. You know, boys have their superheroes, but who do young girls have to look up to? There are few, and those women that reach the heights are often just a mystery to everyone. Susan could speak to an audience in a way that a child could understand. She had that ability. She had cheques, wire transfers, any form of money you could imagine. It all started coming in. And not just locally; from all over the world.

'Of course, there was no way that we could keep it. We weren't a charity. We were supposed to be a legitimate investment fund and we were getting money directly from minors. There are laws about that sort of thing. Also, none of them had filled out any paperwork or read any contracts.

'Peter nearly had a heart attack when he found out! He kept screaming, "Don't open any more of them! Send them all back!" But many didn't even have return addresses. He had spent so much of his time trying to clean up the finance structure of the business and suddenly we had money everywhere. It felt like a casino. It was a disaster. I am surprised Peter lasted as long as he did. He was panicking.

'I kept thinking, "How am I supposed to take all of this money and do good for the world? I'm only one girl". But I also thought about all those beautiful young minds, and how I might disappoint them all if I couldn't. I remember one day going out into the car park where no one could see me and just bursting into tears. I think I may have been there crying for over fifteen minutes before Mathias saw me there and called Susan.'

[Stephen Grace]

'Did she come?'

[Sally Bassett – Social Change Activist]

'She came running. She always did.

'It's funny. I have heard people call her many names over the years. I have heard people call her an actress and a con woman. Plenty of other nasty names. However, the one that upset me the most was when someone once called her an ice queen. I guess, from the outside, I could understand why some might think that. She had to deal with some powerful men, and you can't do that with a soft shell. But they just called her that because they didn't know her like I did. She cared for people in a way that most people would not understand. In a way, most people would never get to see. Not even you, Stephen. It's why she started the fund.

'I think her superpower was her superior understanding of the concepts of care and power. And knowing exactly how to apply either or both for any given situation. Nothing she ever did felt like an act or a performance to me. And she certainly wasn't an "ice queen".'

[Stephen Grace]

'What did Miss Mitchell say to you when she came running?'

[Sally Bassett – Social Change Activist]

'She apologized. She said that her plan was getting off the rails, and she blamed herself for everything.'

[Stephen Grace]

'Did she say anything more about her plan?'

[Sally Bassett – Social Change Activist]

'At the time, I took it to mean her plan for me.'

[Stephen Grace]

'And now?'

[Sally Bassett – Social Change Activist]

'Who can know what is going on in someone else's mind? All I know is that she said that she would get me some help, and, true to her word, she did.'

[Narrator]

We will return to Sally Bassett in a moment. For now, we are going to switch and hear from Mathias Lagrange. You will recall, Mathias was the self-proclaimed mathematical genius who developed the Human Capital Version 2, and one of the original members of Susan Mitchell's team. I asked Mathias what his recollections were of that same time.

[Mathias Lagrange – Mathematician]

'Yeah, I remember seeing Sally in tears. I was never really a fan of Sally, but we had been through a lot, and you still don't like to see a kid cry. So, I fetched Susan. Best to let women sort out their emotional problems with other women, in my experience.'

[Stephen Grace]

'You think Sally was just being emotional?'

[Mathias Lagrange – Mathematician]

'Maybe I'm being a little unfair. It was a very stressful time for all of us. It is just that some, like me, handle it better than most. I find the answer is always in the numbers, so that is where I focused my efforts.'

[Stephen Grace]

'What answer were you looking for in your numbers? What were the questions you were asking of them?'

[Mathias Lagrange – Mathematician]

'How do we scale? Human Capital Version 2, or Cap2 as I came to call it internally, was perfect but never designed to deal with rapid expansion. We designed it for growth in fractions, not in multiples. For instance, it could easily handle a fifteen to thirty per cent growth rate – a growth rate any normal company would be ecstatic about. But that wasn't our growth. Our growth was in a league of its own. The problem was, our systems could not keep up. We never designed Cap2 for two to three hundred per cent growth in an extremely short period of time.'

[Stephen Grace]

'So how did you deal with this new scale issue?'

[Mathias Lagrange – Mathematician]

'I locked myself in a room for three days with my numbers. I told Susan about it and no one else. I only left the room to visit the bathroom every few hours and to shower at the end of the second day. Susan's assistant had food, and anything else I asked for, sent in. On the third day, Susan found me passed out at my desk, so she sent me home.'

[Stephen Grace]

'Did you find the answers that you were looking for? The ones that would allow the business to scale better?'

[Mathias Lagrange – Mathematician]

'I was very close – even Susan said so when she looked over my models. But I didn't quite get there. My mind got caught in a numbers loop which I could not get myself out of. The only way I can think to explain it is like playing hopscotch in a circle. Every number, every calculation, just led to the next, and then to the next. I could not end it. Maybe I was exhausted, or just emotional myself. I write about it in my book. If anyone listening really wants to understand better, they should buy my book.'

[Stephen Grace]

'Did Susan understand it?'

[Mathias Lagrange – Mathematician]

'Yeah, she did. But she said that she had no time to turn her mind back to mathematics with so many other issues happening at once. You can't just take a casual glance at this stuff. She told me to make a list of three people that she could hire to come in and help me, and that she would try to get them. I told her they would be expensive, and impossible to get at short notice.'

[Stephen Grace]

'And?'

[Mathias Lagrange – Mathematician]

'And … she had all three of them in my office the very next day.'

[Stephen Grace]

'How?'

[Mathias Lagrange – Mathematician]

'I have no idea. None of them would discuss the terms of their employment with me or each other.'

[Stephen Grace]

'Were you finally able to solve your scale problem with all that extra brain power?''

[Mathias Lagrange – Mathematician]

'Not initially. It set me back three days just to bring them up to speed, but I guess in the end we found a way. It wasn't perfect, but it just sort-of worked. It wasn't my masterpiece, like Cap2 had been, but it was workable. I'll be honest and say that I felt no pride for it. We called it Cap3, and it was what we used until the day she disappeared.'

[Narrator]

So, Susan Mitchell's company now has more money than it can handle. It has a business and financial structure that is uncompliant by industry regulation standards, and trading on a mathematical formula that 'sort of worked'. There is not a lot in all of that to fill me with confidence. If the outside world would have continued to send them money, would they have disclosed any of these issues? Perhaps if they did, circumstances may have been different for the many people who lost money.

However, not everyone was unhappy. Let's hear from Allison Bailey about how she remembers that time.

[Allison Bailey – Social Media]

'Stephen, we were shining like the sun! If I could go back now, I would resign at that point. At the very fucking peak of my game. Then I wouldn't have had to deal with answering question about the inability of everyone else to do their job.

'I can see that I am becoming the villain of your show, and that's okay with me. But, let me give you a little perspective for a moment. If you look at everyone else on the inside of the Human Capital World Fund – the so-called geniuses, Little Miss Mother Nature running off saving the world, even Peter and all his petty concerns – how many of them could actually say with a straight face that they "crushed their fucking job"? I'll tell you the answer because I'm not here to make friends – I have millions of those online. The answer is: none! Every one of them was a failure, except me!

'That genius mathematical investment formula. Who invented that again? Was it Mathias? No, I believe it was Susan, a woman. I was told that it worked perfectly before he got his greedy hands on it and started making his little "upgrades". After that, I'm told that it was never right again. I notice he is releasing a book on it now. I wonder if there will be an entire chapter on how to take credit for inventing someone else's work, and then stuffing it up.

'And then there is Little Miss Mother Nature back there. Building little bridges, digging wells, helping farmers band together in countries no one has ever heard of. All of it, small time stuff. It would have continued to be, had I not become involved.

'Finally, Peter. That cute little money man. Running about looking like the sky is about to cave in. Seriously, that guy needs to be shown a good time. I even offered it to him once. I'm not embarrassed to say so. We were working back late one night, and I told him I would suck his cock if he just promised to get that miserable look off his face for five minutes.'

[Stephen Grace]
'And what did he say to that?'

[Allison Bailey – Social Media]
'I'm so tempted to tell you he said "yes", but he didn't. And frankly, even though he is cute, I don't want my name tied to him for the rest of my life, so I won't lie. He thanked me for my concern, whatever that means, and scuttled off to work alone again in the dark. Maybe he was married? Who cares? I would have done it anyway. I was bored that day.'

[Stephen Grace]
'So, what are you saying, Allison? That because you were prepared to give a stressed-out man oral sex, you were better than all of them?'

[Narrator]
On reflection, I was not happy with that question. As an interviewer, we strive to carry out our craft without judgement. Judgement is supposed to be reserved for our audience. But over the course of our investigations, I had grown to like Sally Bassett, Peter Lana and even Mathias Lagrange in his own funny way. It was getting hard for me to remain unaffected as Allison Bailey tore them all apart. At the very least, I believed they had all been doing their best under very stressful circumstances.

[Allison Bailey – Social Media]
'No, Stephen, I'm not saying that I'm better than them because I was prepared to blow Peter Lana. I'm saying that I am better than them

because, at the very least, I did my fucking job.

'When I joined, nobody in the world knew anything about Susan Mitchell or that fund, and look at them now. Even before she disappeared, I made Susan Mitchell a household name. Once she had gone, I made her infamous. Seriously, she could come back right now and release a book about her story, and she would sell enough copies to cover all her outstanding debts. I gave her that platform. Without me, she would have just been another hot chick with a funky business plan and a few customers with a boner.

'Sure, Ku-Storm mentioned her in a post one time before I was on board. But if it wasn't for me, they'd have forgotten it the very next day. I took that post and turned it into millions of followers. All those teenage girls who sent in their pocket money to be a part of history. That was a "history" *I* convinced them we were making, not Susan. I had to retell her stories at their level.

'Stephen, that's why I can look at you now, with my head held high, and say, "I did my job". I wonder how many of the others can say that with the same conviction that I have?'

[Narrator]

I will concede that Allison Bailey has a point, to a degree. She can look at me and say that she did her job. But my question back to her is, was it the job that Susan Mitchell asked her to do?

By her own admission, she disobeyed Miss Mitchell's express orders time and time again. We know from multiple accounts that Susan Mitchell blasted her in front of the entire office for acting against her express wishes.

She has countered my argument by insisting that she was just doing the work that they hired her to do. And that she and Miss Mitchell, had an unspoken understanding. But I believe that is where the problem with Allison Bailey lies. If you have an unspoken understanding, how can you be sure that you have an understanding at all? She seems to have taken a lot of liberties while performing that role within the Human Capital World Fund and I, for one, do not believe that she is completely without blame for some issues that arose. That she is one of the few staff members not being questioned by the authorities around the company's mismanagement or the disappearance of Susan Mitchell probably contributes to her cockiness. Her bravado is a luxury that most of her past colleagues who will need to give evidence in court cannot afford. Once again, it seems you can do or say anything you like on social media and not be held accountable for it in the real world.

Next episode, we will hear more from Peter Lana. Peter will share with us the very moment he knew it was all going to fall apart. When you hear about it, you won't believe what happened next.

It is often said 'Not everything is as it seems' but with Susan Mitchell – The Woman Who Stole The World – nothing *was* as it seemed.

Now, a word from our sponsors …

EPISODE 19:
BREAKING POINT

[Narrator]

Who was the mysterious Susan Mitchell – The Woman Who Stole The World? And how was she able to convince so many people to invest hundreds of millions of dollars into her Human Capital World Fund before disappearing off the face of the earth with everyone's money?

Join me, Stephen Grace, as I interview those closest to her to try to answer the questions on everyone's mind. Questions such as: who was she? why did she do it? and where did Miss Mitchell and all that hard-earned money go?

Listeners: welcome back. In previous episodes, you heard about some of the challenges facing Susan Mitchell and her Human Capital World Fund. Challenges such as the ability to scale their investments with their new-found fame, and a business structure that was not compliant with its own industry standard, to name just two. For today's episode, we are going back to Peter Lana. Peter is going to share with us some of the underhanded shortcuts and tricks that funds like the Human Capital World Fund employ when they are trying to generate higher returns for themselves and their clients.

Before the period we are about to discuss, Peter had seen it all but always from the outside looking in through his investigative lens. He was about to experience it firsthand.

It would become something that would eat away at his conscience and have devastating consequences on his mental health.

[Stephen Grace]

'Peter, I know that you have shouldered a lot of criticism around the structure of some of the new deals that were being done around that time. Before we discuss your direct involvement in them, could you give our listeners a little background on the new round of investments that the company embarked on at that point?'

[Peter Lana – Lana Consulting]

'As you know, by this point the money was still flooding into our office. I say flooding because that is how it felt. We would plug one hole and money would simply come in somewhere else. It soon got to a point where we had more money than we had projects we could fund. Having only one Sally Bassett, no matter how wonderful she is, would not be enough to handle all that money. So, we hired a small team to do a similar role to Sally. They would all work with Mathias and his formulas to uncover new investment opportunities for the company to invest in.'

[Stephen Grace]

'How big was the new team?'

[Peter Lana – Lana Consulting]

'It was bigger than just the new people doing Sally's role. We had new people popping up everywhere. Mathias had his new crew of three, and Sally now had her three as well So it was six new heads. Sorry, that means six new people. In business we talk about head count a lot.'

[Stephen Grace]

'Who did the new people report to? Who was their boss? Was it to Sally or directly to Susan herself?'

[Peter Lana – Lana Consulting]

'Well … that was part of the problem. Mathias had no problem shouting orders and telling his gang what to do, but Sally was not built that way. Further to that, her new people were not all built like Sally either.

'I don't think that Sally, or perhaps even Susan, ever had any experience managing people. It was okay when the team was still small, and we were all self-starter types. But when you get a crew, you need everyone going in the same direction and that takes leadership and management. Even I know that much.'

[Stephen Grace]

'Are you saying that it wasn't a well-run team?'

[Peter Lana – Lana Consulting]

'It would be unfair to Sally for me to say that. She never asked for that responsibility, and they did not train her for it. All I'm saying is that perhaps we could have hired an office manager to control everything.'

[Stephen Grace]

'Understood. Would you say that the company as a whole lacked leadership?'

[Peter Lana – Lana Consulting]

'It is probably better to say that at that point we lacked strategy. And not just with our investment portfolio, but with the business. We were flush with money, which most business can never say, but we didn't have enough projects to support the cash. Which means we had a business full of cash which could not perform its core business function. To borrow a cliche, you could say we were all dressed up with nowhere to go.

'It forced the team to look for opportunities that weren't as wholesome as the earlier projects that Sally and Susan had undertaken.'

[Stephen Grace]

'This is not new in your industry, is it Peter?'

[Peter Lana – Lana Consulting]

'No, it is not new. It is a massive problem in the ethical investment market.

'It happens when some investment companies' ethical investments do not perform as well as they would have liked. So, to comply with the expectations of their investors, they go looking for other investments where they can get a bigger return to prop up their portfolios. They might pass that investment off as "ethical" or "sustainable" on some technicality but, in reality, it could be an investment in anything. They call this greenwashing an investment.

'Most investors never take the time to investigate their portfolios. They just accept what's written on the prospectus and go to sleep at night believing that their money is doing good in the world.

'The other issue is that what we may consider "ethical" is subjective to the person making that decision. And to the time frame that the decision is being made. What we could consider "ethical" today might not be considered ethical tomorrow.'

[Stephen Grace]

'Can you give the listeners an example of what you mean by that last comment?'

[Peter Lana – Lana Consulting]

'Sure. Let's argue that an online retailer that hires fifteen people is doing social good by making retail products more accessible to people in remote areas. Perhaps it would make sense to invest money in this retailer and help them expand their operation. To help them help more people. Over the next twelve months, that little business booms, generating a fantastic return on that invested money.

'Then, a year later, we find out that the same online retailer is being criticized for the mistreatment of its workers. Or that, because of its success, three regional shops, who hired local residents as staff members, had to shut down, pushing up unemployment in their towns.

'Do we still consider that online business an ethically aligned investment? That depends on how desperate the investment company is to keep getting their higher returns. They may just choose to ignore the bad news for another year or two before cashing out.'

[Stephen Grace]

'Are you saying that they were not investing the money in how Susan Mitchell told the world that they would? Wasn't Mathias's formula supposed to evaluate that sort of thing?'

[Peter Lana – Lana Consulting]

'I never really understood that formula. It wasn't my part of the business. But I believe they just used it to justify the decisions they had already made. It was like saying to a computer, "Calculate two plus two? But your answer must equal 6". Then Mathias's little brain machine spends three days coming up with a report that says, "Okay, 2+2=6".

'I can't tell you it worked in the beginning, but I know for a fact that it didn't by the end. That is, after Mathias and his friends all got their hands on it. It was like a Frankenstein creation at that point. If it was my decision, I would have gotten rid of him and gone back to the version of it that Susan created. She built it from the ground up for the right reasons. It couldn't have been any worse. Mathias just wanted to show the world how clever he was. It just became an extension of his ego by then. He insisted they made no investments without his machines, or, his personal endorsement.'

[Stephen Grace]

'How did that change things?'

[Peter Lana – Lana Consulting]

'Well, it gave him a lot of power over the running of the business. The new staff members in Sally's team that wanted to get ahead started playing up to Mathias to get him to validate their investments first. Some of them were even bypassing Sally altogether at that stage. I know for a fact that at least one of them was sleeping with him.'

[Stephen Grace]

'How did this all sit with you? You had spent your entire career investigating this type of malpractice, and now you were smack-bang in the middle of it all, with your credibility on the line.'

[Peter Lana – Lana Consulting]

'I had gotten swept up in it all, and now I was watching my entire career go down in flames. I knew it then: they would come to me and ask questions, and I would think to myself, anyone that knew what they were doing would never ask that question of me.

'I was very stressed and upset. I was having a lot of trouble sleeping at night. It was the start of a depressive slump that lasted for some time. You could say I'm still trying to get over it.'

[Stephen Grace]

'Why didn't you just leave?'

[Peter Lana – Lana Consulting]

'It sounds so easy when somebody else says it. My father once said to me, "When you are going through hell, you need to keep going," so that is what I was trying to do. I cared about Susan and Sally, and I could see them both getting swamped by the business. The stress was affecting them just as bad as it was me. I guess I just wanted to help them get through their hell, as well and me getting through mine.

'I also thought that if I could just deliver on my commitments to Susan, at least get them to a legal state, then at least I could argue that I did for them what I said I would. I figured that the public could not blame me for the business's investment decisions. That was never part of my job description.'

[Stephen Grace]

'What effect was that time having on your mental health?'

[Peter Lana – Lana Consulting]

'"I'm not a man who cries" – I could have said that with a straight face before then. I seem to cry all the time now. For anything. My therapist says it's a good thing for me. She says that I am opening myself up to the world. But she has never cried herself dry at 3 am while her career lay about her in tatters. I will admit that I even considered taking my own life at one point. I had invested so much of my life into my career, and it was driving off a cliff. I was a mess.'

[Stephen Grace]

'Knowing what you know now, what should you have done?'

[Peter Lana – Lana Consulting]

'I should have just grabbed Sally and ran. She may not have agreed to come with me back then, but perhaps I could have made her see sense. I should have got her out of there. It was only ever going to get worse; I think I knew it even then.'

[Narrator]

Having watched an interview with Peter before he met Susan Mitchell, it is quite clear that he is no longer the man he once was. Where he was once so self-assured and righteous behind his extensive knowledge of the intricacies of the finance system, he now falters and second-guesses himself. Having said that, I believe this experience has also given him a perspective that he didn't have before. He is no longer cold in his assessments of financial situations. Instead, he now speaks with an inside knowledge of how some of the tougher decisions are made inside a business, having been there himself.

I will say that I somewhat agree with Peter's therapist – that this change may be helpful in his life. If you were paying attention earlier, you would have heard Peter referring to the best interests of Sally Bassett. This was the first time that I had heard Peter refer to Sally is this context. Could it be? A new friendship, a burgeoning relationship, forged in adversity, between Peter and Sally? We answer that question for you, but not in this episode. We need to save something for later.

Before we let you go, I would like to remind you that Susan Mitchell is still at large. We have our private investigator, Dirk Rockford, hot on her trail, but we can still use your help. We are going to hear more from Dirk next episode, and I can tell you now to forget everything you think you knew about Susan Mitchell. Dirk is going to turn this story completely on its head.

It is often said 'Not everything is as it seems' but with Susan Mitchell – The Woman Who Stole The World – nothing *was* as it seemed.

Now, a word from our sponsors …

EPISODE 20: PRIVATE

[Narrator]

Who was the mysterious Susan Mitchell – The Woman Who Stole The World? And how was she able to convince so many people to invest hundreds of millions of dollars into her Human Capital World Fund before disappearing off the face of the earth with everyone's money?

Join me, Stephen Grace, as I interview those closest to her to try and answer the questions on everyone's minds. Questions such as: who was she? why did she do it? and where did Miss Mitchell and all that hard-earned money go?

I will admit that we were excited to record today's episode. We have Dirk Rockford, owner and chief investigator from Ford Investigations, coming back in to our studios to share with us what he had uncovered about Susan Mitchell's past, and potentially her current whereabouts. We were also keen to know if he had tracked down the mysterious Jane with no last name, or even John Hannebery, who had been one of the founding members of the company. There were still so many questions and so few answers.

I suggest you get yourself ready, because today, finally, some questions will get answered, and some answers will lead us to ask new questions.

Without further ado, let's hear the man himself.

[Stephen Grace]

'Dirk, it is great to have you back here in the studio with us. We can't wait to get straight down to business. Have you been able to uncover any new information about Susan Mitchell or her friends?'

[Dirk Rockford – Ford Investigations]

'Thank you, Stephen. Well, I do have some new information to share which I think your listeners will find interesting.'

[Stephen Grace]

'That is great. Where would you like to start?'

[Dirk Rockford – Ford Investigations]

'Why don't we start right at the beginning. My beginning, that is. You may recall that when we last got together, I explained that my job was to find people that either can't be or don't want to be found. After my investigation, I can now tell you that Susan Mitchell did not, or does not, want to be found.

'Let me clarify that a little further. I can't guarantee to anyone that she is, in fact, still alive. Or that bad actors have not already found her. However, I believe that when she disappeared initially, it was of her own accord.'

[Stephen Grace]

'I take it this is very important?'

[Dirk Rockford – Ford Investigations]

'Here it is, yes. Because it is something that I am sure about. And when you have a piece of information that you are sure about, it acts as a foundation for you to build from. It is like how a palaeontologist can find a leg bone of a dinosaur and use it to model what the entire skeleton may look like. I have one of those bones now, and while there are still many theories around what Susan Mitchell's skeleton may look like, so to speak, each new discovery helps to complete that picture.'

[Stephen Grace]

'What makes you so certain that she left on her own accord?'

[Dirk Rockford – Ford Investigations]

'Because she has done it before. She has disappeared. I'm not saying that she didn't have help. I'm convinced that her assistant "Jane" is somehow part of it, and I think that it is highly unlikely that the two ladies acted alone. From what I can tell, these two women didn't just throw their mobile phones off a bridge and drive across the country. They've gone completely off-grid like a professional would. They are not checking social media, no access to banking or credit cards. Basically, nothing that could leave a trace for me or law enforcement to follow.'

[Stephen Grace]

'Earlier you said, "She had done it before". How do you know that?'

[Dirk Rockford – Ford Investigations]

'Because she has no past before turning up to work at that company. I would love to know who her references were, because nobody else knew her from before that time. She is clearly an educated woman, yet I can't find any record of a Susan Mitchell in the education system. That doesn't check out. I had someone call down on one hundred and thirty-seven Susan Mitchells and all of them are verified or certified dead. This is a created identity. Whoever she is, it is unlikely that her original name was Susan Mitchell.'

[Stephen Grace]

'Are you saying that you found out nothing about Susan Mitchell?'

[Dirk Rockford – Ford Investigations]

'No. I'm saying that I found nothing on the name Susan Mitchell from before the day she first entered that building and asked them for a job. This is important because, while we found nothing on her name, we ran her image through a search engine and found her image in a few interesting places.'

[Stephen Grace]

'Such as?'

[Dirk Rockford – Ford Investigations]

'Well, we know that a woman who looks strikingly similar to Susan Mitchell visited a hospital about twelve years ago under the name of Susan Malone.'

[Stephen Grace]

'Do you know why she was there? Will they give you any of her records?'

[Dirk Rockford – Ford Investigations]

'They wouldn't need to. I could get them without asking if I wanted to. The actual problem is that there *are* no records. She was completely wiped out, or was never entered in their system in the first place. We only have one image of her entering, and a signature in a guest book about that time, but no record of her leaving or being operated on. It is interesting, but a bit of a dead end also. She may have just been visiting a patient, or it may have just been someone else closely resembling Susan Mitchell – we may never know. It gave us another name to follow up, though.'

[Stephen Grace]

'Do you have any other leads?'

[Dirk Rockford – Ford Investigations]

'Yes. A young lady in her early twenties visited a shelter for battered women heavily bruised and battling a drug addiction. I will admit that it was not a perfect match, but once again it shows a minor resemblance to the Susan Mitchell we know from her photos. When I asked into it, I was told that the young lady had left a fake name and disappeared days later. I'm sad to say that this is quite common. Sometimes young women in trouble need somewhere safe to hide out for a few days.

'We have a few more of these types of images but none with the same level of clarity, so it is harder to tell if they are just similarities or the same young woman. There are simply too many women in trouble in this world. I see it all the time in my line of work.

'I will say one thing: if it is the same Susan Mitchell that we are looking for, it is unlikely that she had a pleasant background.'

[Stephen Grace]

'How accurate are these image searches?'

[Dirk Rockford – Ford Investigations]

'They are only as accurate as the number and quality of the images that have been indexed into the search engine. If there is no image online, or the system does not index it correctly, then it is not there to be found. The search engine might then look for a match for just the eyes, or nose, instead of the entire face. This leads to false positives.'

[Stephen Grace]

'Right. So, if I might try to summarize what you are saying, you believe that because there are no past images of her online, no education or hospital records, she has either disappeared or erased her identity before?'

[Dirk Rockford – Ford Investigations]

'Yes, but once again, that doesn't mean that she did it alone. In fact, it is highly unlikely. Perhaps she was a just a great candidate for someone to recruit? Someone, or even an organization, who plucked a young girl off the streets, polished her up, and gave her the lead role in one of the biggest scams of the decade. We both know that there is a federal interest in this case, so perhaps they know something that we don't.'

[Stephen Grace]

'If that is the case, what would become of her now that the scam is over?'

[Dirk Rockford – Ford Investigations]

'Well, that scenario is not really my specialty. If I had to hazard a guess, it would be that she might be somewhere where it would be difficult to find her or bring her back into the country. A country with no extradition laws, for instance. She may have a new face through plastic surgery. Alternatively, depending on the risk profile of the group behind her, she could be dead somewhere, with her body in a state that ensures that it will never be recognized. I would think that it would suit these people better if the authorities were still looking for Susan Mitchell herself, and not who her killers may have been. It would be a much cleaner getaway.'

[Narrator]

While we respect the knowledge and experience of Dirk Rockford, who is a professional private investigator, it was still a lot of theory for us to take in. Especially when there was so little evidence. We also recalled Sally Bassett's comments that in all the time she knew Susan Mitchell, she never once saw the woman take an order from any other person. This would suggest that either she was so well drilled in her brief that she didn't require ongoing guidance from overseers, or that she was getting it behind closed doors. Which we do also acknowledge was a big part of Miss Mitchell's office rules.

What we did not get a sense of, however, was how Miss Mitchell never hesitated to consider what the opinions of others might be. To us, and those we spoke to, she was a woman of decisive action. As far as we could see, she called the shots. Having said all of that, when an expert in his field speaks, we listen. And we wanted to hear more.

[Stephen Grace]

'What about her assistant, Jane? Were you able to find out anything about her?'

[Dirk Rockford – Ford Investigations]

'Ah … the mysterious Jane. Yes, I can tell you more about Jane. I could use the image off the video to get a hit on our Jane Doe. You may recall that we had a very short video of her entering a stage to give Susan Mitchell a glass of water. We could only see each side of her face as she entered the video and left it, but we never got a full front forward photo of her because she turned with her back to the camera. Well, I wasn't able to use the composite image of the two sides of her face, but the left side image was enough for us to get a few good hits in our search.'

[Stephen Grace]

'And what did you find?'

[Dirk Rockford – Ford Investigations]

'Her original name was Jana ... Fett. She was born into an abusive household with an alcoholic father and an abused mother. She ran away from home at sixteen, which was probably a good thing because the father shot the mother three months later. No one has seen Jana, now Jane, in over six years.'

[Stephen Grace]

'I wonder if they met at that women's shelter or the hospital you mentioned earlier. You said something about a sighting of Miss Mitchell at those places?'

[Dirk Rockford – Ford Investigations]

'It is a wonderful theory, but just that at this stage. As I mentioned earlier, we do not have a confirmed sighting of Susan Mitchell at that shelter. It was just a low-grade CCTV image that could be a younger version of the woman we are looking for today.'

[Stephen Grace]

'Have you been able to see if Jana Fett was there at the same time?'

[Dirk Rockford – Ford Investigations]

'Not so far, but it doesn't mean that they had to meet there at that precise time. If they were indeed both on the streets, then they could have crossed paths anywhere.'

[Stephen Grace]

'Do you have anything else to share with us?'

[Dirk Rockford – Ford Investigations]

'Nothing I am certain about, but I have a few feelers out still. And I am confident that I will find Susan Mitchell, or what's left of her, soon. I usually do.'

[Narrator]

We checked in with Sally Bassett once again and she told us that Jane had worked for Susan Mitchell since before she had known Susan. Once again, she could not shed any light on where they may have met. As you might guess, Sally was as interested in Dirk Rockford's findings as we were and did not seem at all surprised that Susan may have come from an abusive past. In her words, 'Susan had always had a sadness about her' that led Sally to believe there was a bigger story that may never be told. Not by Sally, anyway.

We are grateful to Dirk for sharing what had learned with us. We hope to hear from him before we finish this series.

Next episode, we will return to Sally Bassett and Allison Bailey who will give us one last update on the so-called love triangle between Susan Mitchell, rapper Ku-Stom and soul singer JC Chains. We will also hear once again, and for the last time, from Peter Lana, who will help us understand how it all unravelled in the days before Susan Mitchell disappeared. If you think that you already know everything then think again, because there are a few twists in our story yet.

It is often said 'Not everything is as it seems' but with Susan Mitchell – The Woman Who Stole The World – nothing *was* as it seemed.

Now, a word from our sponsors …

EPISODE 21: BREAKING POINT

[Narrator]

Who was the mysterious Susan Mitchell – The Woman Who Stole The World? And how was she able to convince so many people to invest hundreds of millions of dollars into her Human Capital World Fund before disappearing off the face of the earth with everyone's money?

Join me, Stephen Grace, as I interview those closest to her to try and answer the questions on everyone's mind. Questions such as: who was she? why did she do it? and where did Miss Mitchell and all that hard-earned money go?

Last episode we heard from Dirk Rockford, the lead investigator at Ford Investigations, and he filled us in on everything that he could find out about Susan Mitchell. Unfortunately, his report was less about what he could find out, and more about what he couldn't, but it was still fascinating. He did produce an image of a potential young Susan Mitchell, which an online image search tool had offered up as a partial match. However, neither myself nor my producer could see any real semblance of Susan Mitchell in that image. We even showed the photo to Sally Bassett, who casually waved it away saying, 'Maybe'.

The one area where Dirk could shed a little light was with Susan Mitchell's assistant, Jane, who at that point had no known last name. It turns out her full, real name is Jana Fett. We now know her to be a teenage runaway from an abusive upbringing. We did our own investigations with this piece of information, and no one that we could find who knew Jane in her childhood had heard from her since her disappearance years ago.

It is unclear how Jane transitioned from homeless runaway to executive assistant to CEO, but we could say the same about Susan Mitchell, who went from assistant to CEO herself. Our guess is that Jane was following in the career footsteps of Susan Mitchell, with Miss Mitchell either her mentor or perhaps a mother figure. We know they shared secrets together, and we believe Jane knew what was happening behind closed doors in Susan Mitchell's office.

In this episode, we will go back to complete the ill-fated love triangle between Susan Mitchell, rapper Ku-Stom and soul singer JC Chains, as told by Sally Bassett and Allison Dailey.

Let's pick up the thread with Sally Bassett.

[Sally Bassett – Social Change Activist]

'Stephen, you can call it a love triangle all you like, but I never did. And I know for a fact that Susan never saw it that way.'

[Stephen Grace]

'Why do you say that?'

[Sally Bassett – Social Change Activist]

'Because Ku-Stom was never in love with her. He saw something he wanted, and when he was told that he couldn't have it he did what many men do.'

[Stephen Grace]

'And what was that?'

[Sally Bassett – Social Change Activist]

'He became obsessed with her. He wanted her captured in a bottle and displayed on his social media shelf for all the world to see.'

[Stephen Grace]

'Do you believe JC Chains wanted the same thing?'

[Sally Bassett – Social Change Activist]

'Look, I don't really know JC. I may have exchanged a few words here or there on Susan's behalf but that is it. I just know what I saw in his face. And I believe he either cared deeply for her, or the two of them were the most amazing actors that I have ever seen.'

[Stephen Grace]

'Do you think Susan felt the same way for JC Chains?'

[Sally Bassett – Social Change Activist]

'I honestly do. I know that some say that she went after Ku-Stom and JC because they were famous, but I can tell you now, when she was with JC, she never once scanned a room to see who was looking. In those rare moments when she was with him, it felt like they were in some sort of bubble together and no one else mattered.'

[Stephen Grace]

'Why do you think it is that everyone involved with Susan Mitchell has either no background or a questionable past?'

[Sally Bassett – Social Change Activist]

'I don't know, you are asking me questions only she could answer.'

[Stephen Grace]

'I concede that it is not fair on you that I need to ask you all these tough questions, but you were as close to the action as it got. There is no one else we can ask.'

[Sally Bassett – Social Change Activist]

'Okay, I will try to answer your question. Why did everyone involved with Susan have a questionable past? Perhaps … because she made us feel safe?'

[Stephen Grace]

'You said "us" just then … what did you mean by "us"? When I asked about people who either had no background or a questionable past, I wasn't referring to you specifically.'

[Sally Bassett – Social Change Activist]

'You may not have known it at the time, Stephen, but you were. I may not be glamourous like Susan, or famous like JC, but that doesn't mean I haven't suffered. Susan knew it the moment we met. She just understood me, like no other person has. She didn't hire me; she was helping me.'

[Stephen Grace]

'Forgive me, but I don't understand, helping you do what?'

[Sally Bassett – Social Change Activist]

'She was helping me break away from my old life. A life that no child or young woman should ever be subjected to. She helped me understand why this is the only job I could ever do. I never came to work to build wells or bridges. I came in everyday to see how many little girls' lives I could improve. And I will tell you now, even though the world may not believe it – not with all that money gone – but we did good things together. I slept better in those early days than I ever had before.'

[Stephen Grace]

'Can I hear a little more about your background?'

[Sally Bassett – Social Change Activist]

'I'm sorry, but no. You didn't believe my background was important before and I would prefer to keep it that way. You have been good to me, Stephen, but this is the place that I will draw my line.'

[Narrator]

Sally Bassett had every right not to answer my questions about her personal life. She is not the focus of this show. However, I will admit that it disappointed me she didn't. I wasn't disappointed in Sally's response, but in how I had assumed that she had been a stable figure to base my interview with. I never checked how stable that foundation was. If I'd had any notion that Sally herself had come from a troubled background, like so many other people associated with Susan Mitchell, I may have changed my line of questioning with her from the very start. To borrow Dirk's analogy from last episode: I had found the leg bone of a dinosaur and fashioned for myself a picture of a giraffe.

I will take this opportunity to apologize to Sally, like I did later that very day, for not respecting her more and taking a better interest in her personal story.

Now we are going to switch across to Allison Bailey, who is going to put the final nail in the coffin of the so-called Susan Mitchell, Ku-Stom, JC Chains love triangle.

[Stephen Grace]

'Can you please tell us about the end of the "love triangle"?'

[Allison Bailey – Social Media]

'Stephen, the death of the love triangle was the true crime of this whole saga. I could have milked that sucker for another six months. I had a third suitor lined up, with the help of Ku-Stom's people, ready to blow the whole thing apart once again. It would have been magnificent. I won't say his name here because I'm lining him up for a new campaign that I'm working on for my current employer.'

[Stephen Grace]

'Didn't Susan have genuine feelings for JC Chains, though?'

[Allison Bailey – Social Media]

'Who she screwed was her business. Who the world thought she was screwing, well, that was my business. She did very well from my love triangle. If it upset her, then she can wipe her tears on the millions of dollars it brought in. Let me say this out loud. "Susan, if you are out there somewhere, listening in and spending those millions? You are welcome! You can thank me any time you like by just sending some more of that cash my way." Anyway, I'm glad it ended. It taught me a lot. My campaigns are a lot more sophisticated these days because of what I learned back then. I've got a whole social media control centre now. It is monitoring thousands of social media statistics across the top one hundred celebrities in the world right now. My new setup could give NASA a run for their money.'

[Narrator]

I don't want to lose the thread of Susan Mitchell's love triangle, but I will ask you to keep one point from Allison Bailey's little speech in the back of your mind. Where did the money for her 'NASA-like social media control centre come from? Getting the data required for a setup like she is suggesting is not cheap. We will get an answer to that question in a future episode. For now, we will return to the issue at hand.

[Stephen Grace]

'How did the love triangle end?'

[Allison Bailey – Social Media]

'Susan put an end to it all. One day she posted this stupid little three-minute video online and her followers shared it over forty thousand times in the first 24 hours. To be fair, not a terrible result, but she should have spoken to me first. I would have strongly advised her not to or, at the very least, not like that. I don't even think she was wearing makeup that day, for God's sake.'

[Stephen Grace]

'Were you angry with her for posting it?'

[Allison Bailey – Social Media]

'I was furious, but not because she posted it. It was a personal message to the world that she felt she needed to post. I was furious because she wasn't just a person by that point, she was a brand. And I was supposed to be in charge of Susan Mitchell the brand.'

[Stephen Grace]

'What did she say to that?'

[Allison Bailey – Social Media]

'She said that, to her, they were the same thing. Of course, she would say that!'

[Narrator]

We are now going to play you the audio from the social media video that Allison Bailey just mentioned. As you listen in, you may like to picture a version of Susan Mitchell who, unless you have seen the video itself, you will have not seen before. If she is wearing her usual designer clothing, then you might be forgiven for thinking that she had slept in it. Her chocolate brown hair, which she had been famous for, no longer plays in curls around her shoulders but seems desperate to get away from her in strands. She looks like a woman exhausted, at breaking point. We know from many sources that there were many fires burning, so to speak, for her. However, it is obvious from the video that the 'love triangle' was a burning fire that Susan Mitchell was determined to put out and to put out once and for all.

We will play it for you now …

[Susan Mitchell – Archive Footage]

'Hello. My name is Susan Mitchell. I guess if you're watching this video, you probably already know that. Over the past six months, much has been said about me, my intentions and the supposed love triangle between myself and the amazing artists Ku-Stom and the man I call Josiah but you call JC Chains.

'I am not in a romantic relationship with either of these men, but I will say I love them both in different ways. Ku-Stom believed in me right from the start. He could see what good my fund could do for the world, and he wanted to be a part of it. He is a man who stands up for what he believes in. He also goes after what he wants and is not afraid to ask the world to help him get it. I respect that about him and hope that you do as well.

'Josiah is a different man altogether, but in every way just as amazing. You know his name as JC Chains, but when you hear him sing you all get a glimpse of the Josiah that I know. He has been an incredible support for me through very trying times. I treasure his friendship and appreciate his love.

'To those who have accused of me, or my team, of fabricating the relationship for fame or glory, let me just say that I never asked for or wanted either of those things. My life is better for knowing both men, but I am my own woman. I existed on this earth before I knew them, and a version of me would still exist even if we ever part ways as friends.

Something I hope we never do. As you can probably tell, I am tired. My workload has been exhausting but I am especially tired of being a by-product of men.

'My name is Susan Mitchell, and I am more than just the sum of the men in my life. I have a place in this world all of my own. There is no love triangle, but there is love. I want to thank both men, and you all, for your incredible support of what we are trying to achieve here.

[Susan Mitchell exhales deeply and rubs her eyes with her hands]

'I … I just felt the need to say all of that before the next stage of my life begins.'

[Narrator]

We have analysed this footage many times and believe that there was a second person in the room during its recording. Perhaps it was Jane. We cannot be entirely sure. We have also had a linguist and body language expert review the footage. Their feedback to us was that Miss Mitchell has been intentionally vague around her genuine relationship with JC Chains and how she refers to her 'next stage of life' with no further detail. Outside of these two specific points, they are convinced she is either an extremely talented method actor, or that she is simply telling the truth. Given her obvious exhaustion in the footage, it is more likely she was telling her truth, or a version of it.

That video would be the last public record of Susan Mitchell before her disappearance. You will hear more about that in our next episode. You will also hear from Peter Lana for the last time. Peter will help us understand how it all unravelled in the days before Susan Mitchell disappeared.

A small warning: if you think that you already know everything there is to know about The Woman Who Stole The World, then think again, because there are a few twists in her story yet.

It is often said 'Not everything is as it seems' but with Susan Mitchell – The Woman Who Stole The World – nothing *was* as it seemed.

Now, a word from our sponsors …

EPISODE 22:
THE DISAPPEARANCE

[Narrator]

Who was the mysterious Susan Mitchell – The Woman Who Stole the World? And how was she able to convince so many people to invest hundreds of millions of dollars into her Human Capital World Fund before disappearing off the face of the earth with everyone's money?

Join me, Stephen Grace, as I interview those closest to her to try and answer the questions on everyone's mind. Questions such as: who was she? why did she do it? and where did Miss Mitchell and all that hard-earned money go?

In today's episode, Sally Bassett will be back to talk to us about the events on the very day that Susan Mitchell and her assistant Jane disappeared. Sally will talk us through the strange conversation she had with Jane right before they disappeared. Sally will also talk about how she alone had to face a room with over three hundred people sitting, eager to see Miss Mitchell. Finally, we will hear what Sally really thinks happened to Susan even after everything she now knows to be true. We have some big episodes for you to finish out our series, so stay tuned and be prepared to have your expectations blown.

Let me take you now to the hours leading up to the big disappearance.

[Stephen Grace]

'Sally, can you please tell us about the day that Susan Mitchell disappeared. What were you doing that morning?'

[Sally Bassett – Social Change Activist]

'Sure, Stephen. I got in early that morning, like I did most mornings back then. I could no longer travel the world like I had been in the early days because I had people management activities to attend to. I had one of my team in Ghana scouting out an investment target and another in the Philippines doing the same thing. I was reading through their trip reports.'

[Stephen Grace]

'So, it was like any other day at that point?'

[Sally Bassett – Social Change Activist]

'Yeah, I guess so. I was a little anxious because Susan had a big presentation planned for later that morning and I wanted to give her some good news that she could take on stage. Those two sites alone would have opened a million dollars' worth of new opportunities to do good for the world. So, yeah, I was looking forward to sharing it with her.'

[Stephen Grace]

'Did she come into the office that morning?'

[Sally Bassett – Social Change Activist]

'No, she didn't. I tried to call her, but it went straight to voicemail, which was not that uncommon. She was a busy woman after all.'

[Stephen Grace]

'Did you leave a message for her?'

[Sally Bassett – Social Change Activist]

'No point in leaving messages because she was often too busy to listen to them. She would typically see my missed call and call me back in her own time. But I had good news, so I called Jane instead. Jane answered. I told her I had news for Susan and said that it would be good if we could talk before Susan took the stage later that morning.'

[Stephen Grace]

'What was Jane's response to that?'

[Sally Bassett – Social Change Activist]

'Jane told me that Susan had a full schedule in the lead up to the presentation, which is again not all that uncommon. So, I told Jane what the news was, and she assured me she would let Susan know between meetings. We both said that we would see each other later that day and we hung up.'

[Stephen Grace]

'Given that Jane disappeared along with Susan Mitchell that day, can you remember what Jane's tone was like? Did you get a sense that she was treating it just like any other day, or was there an edge to her voice?'

[Sally Bassett – Social Change Activist]

'Her words told me it was just like any other day, but when I thought back on it in the days following, her tone told me something else. It's like she was distracted. I got a sense that she was in the middle of something herself or looking over her shoulder. Basically, she was listening and responding, but I didn't have her full and undivided attention.'

[Stephen Grace]

'That didn't ring any alarm bells for you at the time?'

[Sally Bassett – Social Change Activist]

'You have never worked for Susan Mitchell. We worked hard in that place, and often on multiple things at once. Being a little distracted on a call was just part of the job.'

[Stephen Grace]

'Okay, let's skip forward to the moment that you knew she was actually missing. Tell us about that.'

[Sally Bassett – Social Change Activist]

'Well, like I said, Susan had a big presentation lined up for later that day at another financial industry seminar. She had become a celebrity in her own right, so we expected a sizeable crowd to be there. So much so that they had moved her to a bigger room at the conference. To be honest, I think some of them just wanted to see JC Chains' new girlfriend. Perhaps they even thought they might just glimpse Ku-Stom or JC in attendance. But anyway, Susan didn't show.'

[Stephen Grace]

'How did it go down?'

[Sally Bassett – Social Change Activist]

'Usually, Susan turns up fifteen minutes before each meeting or presentation. She and I would then exchange a few words. I would wish her luck and she would take the stage. Once or twice, for whatever reason, she or I turned up late for a meeting and that entire exchange was reduced to a wink across a meeting room, but on this occasion, I couldn't see her anywhere. She never, ever missed a meeting or a presentation, especially one with so many people, so I thought she may be in makeup or something. Then when the time came for me to introduce her, I just went with it. I took the stage and started her introduction. I couldn't see her face as yet, so I added a few extra sentences to draw it out a little. I honestly thought that it would be something that we would laugh about later. But when I finally said her name and held my hand out towards the side of the stage … no one came forward.'

[Stephen Grace]

'What did you do?'

[Sally Bassett – Social Change Activist]

'I froze, Stephen. It is the stuff of nightmares. I had three hundred people all staring at me. I tried to make a little joke about how busy she was, which went down terribly so I started to panic. I will say one thing about Mathias: I never liked him much, but I will be forever grateful to him for stepping in to save me that day.'

[Stephen Grace]

'What did Mathias do?'

[Sally Bassett – Social Change Activist]

'He jumped up on stage, with his phone in his hand, like she had just called him. He then told everyone that there had been some type of mechanical breakdown and that she had asked if he could take over until she got there. None of it was true, of course, but I appreciated it just the same. I couldn't get off that stage fast enough.'

[Narrator]

Sally's moment of panic and Mathias's impromptu speech are available online for anyone that would like to watch. In it, Mathias talks about the Human Capital World Fund and the good it was supposedly doing for the world. They are all things we have already heard mentioned in this show in previous episodes. Never one to miss an opportunity for self-promotion, he also went to great lengths to give himself credit for the Cap2 and Cap3 algorithms. Which he explains was the backbone of the company's success.

To save time now, though, I am going to skip the speech itself and go straight to the aftermath. The first realizations that Susan Mitchell was not just caught in traffic somewhere but, in fact, missing altogether.

[Stephen Grace]

'When the speech was all said and done, and Susan Mitchell still hadn't arrived, what happened?'

[Sally Bassett – Social Change Activist]

'I tried to play it down for all those that had come to see her, but the truth was I was really anxious. We had all the investors there and some of the new staff members had also come along. They had been so excited to see her talk live on stage and now they were very disappointed. Some of the investors were angry. I was telling them all that it was no big deal, but deep down I knew something was terribly wrong.'

[Stephen Grace]

'What specifically was it that tipped you off?'

[Sally Bassett – Social Change Activist]

'We are talking about a woman who was never late. She never skirted a responsibility, never missed a meeting, and here she was completely missing in action. I tried to call her a bunch of times. I tried to call Jane. I even tried to call the driver that she sometimes used for important occasions. But neither Susan nor Jane answered their phones, and her driver didn't know where she was. He could tell that I was concerned, so he offered to drive over to her place and see if she was at home. I accepted and thanked him, but it turned up nothing.'

[Stephen Grace]

'What did you do next?'

[Sally Bassett – Social Change Activist]

'I got Peter to drive me over to the police and I forced them to open up a missing person's case. They were reluctant to do it because she had only been missing for a few hours, but I made them put the paperwork through. They seemed to consider her a celebrity and kept saying things like, "I'm sure a fan will post a photo of her checking into rehab or something". I told them she doesn't drink or take drugs, but they just waved it away like, "what would you know?". I guess they see that type of thing all the time.'

[Stephen Grace]

'At that point, what did you think had happened to her?'

[Sally Bassett – Social Change Activist]

'I thought she had been abducted.'

[Stephen Grace]

'What gave you that idea?'

[Sally Bassett – Social Change Activist]

'She was not the type of woman to let people down. Also, while there were lots of people that loved and admired her, there were also some who didn't.'

[Stephen Grace]

'Like who? Who would want to hurt her that much?'

[Sally Bassett – Social Change Activist]

'It could have been anyone. Maybe one of Ku-Stom's crazy followers. Or one of the male financial elites that didn't like some pretty upstart stealing his investment dollars. She also had that past that I knew nothing about. Maybe there was some abusive husband or something? Who knows? It could have been anyone.'

[Stephen Grace]

'And what about now? With everything you know now, what do you think happened to her?'

[Sally Bassett – Social Change Activist]

'I have not changed my mind on it at all. I knew the woman I knew. I may not have known everything about her, but I knew her. The Susan I knew would not have wanted to let so many people down. I don't believe that her disappearance was by her own choice.'

[Stephen Grace]

'What about all the missing money?'

[Sally Bassett – Social Change Activist]

'My take is, if you have a hold of Susan, it would not be hard to get to her money.'

[Stephen Grace]

'You mentioned earlier that you got Peter Lana to take you to the police station. What was he saying through it all?'

[Sally Bassett – Social Change Activist]

'He was concerned, but he didn't say much. I thought it was strange at the time, but I guess I understand why now. For me it changes nothing, though.'

[Narrator]

Sally Basset is not alone in believing that Susan Mitchell was abducted against her will. You might remember that Dylan Clarke believed the same thing. In fact, many of her followers, as I now call them because of the cult-like nature of her cause, cite the same reasons that Sally does. Basically, that the Susan they knew would never do this.

There isn't a single person alive that claims to be a family member of hers or has even attended the same school that she did. How is it that there is nobody that actually knows her, and yet so many who believe they do? It's perplexing, even to me, and I've lived in this world of conmen and financial tricksters for some time now.

We are coming towards the end of our series now, but we are going to get one more perspective on the events of that day, and the very day before Susan Mitchell disappeared, which may be even more important to our story. If you believe in the goodness of Susan Mitchell's intentions like Sally and so many of her followers do, then you might prefer to give this next episode a miss. Because it may just change your opinion on everything.

I'm sad to say, our time with you is coming to an end, but we have not stopped looking for Susan Mitchell. If you know where she is, it is not too late to do the right thing. Please get in touch with us soon, and we will gladly hear your story. You can tell us anonymously if you wish.

Remember, it is often said 'Not everything is as it seems' but with Susan Mitchell – The Woman Who Stole The World – nothing *was* as it seemed.

Now, a word from our sponsors …

EPISODE 23: THE MONEY – THE VICTIMS

[Narrator]

Who was the mysterious Susan Mitchell – The Woman Who Stole The World? And how was she able to convince so many people to invest hundreds of millions of dollars into her Human Capital World Fund before disappearing off the face of the earth with everyone's money?

Join me, Stephen Grace, as I interview those closest to her to try to answer the questions on everyone's mind. Questions such as: who was she? why did she do it? and where did Miss Mitchell and all that hard-earned money go?

Welcome to the final scheduled episode of The Woman Who Stole The World. I'm afraid to say that without talking to Susan Mitchell herself, we could not answer all the questions that we set out to answer for you all at the start of this show. Often the answers we got about Miss Mitchell were vague, or the new information provided created a new sense of mystery of their own. For instance, we still don't know who she was before her time with the Human Capital World Fund, or where she went after her disappearance.

And while we accept that she was a person of exceptional talents, some of us here on the production team still struggle to agree on what those talents actually were. We also still question if she could pull this scam off by herself or, at the very least, with the help of her junior assistant, Jane.

If you are one of her followers, the people that steadfastly believe in Susan Mitchell's intentions, like Sally Bassett, then you might like to skip this episode because today will not be so kind to the memory of Susan Mitchell. In today's episode, Peter Lana will give a special insight into a conversation he had with Miss Mitchell the evening before she disappeared. Peter's interview might just give you a unique view into what her motivations may have been in those last hours.

Then, finally, we will hear from some victims of the Human Capital World Fund. Not the staff this time, but some of the actual people who believed in their cause. So much so that they invested their hard-earned money into the fund, thinking that they were playing their part in history.

I suggest you hang on tight. We are going to rewind our story back to the day before Susan Mitchell disappeared. It is lucky for us they have given Peter Lana legal clearance to share his account of events. It is the same story that he gave to the police, but few others since. You will hear it here first.

So, with no further delay, let's get straight to the action.

[Stephen Grace]

'Peter, what do you remember about the time when Susan Mitchell released her love triangle video?'

[Peter Lana – Lana Consulting]

'Oh man, that video broke my heart. I guess it just shows you how much pressure she was under. I remember thinking that no man would ever feel the need to release a video like that. It was unfair that she felt the need to do it. Even now, I still feel sorry for her in that respect. The whole thing clearly upset her.'

[Stephen Grace]

'Why do you think she released that video?'

[Peter Lana – Lana Consulting]

'She was a bit of a mess leading up to that time. We had fires burning in the office everywhere. I mean that figuratively, of course. I think it was just one little thing that she could take decisive action on and fix, so she did it.'

[Stephen Grace]

'Given everything we know now about her disappearance, I am curious about the timing of that video. Why do you think, after everything she went through, she felt the need to do it right before she disappeared? If she knew she was going anyway, surely it wouldn't have mattered?'

[Peter Lana – Lana Consulting]

'Maybe she didn't think that she would get another chance. Maybe she wanted to set the record straight once and for all.'

[Stephen Grace]

'Do you think she knew she was going to disappear?'

[Peter Lana – Lana Consulting]

'I have thought at that a lot. I think either she knew she was going to disappear, or she knew someone was closing in. I can't tell you which one. It could be something else again, but she knew something.'

[Stephen Grace]

'Right. Tell me about her state of mind some more. I'm also keen to hear what you specifically told the police. Is it right that you were the last to see her? What was her headspace like at the end?'

[Peter Lana – Lana Consulting]

'To explain that, I need to explain to you the background behind our meeting first. You are right that I was the last of those still around to see her. It was the evening before the no-show, and I was the last person left in the office for the day. Or so I thought. I was in my office at about eleven pm, still working. It had been over two hours since I had heard any sign of life within the office space when suddenly, out of nowhere, there she was, standing at my door. I nearly had a heart attack I was so surprised.'

[Stephen Grace]

'What did she say to you?'

[Peter Lana – Lana Consulting]

'Not much. She giggled a little that she had surprised me. Then she walked around and sat on the chair across the desk from mine. Then we just sat there in silence together looking about the office.'

[Stephen Grace]

'She said nothing at all?'

[Peter Lana – Lana Consulting]

'No, but we communicated. She pulled a little face to say, "How are you going?". And I pulled a face in return that said, "Everything is falling apart" and she nodded. Then we just sat there for a time and enjoyed the silence together. We had spoken so many times leading up to that point that I guess we didn't feel the need to go over it all again. Finally, she actually said to me, "Do you think it is fixable?" and, sadly, I said, "No. I really wish it was, and that I could fix it all for you".

'She thought about that for a few moments before she said, "It's a shame. It could have been magnificent". Then she gave me a wink, and she walked out.'

[Stephen Grace]

'What was happening that made everything so bleak in those last days?'

[Peter Lana – Lana Consulting]

'We had a few things that all contributed to that final day. I was still having issues with the legal entity of the business. You need to remember that it had never been set up correctly, right from the beginning. The structure didn't matter while she was still running a small business, with that little group of questionable investors. Basically, there was no one asking questions of her back then. But then her favour turned, and she met Dylan Clarke. By the time I got there, she still had those initial investors, plus the extra money from Dylan Clarke and his high-net-worth friends. Then the Ku-Stom Trust, and JC Chains, and finally the public, all throwing money around like it grew on trees. It's at this point that people realize how important business structure is. We grew faster than we could fix. If all of that had happened over ten years, I couldn't have fixed it. So, when it all happens in a matter of sixteen months, it's just too much. I think by that point she was also burning money faster than any of the investments could make it. Then the withdrawals started, and it all went to shit.'

[Stephen Grace]

'What do you mean by withdrawals? This is the first we have heard of withdrawals.'

[Peter Lana – Lana Consulting]

'You remember that Ku-Stom crowd-sourced the original money, in the same manner he had used to raise money to make his albums. Well, we never got to see who any of those customers were. We were just given the money as a lump sum, and they posted on social media telling everyone how much money they had raised. We got none of the details of how that money was raised, or if he kept some for himself. Well, eventually some of those people wanted their money back. Not an unfair request, but Ku-Stom's people just pointed them at us. Of course, we didn't know who they were. We never had their customer list, so we had to point them back to him. I mean, we paid a few of them just to keep them happy. We didn't even know how much, but they were screaming so loudly so we had to shut them up. Then, two days before she disappeared, someone posted on the internet that they had tricked us and that we had sent them a thousand dollars in error. They told everyone that the Human Capital World Fund didn't have any records. The next thing we knew, they inundated us with panic withdrawal requests, and letters from scammers claiming to be customers.'

[Stephen Grace]

'So, when she said to you that night that it was a shame, and that "it could have been magnificent", was that her way of saying that it was time to check out?'

[Peter Lana – Lana Consulting]

'Yeah, I guess that's how it felt. It felt like the end of an era. I went home that night, poured myself a drink, then poured another, and another, and another. I had gotten caught up in a dream and taken a risk. It was a risk that I had staked my entire reputation on, and it fell through. I guess people make bigger mistakes in life, but I descended lower that night than I had ever been before or since.'

[Stephen Grace]

'What about when you heard that Susan Mitchell had disappeared the next day, and that the money had gone also.'

[Peter Lana – Lana Consulting]

'To be honest, I wasn't all that surprised. Everyone had given it everything, and it was starting to feel like a house of cards in the wind. It was only a few hours later that I realized I might actually go to jail over it. Then I understood the full ramifications of the missing money. That is when I handed myself to the police and told them absolutely everything. I wanted them to know everything I knew.'

[Stephen Grace]

'But you didn't tell others that part of the story, did you? Why?'

[Peter Lana – Lana Consulting]

'When you run from a crime scene, everyone believes you are the guilty one. Susan disappearing so publicly that day meant that all the press was on her. In the end, her disappearance was a gift to me. After all, I was the financial controller. The one responsible for safeguarding everyone's investment. I hadn't been able to do that. I could have taken the fall for everything if she'd stayed around. I sometimes wonder if she did that on purpose to save us all.'

[Stephen Grace]

'Does Sally know this part of the story, or will she hear it here first?'

[Peter Lana – Lana Consulting]

'I told Sally all of this two nights ago, when we arranged this session. I didn't want there to be any secrets between me and Sally. The only reason that I didn't tell her before is because she believed in Susan so much, I didn't want her to be disappointed.'

[Stephen Grace]

'How does she feel about Susan Mitchell now that she knows the full truth?'

[Peter Lana – Lana Consulting]

'Strangely, her opinion of Susan didn't change. She still says she knew the woman she knew, and that woman was not a thief. Unfortunately, nobody else believes that anymore.'

[Narrator]

We will return to thank Peter and Sally for their contribution to this show before the end of this episode, but before we do, I thought it might be good to hear from some victims of this situation.

You may recall that, when this show first went to air, we invited listeners who had been involved in the Human Capital World Fund and lost money to call in and tell us their stories.

With their permission, I will play some of those recordings for you now.

A quick disclaimer: as there are no records of who directly donated the Ku-Stom Trust funds, we have no way of confirming that they are all, in fact, customers. Given the stories they are about to share and obvious emotion in some of their voices, we choose to believe them.

[Taylor]

'My name is Taylor, and I gave money to Ku-Stom. To be honest, I didn't really know anything about it. He vouched for it, and I love his music, so I pledged a few thousand dollars that I had saved up. It said, "Invest in the future". I thought "invest" meant you get the money back, right? In the end, I got nothing back and had to cancel a holiday because I didn't have enough money to go.'

[Tom]

'My name is Tom. I gave seven thousand dollars to the fund and saw none of it again. I had been saving that money for two years and it was doing nothing in the bank, so I thought, "Why not use it to make the world a better place?". They are all a bunch of criminals.'

[Sarah]

'My name is Sarah. I am fourteen years old. I saw the videos online and just thought Susan Mitchell was amazing. I wanted to be just like her someday and change the world. I sent my money inside a Christmas card to keep it safe. It was one hundred and forty-three dollars. I asked Mum how I could get it back and she told me it's gone. I cleaned cars for three months to save that money.'

[Danielle]

'I don't know what I was thinking. I think I just got caught up in it all. That money I sent in was supposed to be my college money. I just wanted to put it somewhere safe where it could do some good for the world until I needed it back. That money was my future, my entire world.'

[Narrator]

We would like to thank everyone who rang in and shared their stories with us. I'm sorry that we couldn't play them all, but we appreciate your help with our investigations.

Before we finish the show, I will return one last time to Peter Lana.

[Stephen Grace]

'So, what is ahead for you and Sally now?'

[Peter Lana – Lana Consulting]

'I'm back to Lana Consulting. I have my blog now, which I am using to rebuild my reputation in the industry. I'm doing it episode by episode, just like you, Stephen [Laughs]. Sally is working for UNICEF, so she is doing all kinds of good for the world still. If your listeners didn't already know and care, Sally and I bonded after Susan's disappearance, and we have become friends. In fact, I'm sure that I've never had a friend quite like her. Meeting Sally was the best thing to come out of this whole Human Capital affair. I'm so glad it is over now, and we can just create a life together. That life can be as friends or as partners, and I will be happy either way. As long as I still have her in my life, I have a feeling that everything will be okay.'

[Stephen Grace]

'Peter, on behalf of myself and everyone else involved in the show, I would like to thank you and Sally for your honesty and your bravery throughout the show. Given all you have shared, and your clear sense of responsibility and remorse, I'm sure you will be at the top of your industry once again. I also wish you and Sally the very best of luck for your future together.'

[Peter Lana – Lana Consulting]

'Thank you, Stephen. I appreciate it.'

[Narrator]

We would like to take this opportunity to thank you for listening in, and for everyone else who shared their stories with us for the recording of this show, including Mathias Lagrange, Dylan Clarke, Allison Bailey, and Dirk Rockford.

This is the last episode of our show, unless of course Susan Mitchell herself might like to come forward and have her say. So, Susan, if you are listening, please call us. We will be here waiting to hear from you.

The Woman Who Stole The World was brought to you by the National Foundation of Finance and sponsored by Gerald Tilly Auditors, this country's leading fraud investigation firm.

It was written and presented by me, Stephen Grace. Produced and edited by George Tompkins. Script Editing by David Plant and Technical Production by Harrison Carter.

If you would like to know more, head over to our website. There, you will find links to every episode, as well as some previously unreleased footage, photos, and information which you may find interesting.

Wherever you have been listening in, please rate and review us as this helps other find us as well.

We will continue to investigate the big stories about financial fraud and the people that commit them. If you have liked this show and would like to hear more of this type of journalism, please subscribe to our channel and you will be the first to know when fresh stories are available.

Once again, name is Stephen Grace, thank you for listening in.

SPECIAL
ANNOUNCEMENT!

[Narrator]

Who was the mysterious Susan Mitchell – The Woman Who Stole the World? And how was she able to convince so many people to invest hundreds of millions of dollars into her Human Capital World Fund before disappearing off the face of the earth with everyone's money?

Hi, it's Stephen Grace here.

For the past twenty-three weeks, we have told you the story of Susan Mitchell and the Human Capital World Fund. You have heard from all of those that were with her from the very start of this whole saga when she first presented her fund to the world. We learnt about her introductions to the music world elite, and how their endorsement launched her and the fund into the financial market stratosphere. We followed her journey every step of the way. From her humble beginnings with Sally Bassett and Mathias LaGrange, to her last days, where it all came tumbling down with Peter Lana. Finally, we heard how she, and all her investors' money, vanished.

The only person we didn't hear from throughout this entire story was Susan Mitchell herself.

I am excited to tell you, that may be about to change. Somebody has recently come forward claiming to be Jane Fett the executive assistant of Susan Mitchell. We believe Jane may be one of the few people with inside knowledge of who Susan Mitchell really was, or where she might be right now.

This contact has extended to us an invitation to meet with Susan Mitchell herself, in a one-time only interview for one last episode. We were told that we can ask anything we want and that she will answer truthfully and without bias.

To get this interview, we were given three conditions. Firstly, that we will only get the address of the interview the morning that it is scheduled to take place. Second, that nobody else can be present for it other than myself and my editor. And finally, that it doesn't air until seven days have passed since it's recording. We don't know if this is to give her time to flee the location afterwards or if there is an ulterior motive.

These are all conditions we are happy to accept if it gives us a chance to meet The Woman Who Stole The World and get you, our listeners, all the answers that everyone has been waiting for.

So, join us on Monday the 17th of June, for what we hope to be an explosive final episode of The Woman Who Stole The World.

THE NURSE: VISITORS

'We must make preparations,' the doctor said to the nurse.

'Preparations for what?' The nurse had been working for eleven hours straight by that point. She was exhausted.

'For visitors,' the doctor said.

'Who?'

'I don't know,' the doctor replied, exasperated either by the nurse's questions or the situation itself.

'Then how do we prepare?' The nurse wasn't trying to be difficult. She just knew that an instruction can only be carried out if it can be first understood. It is what made her so good at her job.

The doctor threw his hands up. 'I have no idea. Her aid said that she has requested one lucid hour so that she may talk relatively pain-free, and with a clear head, to a visitor. And that she is prepared to forego whatever time she might have left after that hour to get it,' he said.

It was not uncommon for dying patients to have last requests, but some requests were harder to accommodate than others. She was not a doctor herself, but she knew well enough that pain-free and clear-headed were two different sides of the same coin.

You can flip the coin for pain-free or lucid, but it is almost impossible to get both at once. We either get a pain-free zombie, or a patient who is now so completely focused on their own pain that it makes them unable to focus on anything else.

'Which is the priority?' she said.

'She said it is the ability to focus her mind for the visit. Besides, we already know that she can handle an intense amount of pain. To be honest, I'm surprised she isn't dead already.'

'She has something that she needs to do first,' the nurse said, almost to herself.

I shouldn't have said that. That is not the sort of thing a professional says.

She had become so good at remaining silent in their presences that often patients didn't even realize she was in the room with them. She could become a mere machine carrying out its chore in the background when she wanted to be.

Most of the time, the nurse didn't care what was being said between a patient and their visitor. But there was something about these two that captured her attention in a way no other had. They fascinated her. Their whispers, their planning and scheming, their connection. She could not tell if they were the whispers of a madwoman, or the final commandments of a dying leader. The doctor did not need to know any of this. He needed to believe that the nurse was capable. That she was a professional he could count on in a life and death situation. She chose distraction.

She wanted to move on from her comment quickly before he could react to it. 'So, how are you going to achieve this little pain-free mind-clarity miracle?'

The doctor looked to the ceiling and let out a deep breath. 'I don't know yet. A chemical cocktail of some sort. Something to knock her pain receptors out, and then something to slap her across the face. I'm worried that I may end up killing her if I get it wrong. I told her as much. She told me to do it anyway, and she is paying the bills. So, we will do what we are told.'

Nice inclusion of the word 'we'. You're the one about to drug a terminal patient.

She wanted to stop him and make it clear that this would be completely his responsibility. However, they had both signed a contract for this work and she knew it was too late to distance herself from any of it now. If they ever got in trouble for this unsanctioned palliative care arrangement, they would likely go down together. *If he needs a 'we' to ease his conscious, then what more do I have to lose?*

'What more do you know about her? Any name yet?' the doctor asked.

'Nothing,' she replied. She wanted to get back to the patient and her young visitor and see if she could pick up any more scraps of their conversation. 'I'm going to check on her now.'

The nurse turned and started walking back towards the suite. She looked over her shoulder as she left and saw the doctor's frustrated face as he turned back to his own office.

I'm not here to make you feel better, I'm here for the patient, the nurse thought as she left the room. He could have chosen any of the other nurses if he needed a shoulder to cry on, but he didn't. *You needed a professional who could keep her mouth shut, which is why you called on me.*

The night shift will be here soon. Let them prepare for visitors.

THE NURSE: THE MONSTERS

'You don't need to pretend,' the young woman said.

'Excuse me?' said the nurse.

The young woman pointed over her shoulder to the patient. 'She asked me to tell you that you are welcome to listen to our conversations. I think she would actually like some attention from someone other than me for once.'

'I never ...' said the nurse.

'Please don't be offended. You have taken wonderful care of her over these past months. I guess she likes you, or at the least likes to have the attention of someone other than myself. Maybe she just wants one more friend before she goes. Anyway, listen, or don't, it is completely up to you, but you don't need to pretend you are not. We are okay with it. Within a week the entire world will know her business, anyway, so it makes no difference to us.'

The young woman gave a sad, disarming, Mona Lisa smile and returned to the seat that she had been inhabiting for months. The patient was asleep. The young woman placed the patients arm under the blanket and tucked her in. She then reclaimed her laptop and busied herself with other matters.

The nurse knew she wasn't supposed to ask questions – she was being paid handsomely not to – but she couldn't help herself this one time.

'Is she your mother?'

The young woman looked up from her computer and smiled at the nurse. 'She is not, but she may as well be. We have been through a lot together. She has saved me from many dangerous situations over the years and now I am trying to help her do the same. You can hear all about it tomorrow if you are here.'

'Yes, I'll be here,' the nurse said. Perhaps some questions were okay, she thought to herself. 'I was told to expect visitors?'

'Yes,' the young woman said. 'Just one or two.'

'Would you like me to prepare anything special for them?' The nurse replied.

'I don't think so. Two chairs, maybe, a glass of water or two. I expect they will have some type of recording device for the interview, but that is their business.'

The nurse adopted protocol 'I'm not sure we should have recording devices around all of this medical equipment. I would hate for it to interfere with her treatment.'

The young woman gave her Mona Lisa smile once again. 'I hardly think it matters anymore. There is not much life left in her, and she is already giving away whatever is left for tomorrow. Let's just say that it is a price she would be prepared to pay. If you are worried about the equipment, I'm sure that we would pay for any dam—'

'No,' the nurse interjected. 'No … I am only concerned for your friend.'

'Thank you,' the young woman replied. 'She has known that this moment would come for some time now. I'm sure she will be fine.'

The patient stirred. The nurse took her cue to stop talking and get back to the job at hand. She needed two extra chairs, extra glasses for water, and a power cable for their recording equipment. If her patient had been waiting for months to give this interview, then the nurse would make damn certain that a lack of power would not stop it from happening.

As the nurse went about her job, she listened over her shoulder.

'Drink?' said the patient in a whisper.

'Here you go,' said the young woman.

After a few moments, their conversation continued.

'The bank?' Another whisper, but stronger than the last. The patient was preparing herself.

'Yes, they just confirmed that all the transfers went out last night. They should all start seeing the money in their accounts today and tomorrow. That includes the money for our friends here at the clinic.'

'Good. The press release?'

'Yes, two of the big ones have already picked the story up. It is showing on their websites now and I expect it will hit the front cover of most papers tomorrow.'

'Good,' the patient said. 'Do I look okay?'

'Susan, as always, you look beautiful,' the young woman said.

Susan, the nurse thought to herself. *She has a name*.

'So, it is all done. Just tomorrow's interview and it is all over.'

'Yes. Are you scared?'

'I'm not afraid of the interview.'

'Not the interview. Are you afraid of dying?'

'Yes, and no. It will be my second time at death's door. This time I won't even knock. I will just kick the door down,' Susan said. She tried to laugh but her lungs weren't up to it and her voice didn't catch her short breaths.

'Do you still see them?' the young woman said.

The nurse turned around to see the patient scanning the room. She knew from experience that the patients in her condition usually suffered from depleted vision as part of the body's natural shutting down process. She also knew that some close to death often claim to see things that weren't there. She was curious to know which way this patient was leaning.

'Yes. They are still here waiting for me.'

'Tell me again who you see,' said the young woman.

'I see my mother, and I see Isaac. They are both here, smiling at me from different places. I don't think they see each other, so it will be interesting once I get there. I will be like a puppy caught between two masters.' She took a moment to cough once again.

'How about the monsters?' the young woman asked.

'Yes. My father is there, with his friends.'

'Are they still angry with you?'

'Yes. They blame me for everything, and they are right. They started it but I finished it. If they had never touched me to begin with, perhaps I could have been a different person. But too late for all of that. I am the product of my upbringing. They are the only part of dying that scares me.'

'Don't let those monsters scare you. You are Susan fucking Mitchell – The Woman Who Stole The World. You have defeated them once before and you will do it again. Isaac will help you.'

The nurse watched them exchange a moment before the young woman tucked Susan in once again.

'You should get some rest. You will need your energy for tomorrow,' the young woman said.

The nurse left them to each other. She had to find chairs, glasses, and a power cable. She would also phone the night nurse and advise her not to bother coming in. The nurse wanted to stay with them both herself this evening. She had nowhere else to go and no one else to see.

FRONT PAGE NEWS

Human Capital Money Returned!

by Alan Surebridge.

Did 'The Woman Who Stole The World' just give it back?

Over the past 24 hours, we have been receiving reports that some of the missing millions of dollars that investors poured into the now infamous Human Capital World Fund is finding its way back into investors' bank accounts.

'It was crazy!' cited one investor. 'I had completely given up the thought of ever seeing that money again. Then, without warning, I got a message from my bank to say that new funds were in my account. It was everything I invested and some. They even paid interest on my investment.'

'I have withdrawn the money already,' said another investor. 'The moment I saw it in my account, I withdrew it as cash. I didn't want anyone to take it off me again. It was all there.'

Yesterday, this paper received a press release from an unknown source claiming to be acting on behalf of Susan Mitchell. Miss Mitchell had been the fund owner of the Human Capital World Fund until July, when she suddenly disappeared with all the money right at the height of her fund's success. She received the title, 'The Woman Who Stole The World' from a podcast about her life and disappearance produced by Stephen Grace when a young woman who had lost all of her saving through the fund claimed that Susan Mitchell had, 'stolen my whole world.'

At this point in our investigations, we cannot confirm if every single person who invested in the Human Capital World Fund has received their money back, but the press release assures us that if they haven't already, they will within the next 24 hours. So far, we have confirmed over seventy-two cases of customers who have received their refunds, with interest.

Rapper Ku-Stom supported Susan Mitchell right until the moment she disappeared. He even raised money on her behalf. The pair were romantically linked by many of the celebrity gossip sites as part of a love triangle with singer JC Chains in some tabloid press. Today we received this response from Ku-Stom's new head of customer relations, Allison Bailey. 'As this case is currently before the courts, Ku-Stom cannot comment directly. However, Ku-Stom maintains that he always had full faith that Susan Mitchell would make good on their investment. And he hopes that, with her return, regulators will finally understand that he has done nothing wrong in using his crowd funding portal to help her raise money. He would also like to thank his fans for sticking by him over the past month, and to remind them all that his new album, *Apex*, will drop on the 14th of October.'

They refused to answer any more direct questions on the matter of Susan Mitchell.

The whereabouts of Susan Mitchell is still unknown; however, we were advised that there will be a last episode of 'The Woman Who Stole The World', due to air within the week. Its producer, Stephen Grace, has assured his listeners that it will include an extensive interview with Susan Mitchell herself.

This paper will continue to monitor the situation closely over the coming weeks.

EPISODE 24:
THE FINAL EPISODE

[Narrator]

Welcome, listeners. For the last time we ask the questions: who was the mysterious Susan Mitchell – The Woman Who Stole The World? And how was she able to convince so many people to invest hundreds of millions of dollars into her Human Capital World Fund before disappearing off the face of the earth with everyone's money?

Listeners, I want to once again thank you for your support of this podcast. I suggest you pour yourself a glass of wine and make yourself comfortable, because this is one heck of an episode, and it will be a long one.

I will be completely honest with you when I say, I never thought we would ever get to record it. Over the past twenty-two episodes, we have asked many questions, over and over, to those that knew Susan Mitchell best. Questions like: who was she? why did she do it? and where did she and all that hard earned money go? But, throughout that time we never got to ask Miss Mitchell herself to explain her actions. Today we finally get to hear her side of the story. I can tell you now, you won't believe what she had to say.

Before we hear from Susan Mitchell herself, though, there is a minor matter that we have to clear up for you first. You could call it the elephant in the room. Since we spoke last, a lot of the missing money that we keep talking about has mysteriously found its way back to investors' bank accounts; even their mailboxes, for those that had mailed in their investments.

Along with a group of selected journalists, we received an anonymous press release about a week ago which advised us that every cent that had been invested in the Human Capital World Fund was about to be returned to investors with interest. As you can expect, it made front page news around the world. To test the validity of the declaration, we randomly called some people who contacted our show with their stories. And I'm happy to say, almost all of them confirmed they had seen the money returned. While we can't confirm that every cent invested has found its way home, we are yet to find anyone that hasn't gotten their refund. That even extends to the Ku-Stom trust investors, whose individual details were never actually shared with the fund itself.

As usual with this case, every time we got a new answer it just opened a Pandora's Box of more questions.

Before we get to the woman herself, I think it is important that I set the scene on how we found her that day.

As you will recall from our recent announcement about a week and half ago, we were contacted by someone claiming to be Susan Mitchell's assistant Jana Fett. In that email, we were told that Susan Mitchell was alive and willing to talk to us under strict conditions. We could ask any questions we wanted, and that she will answer truthfully and without bias. The three conditions they gave us were: that we will only get the address for the interview on the morning of the interview, that nobody else could be present for the recording other than myself and my editor and, finally, that the episode didn't air until seven days had passed since its recording. We assumed at the time that this would be to give her significant time to make another getaway. After having met her that day, we now know that it was not her intention at all.

The last pieces of information that I will share with you before we get to the interview with Susan Mitchell are the location of the meeting and the condition that she was in when we got there.

As we had arranged, the morning of the interview they sent us a secret address, which strangely enough was only about 3 miles from where we produce this very show. When we got there, we found a three-story beige brick building with no street sign or any indication of what purpose the building might serve. We tried to enter through a fortified glass door, but it was locked and no one was responding to our knocks. We looked for a buzzer to let them know we were there, but there was none. The only thing we saw was a security pad designed for proximity cards. It was quite clear to us that they didn't regularly get visitors to that address. Given we didn't have one of their security cards and there was no doorbell, we could not see any way of getting in. To be honest, at that point we thought that someone had pranked us. We were considering leaving, when the door finally swung open and a young woman called after us. I thought she might be one of tenants of the building confused about why we were there but then she greeted me by name and introduced herself. She must have seen the confused look on my face because she followed through with – *Yes, Susan's Jane, from your show. I look different now.*

It took us a few moments of inspection, but we finally saw the resemblance to the Jane Fett we know from the one image we had. She now wore glasses and her hair had been dyed to lighted shade of chestnut.

With Jane's permission, we started recording from that moment. We will play the recording back for you now.

[Stephen Grace]

'Jane, thank you for reaching out to us. Have you been this close to us the entire time you and Susan Mitchell have been missing?'

[Jane Fett]

'Well, we didn't really know where you were at the start, but when we found out, it seems we have for most of it, yes. We needed somewhere highly secure but flexible enough for Susan to complete her work while her condition deteriorated. The building might not look like much from the outside, but it is a fortress. You could drive a car into that front glass and you still wouldn't get in. It is bulletproof and bombproof. We knew that there would be people who wanted her found for different reasons and we couldn't afford for that to happen before the credits went through. Hopefully now they will be a little more understanding. Soon enough it won't matter either way.'

[Stephen Grace]

'You mention that her condition was deteriorating? Can you tell me a little more about that?'

[Jane Fett]

'You will see her condition for yourself in just a moment, but I can tell you now that she is in the last stages of an extremely aggressive cancer that has spread through her entire body. Five years ago, she nearly died from it, but she recovered. Then, two years ago, it came back. And it is here to stay this time, unfortunately.'

[Stephen Grace]

'Are you saying that the entire time that she ran the Human Capital World Fund, she had cancer?'

[Jane Fett]

'Yes.'

[Stephen Grace]

'How was she able to operate her business like she did if she was sick?'

[Jane Fett]

'We had medical equipment in her office. Out of general view, of course. I was her assistant, but also her nurse. I could give her oxygen, her shots and even blood transfusions right there in that office, twenty meters away from the boardroom. Nobody even knew she was sick. She had a way of crossing that threshold and becoming someone else. Someone strong, and then she would go back in, shut the door, and fall apart once again. Her stamina was amazing, considering.'

[Stephen Grace]

'Why set up the fund at all? Surely she could have just enjoyed what little time she had left?'

[Jane Fett]

'You can ask her that yourself. I have said all I needed to say.'

[Narrator]

Listeners, the Susan Mitchell that I knew from her videos was a woman in her prime. A woman whose intellect, charisma and beauty captivated those who attended her speeches, or met her at parties. And I'm not just talking about the everyday people, I'm also talking about rockstars and titans of industry. People who were famous in their own right, who knew 'the hustle' as Ku-Stom once so eloquently put it. They were all taken in by her. When I walked into that building that day, that was the confident, powerful woman I was expecting to meet. But it was not the woman I met. I'd had so much time to prepare for this meeting, but I was unprepared for the version of Susan Mitchell that I found. To be completely honest, I had never expected to get a chance to meet her face to face. I honestly thought that she had been killed or that we would never see her again.

So, let me set a new scene for you, this time from the inside of a hospital suite. There was a hospital bed in the centre of the room and on it was Susan Mitchell, attached to a drip and a collection of electronic machines that would not appear out of place in a rocket. The best way that I could explain it to you is to say that the Susan Mitchell I saw that day was a bundle of bones loosely wrapped in skin. Her hair was almost completely gone and her eyesight floated about the room like she was struggling to maintain a constant vision or that she continually looking at something, or someone, over your shoulder.

I will give her this, though: there was a flicker of defiance in her still. Whatever she had set out to do, she was not quite done yet.

We were not the only people there. Around her bed I could see Sally Bassett, who was clearly upset, leaning into Peter Lana for support. Dylan Clarke was also by Susan's bedside with a tender hand on her right forearm, resuming his role as the father figure. To my surprise, on her left, sitting quietly on a chair in the corner, was the famous singer JC Chains. I had never met him previously, but his aura was far from being that of an international megastar that day. He had the look of a man in grief, who hadn't spoken a single word in days. Finally, there was a nurse – not Jane – attending. Everyone stood about staring in like they wanted to feel history being created in this moment.

When we arrived, all except for JC Chains looked up and seemed to accept that their time with Susan was over. JC Chains, or Josiah Charnos as he was in that room, simply continued to stare down into his hands which were cupped empty in his lap.

What she had said to them before I got there was their business. None of them ever spoke about it publicly afterwards. And for the record, I never asked. I never felt the need to.

Sally, Peter and Dylan all battled their tears to say one last goodbye and left the room with a slight nod to me on their way past.

Jane then ushered us to some empty seats by Miss Mitchell's bed and instructed us to begin.

[Stephen Grace]

'Hello, Miss Mitchell, I am so sorry to find you in this condition. How are you?'

[Susan Mitchell]

'You thought I would be dead, Stephen. Surely this is one step better? Let's not waste time looking for answers to the obvious questions. Call me Susan and ask me the tough questions while you still can. The only thing I have left to give the world is my truth.'

[Stephen Grace]

'Okay, I'm going to ask you the question that I start every episode with. Are you a humanitarian, a genius or a charlatan?'

[Susan Mitchell]

'You could ask that question to the entire human race. We are all of us, all those things in our own ways. I am certainly no genius in the traditional sense, but I work hard when I need to. And sometimes to be called a genius, you don't need to know everything, you just need to know one more thing than the person you are speaking to. I just knew lots of "one more things".'

[Stephen Grace]

'What about the amazing algorithm that Mathias told us about that was behind the Human Capital World Fund? Didn't you create that?'

[Susan Mitchell]

'I didn't invent it from scratch if that's what you mean. I just took something and reapplied it differently. Mathias loved it because it was already partly his work which he had posted about online. I just gave Mathias the two things he craved more than anything else.'

[Stephen Grace]

'And what were they?'

[Susan Mitchell]

'A mirror for him to see his own brilliance, and a platform for him to project it to the world. Do you see? I am no genius; I just give people what they want.'

[Stephen Grace]

'Were you working alone? There is belief that you must have had a team behind you, for you to pull it all off.'

[Susan Mitchell]

'They are right: I had a team. You have met them all already. Sally, Mathias, Peter, Allison, and everyone else that came to join our company. The people who say I couldn't do it alone are really saying to you they don't believe a woman could pull this off alone. They don't say those types of things about a man. You have done a fine job with this show, Stephen, but you haven't always checked your bias. Or that of your guests. I hope you remember that for next time.' [Coughs]

[Stephen Grace]

'I will … Do you need to take a minute?'

[Susan Mitchell]

'No, keep going. I don't have many minutes left to spare. You have more hard questions to ask me yet, and I don't want you to feel sorry for me.'

[Stephen Grace]

'Okay. Did you purposely target talent agent Dylan Clarke to get to his clientele?'

[Susan Mitchell]

'My upbringing divided my world up into two camps: good men, and wicked men. I have not had the luxury of meeting enough of the in-between. Dylan Clarke was one of the good ones. He saw potential in me that no one else ever did. I wish I had met him when I was younger. But to answer your question directly, yes, I did. I told him so earlier today. But I never put him in a position where he took any sort of responsibility for my actions. I went to great lengths to make sure of that. My father was a monster. I wish Dylan had been my father. Perhaps I would have turned out differently. I told Dylan these things earlier when he was here. He has forgiven me, and I will die knowing we have made peace with everything.'

[Stephen Grace]

'Just before, you said just that in your world there have only been good men and wicked men. Where do you see me on that scale? Are you angry with me for what we have said about you on the podcast?'

[Susan Mitchell]

'I am giving up what little time I have left to live to talk to you, Stephen. I'm, hoping that you are worth it. But I blame you for nothing. I am thankful to you. You have given me an opportunity to tell my story. Well, the final chapter of it anyway.'

[Stephen Grace]

'Why talk to me at all? You could have gone to any of the papers. You would have made front page anywhere.'

[Susan Mitchell]

'You are the person who has invested the most in me. And as they say, the person with the most invested is always the last to leave. You will tell my story through your show longer and better than any other newspaper headline.'

[Stephen Grace]

'Is that why you called me here? To tell your story?'

[Susan Mitchell]

'No, you were already doing that. I just want you to finish it. Life demands nothing of me now, other than that my story be told.'

[Stephen Grace]

'But there is still so much I don't understand.'

[Susan Mitchell]

'Then ask me [coughs] we don't have a lot of time left. I can feel myself getting hazy again, and these wonderful drugs won't last forever.'

[Stephen Grace]

'How did you get the money to pay everyone back?'

[Susan Mitchell]

'That is the most boring question you could ask, but I will answer it because I promised I would. [Coughs] We could never make the returns we needed to make in the time we had available, so I had no choice but to act in another way. I took all the money we had and ran so that everyone was looking for me alone and not the people in my business. I then added all of my own money to it and I took positions shorting tobacco and gambling companies, ahead of those new tobacco anti-advertising laws which were released two months back. It is amazing what you can do with just a little piece of information. I won't tell you how I got it except to say that somebody from my past owed me a favour. Before anyone gets excited, I can assure your listeners that nobody will ever know how I did it, and nobody will ever be able to reclaim the money once I'm dead. Which will be soon enough. The money trail also dies with me.'

Narrator

We had to pause while Miss Mitchell had a coughing fit that in turn triggered some serious internal pain. The nurse came forward and administered a shot into her drip. Those few minutes gave me time to reconsider my line of questioning. I had assumed that I was coming to interview a healthy woman. Instead, I was hearing a deathbed confession. Those are two different sets of questions, but she was right about one thing. The 'how' was not the most important question I could ask. She could have taken it to a casino and bet it all on black, and what difference would it have made to this story? None. She was decaying at a rapid rate, right in front of my eyes, so I needed to move on from the 'how' to the much more important 'why'. But not quite yet.

[Stephen Grace]

'Susan, we are running out of time, and I am still so confused. You say that you targeted Dylan Clarke that day, but then came to look up to him as a father. What was your intention with this whole thing? How much of it was a con and how much of it was real?'

[Susan Mitchell]

'That is a better question. I guess I didn't know what I was getting myself into. I thought that if I created a slick presentation and put on a sexy dress, then maybe some people might take me seriously for once in my life. What I didn't realize until it was too late, was that those people saw something in me I never saw in myself. That look on their faces was intoxicating. It all started with Sally. I tried to send her away. I gave her a test that I didn't think she would do. I told her that if she didn't resign on the spot then I wouldn't hire her. I didn't want her to do it, but she did. Right there at that lunch, she believed in me so much that she quit her job to join me. I didn't have to sleep with anybody. I didn't have to pay anything. I just talked to her. If you ask me, Sally is the actual hero. Without her, I would have just been another slick presentation at a conference nobody can remember. [Coughs] She was the one that convinced me I could actually do it. She believed in me so much she was betting her future on it.'

[Stephen Grace]

'Okay, so you got swept up in all the attention. But why do it at all? You had money already, from what I hear. You could have just enjoyed the time you had left on a beach somewhere. Why put yourself through it? What was to be gained?'

[Susan Mitchell]

'I grew up in an orphanage, Stephen. Men abused me so many times in that place that, by the time I got out, the damage was done. I believed that I only ever had one thing of value that I could offer the world. And so many men had taken it from me for free, that it wasn't very valuable when I finally could negotiate for myself. I settled that score, with those men, long ago. And I thought it would help me forget, to move on, but it didn't. When I look over your shoulder right now, I still see their faces. They are in this room with me, just waiting for me to die so that they can start their torment all over again. [Coughs and wheezes]. When I got sick again, I knew this would be my last fight. I just wanted to hold the world in my hands, to have actual power over men, power where it hurts them most. In their pride and in their pockets. Just one time before I died. I never realized how big it would become.'

[Jane Fett]

'Stephen, Susan won't be able to maintain this much longer. Do you have what you need?'

[Stephen Grace]

'And what about Ku-Stom and JC Chains? Were they just part of the world that you wanted to hold in your hands before you died?'

Narrator

For the record, I was furious at myself for asking that question. It felt juvenile when I listened back to it later. I considered scrubbing it from this record, but that would not be fair to Susan, who had been so honest with me.

This was her response.

[Susan Mitchell]

'Ku-Stom is a child that wanted a toy he couldn't have. Josiah has been everything to me in this final year of my life. I have never lied to him once about who I was, or my situation. He demanded nothing from me and is still here with me today. Does that not tell you something? I only wish we could have found each other earlier. Our lives might have been different. There may have just been some happiness for us both.

You have had your chance to ask me your questions, Stephen Grace. Let me now ask you a question. How many frauds do you need to expose to bring your father back?'

[Stephen Grace]

'What? I ... I don't know what you mean.'

[Susan Mitchell]

'It wasn't his fault. You know that. And yet, you keep trying to undo what was done.'

[Stephen Grace]

'That's not true. I know I can't undo what was done. I can't bring him back. I just don't want the same thing that happened to him – to us – to happen to others. That's why I investigate companies that misappropriate innocent people's money.'

[Susan Mitchell]

'That company needed to answer for what they did to your father. They took his money and left your family with nothing. But he should also answer for what he did to the wife and seven-year-old boy he left behind. I hate to say this to you, but it is the truth. He got greedy and over-extended. Rather than face his actions, rebuild a happy life for you all, he took his own life. You didn't deserve that. If you keep looking for evil deeds, you will keep finding them, and you will forever see his image in the victims that you so diligently seek out. But it will not help you deal with what happened to you and your mother. Perhaps it is time for you to move on. I'm sure it is what he would want.

'If I see him on the other side, I will send him your love. You can send him your forgiveness yourself.'

[Stephen Grace]

'Why are you saying this to me?'

[Susan Mitchell]

'Because my life has been bound by suffering also. I looked away from it, but you, you look back into yours. I'm sorry, I just don't have enough time to say it any nicer. Wrap this show up and go find some beauty in the world. Find something worthy, under that magnifying gaze of yours, for the world to see. [Coughs and wheezes] I'm sorry, but our time together is coming to an end [laboured breathing]. If you have any more questions, ask those that knew me best. They will be the ones to tell my story now.'

[Narrator]

Susan Mitchell descended into another coughing fit. We were ushered from the room by the nurse, and the doors were closed behind us. Just like the rest of the world, we never got to say goodbye to Susan Mitchell, but like so many others we are thankful for the short time that we had with her.

So, for the very last time, I am going to try to finally answer the question that has dogged us from the very beginning. That question again, was she a humanitarian, a genius or a con woman? I'm sure you will all have your own opinions on that matter. But for me, she was all of those things, and more.

I believe that Susan Mitchell did 'steal the world', but she gave it back, with interest. I can tell you now that, after speaking to those closest to her, I can see their world was better for having had her in it. They got to do the things they loved most and, for a short time at least, they got to be the people they had always wanted to be. Even poor old Peter Lana enjoyed his time at the start. And, as they always say, 'those with the most invested are always the last to leave'. He was there right to the very end, trying desperately to keep their dream alive. When I spoke to him this week, he said that he still would take none of it back. He got to meet Sally, and that in itself was enough for him.

As you may have heard, Sally now works for UNICEF, where she continues to do the thing that she loves. She would never have gotten that chance had Susan Mitchell not taken her under her wing. And while Sally confessed to me that she enjoys being part of a team much more than trying to lead one, she now has a knowledge of both sides which she never had before. She said that whenever she has a hard decision to make, or needs a little courage, she simply thinks to herself, 'What would Susan do?' and, in some miraculous fashion, she finds a path.

I have not been able to speak with Dylan Clarke or Mathias LaGrange over the past week; however, both have sent messages. Neither man harbours any grudges against Susan Mitchell. In fact, part of the reason I couldn't speak to them was because new and exciting talent has overrun Dylan Cark's agency. Young excitable faces keen to work with an agent who cares so much about his clientele. Something that they learned about him from this very show.

And the reason we couldn't get hold of Mathias Lagrange is because he is currently touring this country on a book speaking circuit. It seems that he now gets paid thousands of dollars to tell people how clever he is. He shares his story about working for the famous Susan Mitchell and the Human Capital World Fund that he helped to create. I have it on good authority that the stories are embellished every time that he tells them, but they become more entertaining in the process. I wonder if the history books will eventually cave into his relentlessness and record his version of the history of his Human Capital World Fund as the true account.

I am also pleased to say that Susan Mitchell's influence doesn't stop there. We now have young women all over the world looking up to her as a role model of how they might one day 'steal the world' for themselves and make it better. Her legacy will live on and, if this show has played a part in that – even if we didn't always believe in her ourselves, I can say that the team and I are proud of the body of work that we have produced for you.

Now, the sad news. We were told that Susan Mitchell died four hours after we recorded that interview. She never quite recovered from that last coughing fit and eventually passed out, never to reawaken. We would like to thank Jane for reaching out to us and allowing us to hear Susan's last words but, unfortunately, it seems she has disappeared once again.

If you are out there, Jane, thank you. Out of respect, we will not come looking for you.

To all of you at home, or in your cars listening in, we thank you all for your time and attention. We could not have made this show without you.

As for me, I think I might take a well-earned break and then hopefully I'll be back on your airways. Back with another tale of mystery and intrigue, and maybe just a little beauty as well next time around.

I send you all, for the last time, my warmest regards.

Stephen Grace.

Now a final, final word from our sponsors …

THE NURSE: CLEAN UP

The nurse had allowed herself a few hours' sleep in the lead up to the visitors and the interview that followed, but that was all the sleep she'd had over the past day and a half. She had a strong temptation to go online and do some research on Susan Mitchell, but that could wait.

When her head had finally hit her pillow, her exhaustion washed over her like a wave. She smiled in sheer delight as she surfed that wave into her dreams.

She would have been at home still curled up in her bed right now had she not received the phone call that ripped her back from her dreams.

'Yes?' It wasn't a greeting, just an invitation to say what needed to be said and leave her alone.

'Hi, Jackie, it's Sarah from work. We just thought that you would want to know that your patient just died peacefully in her sleep. Her people asked me to thank you for everything you have done for her over the past few months, and to advise you that your contract is now over. The money should already be in your account.'

Jackie didn't know this 'Sarah from work' but it was hardly a concern. She cared for patients in a terminal condition every day. It was her specialty. Mostly, she cared to ease their suffering of the patient, but didn't get involved with the patients' personalities themselves. With the amount of death, she had been exposed to it was the only way to protect herself from having to grieve every death. With Susan Mitchell, it had been very different. She cared and felt something for the woman herself and her story, and that of her young companion as well.

Jackie thought back to the moment the doctor had patted her on the shoulder at the hospital and ushered her into a supply room to talk.

'If you think that I'm coming in here to,' Jackie started before running out of the precise words. 'To do things, then …'

She was not 'on the market' and she was certainly not 'up for a good time' as they had liked to snigger in her younger days. She was a professional, she did what she was told, and she kept her mouth shut.

'Oh, no. Nothing like that,' the doctor had replied indignantly. 'A rich patient has contacted me. She is terminally ill and needs care. The patient wishes to remain anonymous throughout her dying process, so she cannot go to a standard hospital for her treatment. She is prepared to pay handsomely for premises, equipment and people, but it has to be people she can trust.' The inference was *to keep our mouths shut.*

'Why does she think she can trust you?' the nurse had said. It wasn't meant as an insult, but he clearly took it that way.

'Because I need the money. I need it badly enough to agree to almost anything. How she knew that I don't know, but she knew.'

'And why do you think you can trust me?'

'Because you do what you are told, and you keep your business to yourself. I figure it is easier for someone to keep a secret if they don't have friends ... or talk.' He hadn't meant it as an insult, but it had a sting just the same.

Jackie could have said yes right there, just out of morbid curiosity, but she didn't.

'We both have jobs here. How would this work?' she had asked.

'We both give notice today and we start work at the new location in one week. I'm told it is within a few miles of this hospital.'

'They will think we are having an affair if we both give notice on the same day,' she said, pointing over her shoulder. 'If they saw us walk in here together, they probably are talking about us together already.'

'I don't think you really care what they say. And even if they do, if you take this job, it won't matter. Not with the amount of money they have agreed to pay us. Neither of us will have to work here, or anywhere else, again.'

'Okay, I'll do it. I need a change of scenery.'

'Don't you want to know how much they are going to pay us, or why I need the money so badly?' the doctor asked through a grin.

'No,' she said.

'I knew you were the right person to ask,' he said.

She knew it made little sense. Rich and famous people had rich and famous hospitals that they could go to where their identities would be protected. She could think of no reason for this level of secrecy unless this was an underworld figure, but even if it was, to her she would just be another patient needing a nurse. Jackie was a professional.

If there is someone in need and I'm available, it is my duty to help.

She also knew that she would work again in any hospital. No matter how much they paid her for this contract, she would work again. How could attending to one person, no matter how rich they might be, stop her from attending a lifetime of patients? She would help this patient, and then go seek another patient somewhere else. Nurses are always needed, and they resign for many reasons.

I will just pass myself off as another nurse that went through something at my previous job that I don't want to talk about. They will just assume it was some type of sexual harassment and they won't want to talk about it either.

It wouldn't take much to talk around it.

Now, three months later, when it was all said and done, Jackie was sad it was over. She was sad for Susan Mitchell the woman who had been in her care and she was sad for her young friend, but she was also sad for the work. She had enjoyed it. It had made her feel part of something. Like she was playing her role in one of history's major events. From a professional perspective, the fact that she had been required to devote all her time to just one patient had been liberating. She was no longer divided across seventeen wards, with patients pressing their attention buttons for her to change the channel on their TV sets because none of the remote controls worked or laying towels down over patients because there weren't enough blankets to go around. This had finally been the type of nursing that she had dreamed about growing up.

As she entered the building where she had been working, Jackie saw workmen in hardhats and high visibility vests everywhere. They were carrying furniture and medical machinery out of the building. One of them accidentally knock the side of the hospital bed her patient had been lying in only hours before on the front window on the way out. The window's pane split, and a small piece of glass fell to the floor in front of them.

'I didn't see nothing,' he said with a grin to the man at the other end of their load.

The other man replied, 'Don't sweat it, mate. The whole place is being pulled down.'

They paid no attention to Jackie as she squeezed past them through the door frame. From the inside, the place looked completely different again. In the space of only a few hours, they had stripped the interior right back to its shell. She looked about but no one that she recognized. They were all laborers going about their jobs automatically, like a pack of ants pulling apart a meal and carrying it back to their nest. Jackie looked about once again just to be completely sure she hadn't walked into the wrong building, but this was the one. She grabbed the arm of one of the passing men.

'Excuse me, where is the patient?' she asked.

The man wiped his brow and looked at her. 'There're no patients here, love.'

'I mean the body. Where's the body?'

The man shook his head once again. 'I don't know what you mean. You see that man over there, in the green vest? Talk to him, he is the supervisor here. Maybe he can help you.'

Jackie thanked him and made her way across the room to the man in the green vest. He was issuing instructions to another man but watched her out of the corner of his eye. He stopped talking the moment she was within range to address her directly.

'You can't come in here. This is a worksite, and you don't have a hat,' he said, pointing to the hardhat on his head. 'It's not safe in here for you.'

Jackie peered over each of her shoulders looking about for a hat of her own, but there was none readily available. 'Look, I just need to know—' she started, but the supervisor cut her off before she could finish.

'It doesn't matter what you need, you can't be in here without a hat,' he said.

Jackie then lashed out and stole the hat from the man that the supervisor had been speaking with then put it on her own head.

'Hey! What the …' the man said.

'I just need a moment. It is important that I finish my job,' Jackie said.

The supervisor looked mildly impressed by her conviction. 'Okay, you have a hat but you really can't be here, ma'am, this is a worksite.'

'I can see that! I work here,' the nurse said. 'Where are the staff? Where is the body of my patient? I need to prepare it.'

The supervisor waved a hand in front of her. 'I know nothing about any of that. We got contracted one week ago to come in at 8 am today and demolish the whole place. I haven't seen any dead bodies, and I don't know what you are talking about.'

'What do you mean they contracted you a week ago? I have been working here for the past week and nobody said anything to me about closing today. I was here just last night with a dying patient, and nobody mentioned anything about this. Who contracted you?'

The man seemed suddenly concerned about volunteering any further information. 'Look, I don't have any names. We were just paid triple our normal rate to drop whatever we had planned and turn up here this morning and bring the place down. I saw a few people leave earlier, but I do not know who they were.'

'Were they men, women, doctors …?'

'One man, two women. A young one and an older one. That's all I know. Now, I'm sorry, but I'm going to have to ask you to leave.'

Jackie nodded to thank him for the information. Her mind was racing with question that she was quite sure this man didn't have the answers for. She returned the stolen hard hat to its rightful owner reluctantly. On her way out of the room she allowed herself one final good look around for posterity.

It had never looked like much from the outside, but on this day, it seemed even barer.

Perhaps I'm still asleep, and all this is just a dream.

She chuckled to herself, but the detail of the world about her left her sure she was on the right side of reality.

My pay?

Jackie almost dropped her phone in her rush to retrieve it from her bag. She logged into her banking application for her balance. Staring back at her was a bank balance that she would have never thought possible for one of her own accounts. It was a figure that she could build a wonderful future on. The name for the depositor of that money was a company called 'the Human Capital World Fund' and the only comments about its nature read 'With our thanks'.

Jackie smiled. She would never have to work again if she didn't want to. She considered that concept for a moment. Of course, she would return to work at some point, but maybe not right away. First, she needed to get some sleep. Then, perhaps a break might be okay. It had been so long since her last holiday, and she had been working six days a week for months now. She could go somewhere nice. Spoil herself a little. She would tell no one about her new money, or her experiences with The Woman Who Stole The World, because she was a professional, and she kept her mouth shut.

After all, isn't that why they had hired her in the first place?

THE END

THANK YOU!

To my readers, a massive thank you for investing your time, money, and attention into reading this book. I sincerely hope that you enjoyed it.

I know this book has differed from my previous two novels. If you liked my darker books, like the first two books, then don't fear because there will be more to come in the coming years. However, if this book was more your style, then I'm hoping to bring you more like it soon. For now, I just needed a break from the darker things in life and wanted to get back to good old-fashioned storytelling.

I hope the podcast format that I wrote this book in was not too jarring for you all. Hopefully you would have seen past the format after the first few chapters and just enjoyed the story for what it was.

If you liked this book or any of my books, then please tell your friends and family about them. I want my books to have a positive impact on people's lives and they can only do that if people read them. I often find that the best books are the ones that are recommended to be me by the people whose opinion I respect. So, if you liked it, then they most likely will as well.

Also, if you would like to come on this journey with me, please subscribe to my newsletter at Andrewhoodauthor.com and come follow me on Facebook at @andrewhoodauthor.

Once again, thank you all for your support.

Andrew

INTERVIEW WITH THE AUTHOR - ANDREW HOOD

Firstly Andrew, how does it feel to have finished your first trilogy?

Oh my gosh, it feels amazing. When I started writing, I only ever thought I would write The Man Who Corrupted Heaven. But in writing that book all three of my characters came to life, and I soon realized that, to tell this story right, I needed a book on each character to explore their backstories and what they might do next.

What made you decide to end your series with Susan Mitchell's story?

Susan's character really upstaged Isaac's character in many sections of the first book. It came completely by surprise because she didn't start out well in that book and I did not know what part she would end up playing. But it soon became very obvious to me that her character would be the lead character in my final book in the trilogy, and I couldn't wait to write it.

What made you decide to use the podcast format for this book?

I wanted to hear some stories about infamous women and conmen and ended up listening to some wonderful true crime podcasts on the topic. I just loved the documentary style of it all and how at the end of each episode they got you excited about what you will hear on the next one.

It also worked well because it meant that I could build a real mystique around Susan, the character in the podcast, and then play it off against Susan the woman at the end.

Was this the story you set out to write when you first started writing this book?

Not exactly, no. I don't know what exactly I was expecting to write, but during its creation the *Me Too* movement really took off and it got me thinking about a lot of things. I decided I wanted most of the people that I interviewed in the book about Susan to be men. You may notice that it is almost always the male perspective on the woman. None of them believe that a woman alone could pull this off, so they fill in the blanks in their expectations of how she must have had outside (male) help, or that she just got lucky. It is only Sally who really sees her for the incredible woman she was in the story, but everyone just thinks Sally is unimportant in the grand scheme of things.

Is this the end of The Man Who Corrupted Heaven series? You left it a little open at the end.
For now, yes. I have already started on a new series, but this doesn't mean I won't be able to dive back in later if I ever want to. I have built some amazing characters in this series and there is still so much more I could say about them. There are lots of little avenues I could pursue with those characters, but yes, for now this will be the last book in that series.

What are you writing next?
I have two separate books I'm working on at the moment. One of them is something new that I am just having a break from because it is quite a task. The other book is a lovely story that I started about fifteen years ago. My mother read it back then and has been begging me to go back and finish it ever since. I figure that if she can still remember it after all this time, then it is probably worth going back for.
You will have to wait and see which of those two books comes to market first.

Do you have any last words for your readers?
Once again, thank you! For being my witness, and for seeing my tree fall in the woods! (A reference from my first book)
Your beautiful comments keep me writing even when I don't want to. I will always be grateful to you all for that.
You have my warmest regards.
Andrew

Shawline Publishing Group Pty Ltd

www.shawlinepublishing.com.au

SHAWLINE
PUBLISHING
GROUP